To Kill a Shadow

To Kill a Shadow

Nathan Ronen

Editor :Dr. Amnon Jackont
Translated from Hebrew by Yaron Regev
Copyediting by Adirondack Editing

Contact: natek7474@gmail.com

ISBN-13: 978-1539777571
ISBN-10: 153977757X

A Personal Note

"Espionage is the world's second oldest profession and just as honorable as the first."

Michael J. Barrett, Assistant General Counsel of the CIA, Journal of Defense and Diplomacy, February 1984.

The book you hold in your hands tells the story of unique individuals who pay a heavy toll for their dedication and commitment. They do it not only out of commitment to their country or for their livelihood; they are addicted to adrenaline, control, action and the fact that their actions which, on other circumstances, would be forbidden are sanctioned and authorized.

These people live in the shadows, work under false identities and behind masks, and, like the common man, are petrified of loneliness.

It is a fictional tale. Its name, *To Kill a Shadow*, hints at the different levels at which the intelligence system operates above and below the surface, the interpersonal and international relationships, and the complex considerations the people who operate in it need to face on a daily basis.

I concocted the plot from various autobiographical and historical events, rare people, dreams, and fantasies. Part of the book's plot was inspired by people I've met and events that took place while I had served as a senior officer in the Israeli defense forces.

The book is dedicated to the memory of my late sister, Naomi Sharon, whom I miss dearly. Naomi passed away from blood cancer in 2008 at the young age of fifty-seven.

Nathan Ronen. Yavne, Israel. May 2016

Prologue

February 2003. La Triple Frontera—The Triple Frontier

It was the end of a summer weekend in the southern hemisphere. Twilight time. A drizzle washed away the dust from the leaves of the tall *cupuaçu* trees. At the border junction of Paraguay, Argentina, and Brazil, the wide Paraná River flowed serenely, its water tinged with the brown-reddish hue of erosion. Colorful parrots sought a place of refuge for the night at the top of the canopies of the trees, and their screams muffled the sound of the UCAV drone hovering above Aiman Juma's mansion in the suburbs of Ciudad del Este in Paraguay.

On the other end of the border, in the Argentinean town of Puerto Iguazú, a small group of men wearing faded khaki uniforms sat and closely watched the images transmitted by the drone onto a computer screen.

"Here he comes," said a young, crop-haired remote pilot operator in Hebrew.

Arik Bar-Nathan, head of Caesarea Division,[1] sipped from his umpteenth cup of coffee. "Zoom in on him."

---

[1]Caesarea is the name of Mossad's special operations division in the prime minister's office.

The young man's fingers fluttered commands on the keyboard, and the drone camera focused on a racing boat approaching the mansion dock from the Brazilian side of the border. A fleshy, bearded man wearing a baseball cap stood at the bow of the boat, wearing a heavy pistol. Behind him, in the wider part of the boat, stood several men. The drone camera zoomed on each of their faces in turn.

"I recognize Imad Husniyah, Hezbollah's chief of operations," said the young man, "and that's Omar Mussawi, Chairman of the Da'wah foundation, which assists the Hezbollah's charity organizations. Next to him is Asaad Ahmed Barakat, a businessman and one of Hezbollah's primary donors. There's another man there I don't recognize…"

"Aiman Juma," observed Dr. Alex Abramovich, Head of Mossad's Research and Intelligence Division, "the biggest drug dealer in the area."

"The two behind him are bodyguards," added the young man, "both armed with submachine guns."

"Why only two?" asked one of the men present.

"They feel safe here," explained Arik. "They're bribing the district governor, the chiefs of police, and the generals of the army camped in the area. One couldn't wish for better defense…"

The boat kissed the dock, and the company exited it and entered a minibus that awaited them. Two heavy motorcycles manned by Paraguay Police officers accompanied the minibus on its way to the heart of the mansion.

"Who else are we waiting for, Alex?" asked Arik.

"This is a gathering of Hezbollah donors, and more stakeholders are supposed to arrive. Men like Ramzan

Akhmatov, head of the Chechen Mafia in South America, and his younger son. They're both making huge profits smuggling drugs and weapons and laundering money. The heads of the Triads in Hong Kong, specializing in human trafficking and brand piracy, are also going to be there along with representatives of the Columbian drug cartels. Others will probably join them later on today, people who donate profits from their businesses to the Hezbollah in order to ensure the continuous flow of drugs into South America from Afghanistan through Iran and the Beqaa Valley in Lebanon."

Arik Bar-Nathan exhaled impatiently. "If we have a chance to nail them all in one shot, that's even better. I'm certainly not going to cry at their funeral."

Their eye in the sky followed the minibus, which stopped at the entrance of a large house. The passengers disembarked and went inside. Only the bodyguards remained outside and chatted with the drivers of the armored limousines.

"Kidon task force, are you ready?" Arik asked on the encrypted radio.

"T-minus five minutes," answered the commander of Mossad's commando unit from the other end of the border, close to the mansion wall.

"You're clear to go," he whispered into the mouthpiece. "Nail the motherfuckers."

The UCAV remote pilot operator navigated the aircraft toward the center of the building and homed in on the laser designators of the Kidon. Arik was pleased. Everything progressed according to plan.

In less than a minute, the drone crashed into the center of the villa with a huge blast. That was the signal. The Kidon detonated charges, planted in advance, inside the villa's wall and broke into the garden, riding ATVs. They opened fire from short range on the bodyguards with their submachine guns and hurled grenades into the spacious ballroom. Some of the participants died on the spot, among them Ramzan Akhmatov. His younger son had only been lightly injured and was dragged outside as the fire subsided by his bodyguard.

The local rescue and police forces were busy putting out fires, started by Mossad agents and local collaborators using incendiary bombs, and delayed from getting to the mansion. Under the cover of those actions, the Kidon retreated to the Argentinean border, where Arik and his Caesarea unit were already waiting to be debriefed.

It was only then that Arik learned about the telephone call Imad Husniyah had received seconds after he'd arrived at the mansion, a call intercepted by the listening station. "Get out quickly, the Israelis are here!" the local chief of police warned in English. Arik reviewed the drone footage one more time. He had to examine it closely before he discovered the figure of a man breaking out through a back window, crossing the yard at a run, and throwing something over his head. Arik knew exactly what it was: the baseball cap, Imad Husniyah's trademark.

"Who leaked information to the local police?" Arik shouted with frustration, knowing he would never receive an answer. In the nearby town of Foz do Iguaçu lived a large community of Lebanese Shiites, the tenth largest and richest community in South America. The police, like the rest of the authorities and government institutions, were eager to please. Someone there must have known something.

"This just came in." Alex Abramovich presented him with a piece of paper scribbled with a name.

"Ramzan Akhmatov," Arik called.

"He's been killed," said Alex with a grim face. "The Chechens won't let it go without retaliation."

"I know," said Arik, his heart filling with foreboding.

Chapter 1

Spring, 2003. Beehive on the Cliff Neighborhood in the Palmachim Air Force Base

Sunday at dawn. Arik woke to the sound of birds chirping among the branches of the *erythrina* tree outside his bedroom window. The digital clock gleamed with a green luminance. It was four forty-five AM. His hangover caused him to toss restlessly in bed. He gently removed the arm of the woman sleeping next to him from his chest and covered her tanned, shapely body with the satin sheet. All he remembered was that her name was Eva, and she had a PhD of some sort. She had a long German last name Arik had forgotten, perhaps because of the influence of the fine Zachlawi *arak* one of his agents had brought back from Lebanon. He had drunk the strong alcoholic beverage to the last drop. After all, it was his surprise party, thrown for his fiftieth birthday.

Arik brushed his teeth, dressed in a gray track suit, put on his battered New Balance running shoes, and headed down to the first floor. From the large glass window, he could watch the Mediterranean Sea below the cliff, peaceful and smooth as the surface of a mirror. The first rays of dawn broke through the veil of clouds and swirled with green, gray and black. The porch was littered with last night's surprise party's leftovers: plates with salads, half-eaten fruit, half-filled glasses of alcohol, bread the wind had managed to dry and cakes snatched by a company of screaming seagulls. Arik ignored the chaos. Others were in charge of organizing and cleaning the house. He preferred to focus on life's pleasures. "Life's too short and there are no reruns," he often said. Arik enjoyed good wine, exquisite food , thrillers, and espionage novels. His kicks came from fast cars, renovating old Harley Davidson motorcycles, off-road riding, and strong women who felt comfortable with short-term relationships. His job—Mossad's Chief of Operations— had made him addicted to adrenaline rushes. He enjoyed the stress and ambiguity offered him by his line of work.

Arik wasn't liked by everyone, and he knew it. There were those in the office who called him "Arik the Smiling Bastard" behind his back for being a control freak and a perfectionist. Others claimed he was a *nouveau-riche* because of his love of designer brands. Only few soul mates experienced rare moments of grace in which he relaxed and showered everyone around him with charm and witticism.

Arik activated his Rolex stopwatch, shoved the Blackberry into the cell phone armband, and put on the earphones. He began his six mile morning run by going down the 120 steps leading to the rocky beach beneath his cliff house at the edge of the Palmachim military base. When he reached the sand strip, Arik pressed the activation button on his cell phone. The unique *contratenor* voice of David D'Or singing *Che Faro Senza Euridice* rose from the earphones. Arik increased his pace and leapt between the rocks and reefs in the shallow water, slaloming through the scattered metal husks of burned tanks used as target practice aids for combat helicopters stationed at the IAF base.

The sleepy soldiers waved hello from their stations. The watchdogs, tied to a rail or running along the fences, barked at him and bared their teeth. He growled right back at them and laughed. Arik Bar-Nathan took pride in the fact he had transformed over the years from an overweight, asthmatic kid from a poor neighborhood in Haifa to a strong, muscular, and handsome man whose military position awarded him in a luxurious and cultivated villa situated in an upscale neighborhood on the cliff in the midst of a military base.

He recalled his childhood with loathing, the frequent asthma attacks, the wheezing, and desperate attempts to gulp air. As the son of Holocaust survivors, Arik couldn't possibly show any outward signs of illness. "Those who were sick were the first to be taken to the gas chambers," his mother used to whisper to him. In reply, he began a series of self-inflicted tortures. He beat his breast with a clenched fist and encouraged himself by saying, "I mustn't be weak, I must be strong!" But the wheezing and panting merely served to worsen his bodily weakness and brought him a terrible tiredness mixed with unbearable helplessness. As the years passed, he realized that the asthma attacks had been a sort of desperate plea for help, an expression of his need for his parents' attention. It was also an expression of annoyance with the forced role his parents had burdened him with of caring for his younger sister as a parentified child.

His anxious mother, who had already lost a husband and a son during the Holocaust, stayed home with him during the days he was sick and did not go to school. She sang him Yiddish songs, hugged him, and whispered in his ear secrets and stories about her far-off childhood in the little village of Sarnaki in Poland. She used to spoil him with Swiss chocolate bars or expensive, red-cheeked Italian apples she bought in the black market with money she saved and hid deep within her lingerie drawer.

From his father, Arik had known only anger and resentment. He was a short-tempered man who grew up in a God-fearing, hunger-stricken Hassidic family. As he failed as a *yeshiva* boy, Arik's father was sent to study and work as a shoemaker's apprentice in a far-off city. He always bemoaned his lost childhood but believed he mustn't spoil his children so they wouldn't turn out to be too soft in a harsh world.

As a weak, sickly child, Arik needed a loving, protective father figure. Devoid of such a father figure, and for lack of any other choice, he'd learned he must toughen up, put on a hard shell, and wear a mask of indifferent criticism on his face. He protected himself with an impenetrable armor of anger often mixed with cynicism, but deep inside remained that sick little boy who lay in bed, yearning for his parents' embrace.

After an hour of running, Arik turned back. His pulse rose to a 120, his warm body drenched with sweat, and he longed for his morning shower.

When Arik arrived at the door of his house, he heard a strange noise inside the kitchen, and his senses tensed. He knew from experience that the least likely event could take place in the least expected moment. Arik froze and listened, then crouched silently beneath the kitchen window. The noises became louder. He threw himself to the ground, crawled toward a large jasmine bush, dug beneath it, and removed a sealed metal box. The oiled cover opened silently on its hinges. Arik took out a Glock 17 pistol he'd buried there with two cartridges for emergency cases. He lay on his back for several minutes until he regained his breath and his body relaxed. Then he cocked the gun and advanced, crawling on all fours to the basement of the house where his service car was parked. Behind it, the Harley Davidson motorcycles he'd collected over the years glinted in the sun, a fully equipped repair shop beside them.

Arik crossed the garage on tiptoe until he reached a steel door. He tapped the entry code, and the door silently slid open. The noises were distinct now, coming from the floor above. Someone opened a faucet and turned on the radio. Arik slunk up the stairs separating the basement from the ground floor, his loaded gun at the ready. When he peeked around the corner, he relaxed at the delightful sight revealed to him. His nightly guest stood with her back to him, singing and moving to the sound of a Bruce Springsteen song, dressed in her underwear and one of his denim shirts.

Arik smiled. His suspiciousness, which had saved his life on more than one occasion, had turned out to be unnecessary this time. He hid the gun in the fuse box and went into the kitchen with a loud "good morning." Eva jumped and turned to him with a smile that revealed tanned Nordic features and a pair of large blue-green eyes. Her dirty blond hair was tied in a ponytail.

"I watched you through the living room window when you went down running to the beach and decided to shower and wait for you. Meanwhile, I've prepared us a little breakfast. I found some croissants, orange juice and a couple of eggs in the refrigerator, and strawberry jam in the pantry." She spoke fluent English, almost without a German accent. Her smile conveyed an air of confidence and unceremonious openness. Arik could tell she had used his *ylang-ylang* soap. It smelled good on her.

An itch crawled down his spine. It had been a while since a woman stayed in his house. His casual affairs normally ended at the lover's house or a hotel room with him apologizing at the end of the act and running back home by using various excuses.

Arik lightly kissed her forehead and headed upstairs to shower. When he came back, the rich scent of strong Arabica espresso rose from the kitchen, mixed with the smell of butter melting on the croissants warming in the oven. Scrambled eggs sizzled in a frying pan. The table was set for two, and a pitcher with orange juice and ice was placed at its center. Eva was curled in a black leather armchair, waiting for him. He smiled at her and they sat down to eat.

When did she manage to do all that? He thought with appreciation while sipping from the fine coffee and munching his croissant. Eva looked thirtyish, the age *When* at which women begin to seek their nesting place. After a night of lovemaking, she stayed in his bed and now had even prepared breakfast. How could he stop her from settling in his house?

"Arik..." She disturbed his thoughts. "You said you'd be going to Jerusalem this morning. Could you take me with you and drop me off somewhere I could easily get back to my hotel?"

"Sure," he answered reluctantly. "But you'll have to be ready in ten minutes."

"How about five?" She teased him with a smile.

He followed Eva with his eyes as she climbed the wooden staircase. His cell phone vibrated, the caller ID identifying it as the personal assistant to the director of Mossad.

"Yes, Itzik," Arik said. He didn't especially like the man who had arrived from the Administration and Human Resources

Department and attempted to impose bureaucratic order on the creative chaos that typified Mossad's work.

"The chief is not feeling well this morning. He injured his back again and needs to go to the hospital. He won't be able to attend the Heads of Intelligence and Security Services meeting with the prime minister and asks that you represent Mossad. Your job is limited to listening and reporting back, is that clear?"

Arik shrugged and hung up without saying good-bye.

Eva returned barefoot and wearing the black evening dress she had worn on the previous evening. In one hand, she held a red jacket, and with the other, she waved a pair of black-lacquered, high heel shoes. Arik's face was expressionless as he walked her to the garage's staircase. She followed him without saying a word, as if she were watching his back. Arik activated the alarm system and opened the car door for her. He raced the car outside, just the way he liked it, as the garage door closed behind him.

Arik brooded. He had never participated as the chief representative of Mossad in the Heads of Intelligence and Security Services weekly meeting. The job assigned to him by the head of Mossad—listening and reporting—did not fit well with his personality. As they drove east on the No. 1 Highway toward Jerusalem, it crossed his mind that a polite host should probably indulge his companion with a bit of conversation. "Tell me a bit about yourself, Eva. You're a doctor of what exactly? What was your thesis about? What are you doing in Israel?"

"I come from the Von-Kesselring family, a German junker family who lost our fortune. My father was a Protestant priest, so I've always been drawn to religion. I studied philosophy and theology at the university, my PhD thesis was called *Guilt, Compassion, and Forgiveness.*"

Another German trying to atone for the crimes of her father or grandfather, thought Arik.

"It's exactly what you think." Her candor and perception surprised him. "When in high school, I was exposed to the horrors of the Holocaust. To my great sorrow, I discovered my grandfather was a major in a Waffen-SS unit that operated in France and banished Jews. I've always asked myself how such a nice man was able to separate his work and personality so completely."

"And what exactly *were* you doing at my party?" asked Arik.

Eva looked at him with concentration, as though trying to read his thoughts. "When I was a student, I came to Israel to volunteer on a *kibbutz.* I was given adoptive parents—a German-speaking family. We remained in contact even after I returned to Germany, and I still visit them from time to time. Their daughter was the one who brought me. Her husband is abroad, and she was lonely. He has a senior position where you, yourself, work, right?"

"And what business do you have in Jerusalem?" Arik asked without answering.

"I'm a professor of theology and a faculty member of the German philosophy department in the Heidelberg University. I've conducted some research regarding Nietzsche and was invited by the Spinoza Center at the Van Leer Institute in Jerusalem to give a lecture series. I start tomorrow and found a nice hotel in the meantime: the American Colony Hotel. Are you familiar with it?"

Arik tensed. That hotel was favored by representatives of human rights organizations and foreign journalists who preferred to stay in the Palestinian eastern part of Jerusalem. Two bothersome thoughts now pecked at his mind: the meeting with the prime minister and the nature of the woman beside him. At least one of them could be dealt with immediately. He pressed the blue button on his cell phone and said, "Office," with emphasis. The voice recognition software repeated his command and within seconds he heard the voice of Claire, head of his bureau.

"Good morning, Arik. Are you on your way to Jerusalem?"

"Yes, and I'm not alone. I have a guest here, so please speak in codes and abbreviations. I need you to fax me the schedule and subjects to be discussed in today's meeting. The director of Mossad is not going to attend."

"Yes, I know," said Claire. "Talk to me when you can. There's an urgent personal matter you need to take care of."

"All right," Arik answered impatiently. "Send the fax."

The car printer emitted a feeble *bleep* and spat out a document with a *menorah* logo and the headline "Prime Minister Office—Top Secret." Arik took a brief glance, tore out the page, and shoved it deep into his left jacket pocket.

"I see that you, like most men, like your toys," said Eva. "You have a motorcycle collection in your house, and your car is equipped with all the latest gadgets. What are all these phones and antennae for? Do you work for the security services?"

"You must have been with a lot of men if you know so much about what most of them like."

Eva blushed. "Sorry. I'm being terribly nosy this morning," she said, sounding like a scolded child. "The Israeli mentality must be influencing me." Silence lay in the car from that moment on, though Eva's expression indicated her wish to continue the conversation.

When they reached the capital, Arik stopped next to a taxi stand. "You can get a taxi to your hotel from here."

"I'll be here for another week. I assume you wouldn't be interested in coming to the Van Leer Institute to hear a philosophical lecture about guilt, compassion and forgiveness, right?"

Much to his surprise, Arik discovered he wasn't so sure. Eva attracted him, but he also felt a vague sense of danger he couldn't put into words. Intelligent women aroused him, and Eva was a highly intelligent woman.

"In other words, will I see you again?" she asked directly.

"I'm a little busy, but don't worry, I'll know how to reach you," he said and sent her the friendliest smile he could muster.

Eva gave him a penetrating stare. "Sounds like a targeted kill," she said and exited the car.

Arik continued with his drive and caught a glimpse of Eva leaning toward the window of a taxi. The professional expression, "targeted kill," slipped from her mouth a little too easily. He made a mental note to find out anything he possibly could about his overnight visitor.

Chapter 2

The guard sitting in the booth outside the prime minister's office glanced at the monitor of the computer that automatically identified Arik's vehicle and raised the gate. Arik passed three more checkpoints before entering elevator that brought him up to the conference room in the prime minister's office. The office was ironically nicknamed "The Aquarium" because of the predatory piranhas that regularly swam in its waters.

The chiefs of the security services already sat around the large, round table and greeted him, some smiling, others grimacing with distaste. There was constant professional rivalry between the heads of Mossad and the Division of Military Intelligence at the IDF regarding assessments and analysis of raw intelligence from classified sources. The two organizations were united only by their dislike of the Foreign Ministry Office (whose people sat on the other end of the table) and their determination to hide sensitive information from them for fear of leaks.

The prime minister, a heavyset man who was chronically late, came into the conference room like a whirlwind. His military secretary and a trio of security guards ran right behind his plump buttocks. The prime minister's facial expression clearly indicated he was preoccupied with other matters. He examined everyone with his little, pale-blue eyes, gave them all half a smirk, and opened with a typically sarcastic remark. "They say the test of intelligence is its ability to create shortcuts. The weekly cabinet meeting is about to start in half an hour, so I want each of you to give me a brief, but thorough overview of what is new. Do not bother to repeat your reports."

The representatives of the intelligence services reported one after another, and it took just a few minutes for the prime minister to start scolding them for repeating and quoting information he'd already read in the daily intelligence report he received at his farm. The only subject he cared about was Iran and its progress toward achieving nuclear weapons.

"Where's the director of Mossad?" he spat at Arik.

"I'm sorry, sir. He's been hospitalized with a herniated disk—"

"I'm sick and tired of your bullshit excuses," the prime minister interrupted him angrily. "I want results, you hear me? Results!" He hit the table with his large fist and examined Arik with a chilling expression. "What's new with Ahmadinejad and the elections in Iran? What's going on with the centrifuges and the underground Fordow nuclear facility? What's going on with Hezbollah in Lebanon and the threat on our northern border?" His lower lip trembled with anger.

"Sir, with all due respect, may I suggest that the director of Mossad give you a face-to-face report about activities relating to these issues?" Arik tried to appease him in a soft tone that wasn't very typical of him.

The prime minister looked around the room, and his nose wrinkled in a nervous tick. He turned to his military secretary and spat, "This meeting is a waste of time."

He rose from his chair. "You,"—he addressed Arik—"you represent the director of Mossad here, right? I want you to report at my office in two hours and give me all those face-to-face details you think I should know." He finished the sentence with a snort of contempt and raced out of the room, accompanied by his entourage.

Arik left the conference room and retrieved his gun and cell phone from the security officer's safe. His cell phone showed seven unanswered calls from his sister, Naomi, and three from the office. He called Naomi as soon as he got into his car. "What's up, sis? What was so urgent you had to call me seven times and didn't even leave a message!"

The silence on the other end of the line did not bode well. It was apparent she was choosing her words carefully, and that made him very nervous.

"What happened? Is it Mom?" he asked with concern.

"Listen. I love you. You're the only brother I have. I've always respected and appreciated you, but you're so wrapped up in your own affairs, your divorce, and your trips abroad."

"If it's a question of money—"

"Cut it out right now!" she stopped him angrily. "You think you can solve every problem with money and connections? We're talking about people's feelings here. You never ask what's going on with me and Mom!"

"I'm sorry. I was only trying to help," said Arik, humbled. "Actually, Naomi, I've no idea what you expect from me. Tell me what the demands and requirements are, and I'll try to make the necessary adjustments."

"Here you go again. Demands, requirements, and adjustments… We're your family, not a part of some military operation! Where the hell did my big brother disappear to? The one who was so sensitive and caring, who meant more than my mom and dad to me…"

Her outburst shocked him. That was the first time he had ever heard his little sister speak with such rage and authority. He was struck with the realization that something new and intimidating had now entered his life.

"I'm in Jerusalem at the prime minister's office. I'm willing to cancel the rest of my appointments for the day and come to Haifa to meet you and Mom. Do you have time today?"

"Sorry, I'm at the airport, waiting for my flight. That's why I've been trying to reach you for several days. I left messages on your home phone on Saturday. I called you on your cell this morning and also left a message with your secretary— what's her name? Claire?—I'm going to Geneva for a week. There's a convention I need to attend. I need you to keep an eye out for Mom. She's starting to be dangerous to herself. The neighbors keep complaining about her leaving the gas stove on. She can't really smell it. If there's a gas leak or a fire, she won't notice until it's too late."

"So where is she now?"

"At home. Her nurse is on vacation today, and the neighbor said that she'll take care of her—"

"Mom has a nurse?" he interrupted her with amazement.

"Arik, now's not the time to bicker, but there are a lot of other things you just don't seem to remember. I'm not even sure you remember what I've told you about your own children, but we'll talk about that another time."

Arik fell silent, and Naomi continued, she almost sounded pleading. "Would you come to be with Mom so I can travel with a clear mind?"

"All right, now I finally get it. I'm a little slow. Sometimes I just don't get it when people talk too fast." He tried to make her laugh. "You go to Geneva and enjoy yourself, and don't worry about a thing. I'll be leaving for Haifa right now. Be available on your cell phone, and I'll keep you posted, all right?" he said.

"All right, and if the door to Mom's apartment is locked, there's a key at my place. It's hanging behind the front door. I need to go; they're calling us to board the plane."

"Good-bye. Have fun at the conference." Naomi hung up before he finished speaking. Arik then hurried to call Claire, "What was so important you couldn't wait telling me about?" he asked without greeting her.

"You hung up on me."

"All right, don't make a fuss. Now's not the time to educate me. What's it about?"

"You're not going to like it, but the Haifa Police called a few minutes before you reached Jerusalem. They've found an old woman wandering the streets of the Nesher neighborhood. She was pretty confused and spoke to them in broken Yiddish. The cops said she was wearing a chained tag engraved with two phone numbers: yours and your sister's. They couldn't reach your sister, and they've been calling you since morning."

"Tell me, have you lost your fucking mind?" Arik erupted. "*Now* you're telling me all that?"

"You should be ashamed of yourself! You're the one who kept interrupting me—"

"Well, you should have told me."

"Should have told you what? You wouldn't listen. You were too busy thinking about covering for the director and meeting the prime minister. I tried to reach your sister, but I understand she's abroad."

"You should have insisted. You shouldn't have given up," he screamed. "You completely fucked up!"

The sound of weeping immediately followed on the other line, and Arik hung up. He hated tears because they forced him to seal the tiniest cracks in his protective emotional armor. This phone call, added to the previous one with Naomi, threatened to infiltrate that famous armor of his. The surprising ease with which his emotional balance had been compromised both surprised and concerned him. Was he becoming soft in his old age?

A call came in on his secure line. The nasal voice of Dr. Alex Abramovich, head of the office's Intelligence and Research Division rose from the speaker.

"Have you heard the latest news about the chief? He's about to be promoted to become the Israeli Ambassador in the United Nations Office at Geneva. It looks like they're going to replace him with Major General Ben-Ami Cornfield, the prime minister's watchdog."

"Cornfield is going to be the new chief? Isn't he considered a has-been? He's a disabled veteran who had a car accident recently and can barely even walk with a cane."

"He's alive and kicking." Alex chuckled and continued in a more serious tone. "Which is bad news for all of us. Do you know what they used to call him back when he became the head of operations for the General Security Services? The Butcher! He's a sort of a sadist who's addicted to action. All he cares about is getting the job done, no matter how many casualties it takes."

"As usual, you're grossly exaggerating," Arik chided. "It's true that Cornfield has a reputation for having no patience for details and for being one who cuts straight to the chase, but still—"

"Don't be childish; it's the classic case of putting the wrong man in the wrong place. They didn't allow Cornfield to become Chief of Staff because they were afraid of him. Now they're going to appoint him Director of Mossad as compensation. Don't forget: he's more dangerous in this new position. He's going to operate from an environment that involves lots of money and power. That nurtures dictatorial and predatory qualities, especially with those already inclined to act that way. Add the fact that most of his moves are going to be covert and veiled by censorship, and you'll reach the same conclusion I have: all we can do is greet the master of the new world we'll all need to live in from now on."

"But how can the prime minister appoint an outsider? A man who didn't grow up within Mossad is going to have a very hard time taking initiatives without being familiar with the system and the way it works. He'll also need to approve operations suggested by the lower levels; operations he doesn't even imagine are possible. He has no idea the unique methods of operation we've developed here over the years. There are things that would seem unreasonable or improbable to an outsider," Arik muttered.

"Don't forget, people from outside the system have been appointed before," Alex reminded him.

"Only during times in which we've experienced a crisis of confidence. Bottom line, this position is all about mutual trust between the prime minister and the director of Mossad. Bringing in a character like Cornfield will only create unnecessary chaos and bring down the morale of employees all across the chain of command."

"You've worked with him before, haven't you?"

"Yes." Arik sighed. "I've worked with him when I was a Naval-Commando Company Commander, and he was Chief of Operations for the Israeli Defense Forces General Staff."

"So you know what I'm talking about. Who knows, he might appoint you as his second!" Alex burst into laughter and hung up.

Arik felt a terrible tiredness weighing his body. There was a lot of bad blood between him and Cornfield. He knew working with him was going to be an ongoing nightmare. Arik also felt the influence of his sister's emotional blackmail. He kept seeing an image of his elderly mother wandering the city streets aimlessly. Arik's mind raced. He knew he must talk to the Haifa Chief of Police and get details about what had happened to his mother, but before that, he needed to speak with Claire and apologize for his outburst.

Arik said, "Office," again, and the phone dialed the number for him. Claire picked up the phone.

"What do you want now?"

"To apologize for being an idiot. I'm going through a lot of things I need to think about right now, and I need you to be on my side. All right?"

Silence.

"I need three things." He interpreted her silence as consent. "First of all, I need you to arrange a conference call with the Haifa Chief of Police. Second, I need you to cancel all my appointments for today and tomorrow. And finally, I need a vacation; I need some time to think about a few things and take care of personal stuff. Please let the director's office know."

"Be available!" said Clair in a commanding tone.

Chapter 3

The Transaero flight from Moscow landed at the Ben-Gurion Airport. Businessmen turned on their cell phones as soon as the airplane had touched the ground, and a few elderly nuns and a flock of grim-faced priests stepped down the gate sleeve. The few Israeli tourists among them pushed their way through, wanting to be first to the passport booths. Ruslan moved closer to the wall to let them pass. A conflict with an Israeli was the last thing he needed at that point of time.

At the passport booth, he handed the police officer his Russian passport and immediately pulled his hands from the counter. She gave him the usual, brief glance, which lingered as she examined his flat features; slanted eyes; long, black robe; the black velvet hat on his head; and the large, silver crucifix that adorned his chest.

"Sir, what's the purpose of your visit in Israel?" she asked in fluent Russian.

"I'm a neophyte. I came to the Holy Land to study at the Russian Orthodox College in Jerusalem."

"Do you have a student visa and admission documents from the school?" asked the police officer.

She examined him again and typed his name into the computer. The biometric examination conducted by the camera hidden above matched the details of the photo in the passport. A comparison with the Interpol database had yielded no results as well. Still, the young border police officer hesitated.

"I have an invitation letter from the Archimandrite Tihon Pavel Gremidar, head of the Russian Orthodox Mission in the Holy Land," said the young priest with a bashful smile and lowered eyes.

The police officer looked at the document that carried the official seal of the Israeli Consul in Moscow, and stamped Ruslan's passport with a student visa for a full year.

Ruslan silently passed his colleagues, avoiding their attempts to make conversation. He took an old-fashioned hand-carry suitcase from the baggage conveyor belt and went out to the passenger reception hall where his eyes wandered until they found the public restroom sign. He entered one of the booths and came out dressed in a faded pair of jeans and a t-shirt.

He exited the Terminal and headed to the Public transport stations.

"Daniel Hotel in Herzliya," he said to the taxi driver in English.

"Tourist?" asked the driver.

"No. Scientist."

Ruslan kept silent all the way to the hotel, much to the dismay of the driver who was eager for an opportunity to detail his thoughts and opinions about the political and security situation in Israel and share his life-changing decision to stop hitting on Israeli girls because only European girls were in his league.

Ruslan entered the hotel lobby, filled out the guest registration forms, presented his passport, and received a keycard for the room he'd reserved.

The receptionist examined him. "Ruskie?" he asked.

Ruslan answered with a noncommittal murmur.

The receptionist, who insisted on being friendly, added in Russian, "A little something to eat? Our room service closes in fifteen minutes."

"No, thank you," Ruslan answered curtly and turned to the elevator.

Ruslan, eldest son of the late Ramzan Akhmatov, had arrived from Chechnya to perform a duty and fulfill a destiny.

Chapter 4

Highway 1—West of Jerusalem

The drive to the Judean foothills was long and tedious. Arik silently cursed drivers who ran traffic lights or cut him off.

His cell phone rang, and he slammed the button to answer.

"I'm conferencing you with Police Commander Solomon Toby, Chief of the Haifa Precinct," Claire let him know in a frosty voice. "Patching through!"

"Hello, Commander Toby. This is Arik Bar-Nathan from the prime minister's office. I understand you have a Yiddish-speaking elderly lady who's a little confused at your station? I was happy to hear your vigilant police officers recognized the fact she was wearing a nametag with my details on it."

"Excuse me, but who are you, and how are you related to her?" asked the police chief suspiciously.

"I'm her son, and I'm a little worried."

"I am sorry, but she's no longer here. She was sent to the hospital by ambulance about an hour ago," said Toby sympathetically.

"Could you please tell me more about the circumstances?"

"Of course." Toby began to read. "Mrs. Ethel Rechtman was found wandering in the Nesher Central Bus Station, muttering to herself in an unintelligible language. A patrol car that had been called by passersby was unable to ascertain her identity, as she didn't carry any identification papers. When a patrol officer approached her, the lady started screaming, 'Nazis! Nazis!' and ran away until she got tired, sat on a bench and allowed the patrol woman officer to approach her. At first, the officer thought she was mentally disabled and suspected she had escaped from the nearby psychiatric hospital. Then the officer noticed a gold medallion hung around her neck, engraved with the names Arik and Naomi as well as their phone numbers and the lady's blood type. The officer called Naomi, who didn't answer. Next she called Arik next and was answered by his secretary, who was given the details of the incident event and told the officer she would take care of it." Toby finished and took a deep breath.

"Thank you commander. I'll be taking care of everything. I'm on my way to Haifa right now."

"Good luck!" said Toby.

Arik hung up and keyed up the voice recognition once more. "Office."

Claire answered. "Your schedule is clear for the next two days," she said before he could even ask. "They're worried about you here, so I said you were going on a two day vacation. Everyone is rooting for you and jealous at the same time. By the way, I heard you've found yourself a German bombshell at your birthday party. Good for you. Have fun."

"Thank you, Claire. It was an amazing surprise party. Thank you from the bottom of my heart for organizing it," said Arik, who suddenly remembered he hadn't even bothered to thank her.

Claire muttered something and hung up.

The traffic dwindled out after the Sha'ar Hagai interchange, and Arik made good use of his 3,500CC BMW engine. He put the flashing red and blue police strobe up on the vehicle's roof to prevent unnecessary hassles from the national traffic police and looked at the speedometer needle, which leapt all the way to 100 mph. After that, his driving became instinctive, and his mind was overtaken by doleful childhood memories.

In one of the alleyways of the Talpiyot Municipal Market in Haifa there was a small greengrocer shop where his parents had worked for their living from dawn to dusk. The shop had served as their refuge from all the memories and traumas of the Holocaust. Taking care of merchandise, sales, and customers, along with the busy routine of daily labor, suppressed the painful recollections of two brokenhearted people who had both lost their first families, including spouses and children. At the end of each tiring day, they dropped on the sofa in their little dump of a flat under the Ottoman Bridge, turned on the radio, and listened to *The Voice of Israel* in Yiddish. It was a radio show they religiously listened to, intended to help Holocaust survivors reunite with their lost family members, refugees who wandered abroad, or those who had never managed to reached Israel.

Arik and his sister Naomi were substitute children. They filled the place of their parents' beloved first children, born from a previous marriage of love and happiness in another era. People who had been annihilated in the Holocaust. As substitute children, they lived in a suffocating atmosphere in an overprotective house. They grew up under the shadow of terrible memories and had to deal with constant emotional blackmail that expressed itself in their responsibility never to become sick, injured, or (God forbid) die. In addition, Arik needed to be responsible both for himself and his sister who was three years his junior. He wasn't expressly requested to do so, but he realized his parents expected him to act that way. Arik was charged with bringing his little sister back home from kindergarten or school, feeding both her and himself, washing the dishes, and taking care of the house.

The coming meeting with his aging mother made Arik shudder. He and his sister weren't closely familiar with the ravages of old age. There weren't many elderly people left around them during their childhood, as most of their extended family members had been murdered in the Holocaust. Their father passed away when Arik was thirty-eight and too busy to care for his mother. His sister, Naomi, was the one who had assumed that responsibility. She stepped into the shoes of being her mother's caretaker, taking her to see doctors, doing all her grocery shopping for her, and renting out the apartments their parents had bought as an investment. His mother, a very active woman by nature, used all the spare time she suddenly had to volunteer in various organizations and feverishly cook for Friday night meals to which she'd invite her children and their families. He couldn't understand how that vital woman had turned into the confused old lady the police had found at the Nesher Central Bus Station. And she had a nurse! When did *that* happen?

After arriving at the hospital, Arik strode into the Emergency Room and immediately looked for the doctor in charge. In front of the entrance door, he saw an information desk with two receptionists. A long line of people stretched from the window, all of them waving forms and paperwork impatiently. Arik walked past them straight into the emergency ward. He strode past gray curtains and glanced at the beds behind them. His mother wasn't there. A male nurse wearing a green robe instructed him to get out and added, "Or I'll call security."

Arik nervously replied, "I *am* security, and I'd like to speak with the person in charge."

A young doctor in the final weeks of her pregnancy popped out of nowhere and approached him. "Hello, my name is Dr. Orly Sharon. Can I help you? You seem a little lost."

"Yes, thank you." Arik lowered his voice. His anger suddenly subsided and was replaced with horror. He recalled he was supposed to personally report to the prime minister in Jerusalem at that very moment.

Chapter 5

The Coastal Highway—On the Way to Palmachim Air Base

The highway was jammed with traffic in spite of the late hour. The image of his mother lying in a hospital bed and mumbling to herself refused to leave his mind. He drove nervously, almost wildly. His thoughts kept wandering back to the things his sister had told him that morning, especially to one sentence: "I'm not even sure you remember what I've told you about your own children." Mixed feelings he wasn't familiar with swirled in his mind along with existential thoughts about the meaning of life and family. He felt deeply ashamed for the fact he couldn't recall the last time he had spoken with his children.

His son, Michael, was in India, and he didn't really know how to contact him, but Nathalie was in Jerusalem. Arik sent a hand to his phone, hesitated, then changed his mind. Before he called his daughter, he needed to speak with someone who understood more about such matters. He dialed Claire's cell phone number and was answered with a businesslike, "Yes?"

"Please forgive me again for being so aggressive this morning. I have a lot of things on my mind. My mom's in the hospital."

"So, as usual, I need to serve as your lightning rod until the storm passes."

Arik ignored her sarcastic remark. "Can I ask you a personal question?"

"That depends. How personal?"

"It's about my girl. You've raised two wonderful daughters. Tell me, why am I such a failure as a father? Why can't I have a decent relationship with my children? I want to make it right before it's too late."

Claire was silent, surprised by his candor.

"I have no one else to talk about it with," explained Arik and continued to unburden his heart. "Nathalie and Michael grew up with Rachel my ex-wife, and she's poisoned them against me."

"You gave her every possible reason to do that."

"To her, maybe, but never to the children. They're all grown up, and they need to understand. Anyway, Michael ran away to some *ashram* in India, and Nathalie just keeps avoiding me. Tell me, what have I ever done to deserve this?"

"Arik, you should be the first to know everything in this life is a matter of perspective. The only question is what kind of story you choose to tell to yourself."

"I'm not buying this cliché. The truth is not a story; it is based on facts. What actually happened is the only question one should ask himself."

"Try telling yourself the story of your divorce from Rachel's and from your children's perspective."

"What does it have to do with them? It doesn't concern them, and they're not a part of it. Their mom and dad didn't get along and got divorced. End of story. Then their mother poisoned their minds, and they ended up inventing a twisted story under her influence!" Arik said heatedly.

"It's not necessarily like that," said Claire softly. "But I don't think I'll convince you. By the way, you've never told me what Nathalie is doing."

"She's a student at Hebrew University." said Arik. Pride mixed with his words, but he added bitterly, "She's studying psychology and already uses all the professional lingo to explain how I've abandoned her when she needed me most as a teenager. She accuses me of being unfaithful to her mother. She hates me and avoids speaking to me. But that doesn't prevent her from regularly demanding money, giving me shopping lists, and asking for gifts from abroad."

Claire sighed. "That's only to be expected. Don't you get it? She's punishing you."

"As it happens, I *do* get it! She's not even trying to hide it."

"Arik, what exactly do you need from me?" Claire asked in a sympathetic voice.

"I don't know, but I was hoping you'd give me some sort of a possible way out. Some good advice, a key, something. Anything. I'm looking for a way to get closer to my kids and to make amends. When it comes to these matters you are much better than me."

"Can you get Michael on the phone?" she interrupted, as efficient as always.

"No. I think he has a cell phone, but he never gave me the number. And his mom… You know."

"What about Nathalie?"

"I don't have her cell number—just the phone number in the dorms."

"Call her."

"What should I tell her?"

"Just tell her how you feel. Let yourself be off-duty for once, and set the inner Arik free. Be the sensitive dad and loving person you are when you allow it."

Call her dorm room? Arik was pretty certain she would slam the phone as soon as she heard his voice. Best case scenario, she'd conduct a polite conversation with him then give him a full report about all the things she needed him to buy for her and how much money she needed to deposit in her bank account."

"You still there?"

"Yeah, I was just thinking. Thanks, Claire. You know I love you, right?"

"Flattery will get you everywhere. See you after the vacation." She hung up with a smile, and Arik knew she was no longer angry about the morning incident.

Arik went over the list of contacts in the cell phone placed on his knee. A passing vehicle honked when his car drifted across the lane, and he swerved back. Then he tapped his daughter's phone number, guessing no one would answer; she was supposed to be in class that time of day.

"Hello?" her voice drifted hesitantly across the line.

"Hi, daughter of mine. It's Dad. I have some spare time today, and I wanted to spend it with you. If you're available, that is."

Silence.

"Nathalie?"

"All of a sudden you remember I exist?"

"I missed you. I know I'm not exactly father of the year, but I care for you deeply."

"You never call just like that. There's always a reason."

"I was with my mom today," he said sadly. "Grandma's in the hospital, and her condition is not good. She's suffering from Alzheimer's. When I got out of there, I decided I need to dedicate more time to my family."

"So why are you saying that to me? You finally have a moment to spare, so you called to emotionally blackmail me?"

"No, Natush. Family is the only thing a man has. I've been trying to find a way to reach out to you for a long time without knowing how. I suppose it's all up to me, and I'm sorry for not doing more."

Once more, silence.

"So tell me, what's up with you? How's school?"

"Since when do you care?"

"I've always cared. Right after you, Michael, and your mother had left the house at the air base and moved to Jerusalem, I tried to schedule joint therapy sessions with you. You agreed in principle, but never really cooperated."

"What did you expect? I was starting my teens when I found out my dad was cheating on my mom with her best friend. As a teenager, I needed a father figure, but you were never there for me."

"Nathalie, I don't want to start another war of accusations, but your mother wasn't exactly the perfect wife either. I don't know what she's told you—"

"I don't care about your bullshit!" Nathalie shouted. "That's between you and Mom. I'm talking about you and me. I'm talking about what you did to Michael when he was a little child who looked up to you as a hero. Forget about me—why weren't you there for *him*?"

Arik considered whether he should tell her his ex-wife had issued a restraining order that prevented him from coming to visit whenever he wanted to, and his sort of job prevented him from coming to see them on the visiting hours the court had set for him. Finally, he decided silence was the better policy. He recognized a glimmer of hope in the conversation. Perhaps the fact she had actually confronted him, for the first time, marked the beginning of a relationship.

"Maybe we should meet and talk about it?" he suggested. "I'm driving from Haifa back to the Tel Aviv area now. I can drive up to Jerusalem. Maybe we could go to that seafood restaurant you like so much?"

"I don't go there anymore. I only eat kosher food now."

"You're tired of eating shrimp and calamari with basil and tomato sauce?" he asked smilingly.

"Yes. My faith has been getting stronger this past year. Anyway, I can't do it this evening. I'm going to study with my rabbi's wife."

"Don't tell me you're thinking about becoming religious."

"Why not? They accept me for who I am in the rabbi's house. At least I have a spiritual father there."

"Do you want me to get you something from abroad if I need to go in the near future?" Arik tried bribery, a policy that had never failed him before.

"No thanks. I'm trying to learn to settle for what I have."

"Do you need money or anything else?" He tried again.

"No, thank you. I have everything I need, praise the Lord."

"See you soon, then?" Arik tried hopefully.

"Have a good month," she answered and hung up.

He couldn't help himself. Arik stopped at the nearest bus stop and checked the calendar in his cell phone. Indeed, it was the first day of the Hebrew month. Apparently her faith really *was* getting stronger.

"You have a good month too, daughter of mine." Arik released a short, sad sigh .

Chapter 6

David Fischer, director of Mossad, entered the conference room. As usual, he was dressed in a tailored three-piece suit and wore an Oxford alumni tie.

"Before we begin," he said, speaking with a pronounced Anglo-Saxon accent, "I want to thank all of you for calling to inquire about my health. As you know, I've been suffering from backaches for many years. The pressure I've been getting from the prime minister's office is not improving my condition."

The men sitting around the large table all stifled smirks. Each of them had been exposed to that pressure in one way or another.

"Don't get me wrong," added Fischer, "the prime minister has every right to demand we sabotage the Iranian president's plan to turn his country into a nuclear superpower. It is also his legitimate right to limit my term as the head of Mossad to four years, a term which, as you have probably already heard, is coming to an end in a few weeks."

"There were rumors," replied one of the men, "but we still don't know who is going to replace you."

Fischer ignored him. "Let's get back to the subject of Iran." He pressed a button and the photo of a woman wearing a *hijab* appeared on a large screen. "This is Mariam Halachi, head of the Mujahideen al-Islamiyya organization. Alex, please give us all the information you've accumulated about this organization."

"Mujahideen al-Islamiyya is a terrorist and guerilla organization that's been operating in Iran since the sixties of the previous century," Dr. Abramovich read in polished Hebrew that a slight Russian accent still clung to. "In its first years, the organization united the resisting factions against the Shah's regime and even fought side by side with Khomeini. But after the Iranian revolution of seventy-nine, it wasn't allowed to take part in the rising new regime because of its leftist inclinations. Many of its members were arrested or even executed by the Ayatollahs, and the others were exiled. From the beginning of the eighties, they have been located in various countries in the area and operating against the clergy regime."

"Real saints," Fischer hissed.

Alex smiled. "Saints suffer more. Isn't that written somewhere in the Scriptures? Anyway, in spite of its political views, the Mujahideen al-Islamiyya has been declared a terrorist organization in the United States and Europe. Right now, the organization is in dire straits. I think we should take advantage of their situation. All members of the organization are Iranians who are very familiar with the area. They have agents and supporters scattered among the educated elites in universities all across Iran. We can assist them in their attempts and even help remove their organization's name from the list of terrorist organizations. We can also offer them financial, perhaps even military, support in return for cooperation that could greatly benefit both parties."

"What influence could such a small organization have on the Iranian empire?" asked Fischer.

"The Iranians are much weaker and more vulnerable than they make themselves out to be. The way they're running their country is a part of Shiite culture, the culture of a minority operating within a Sunni majority. They've always used fraud and psychological warfare in order to survive."

"Hmm… Interesting," Fischer said. "We'll still need to check how much we can trust them." He turned to a tall, slim man sitting at the end of the table. "Jonathan, do you have an agent that could thoroughly look into this?"

Jonathan Soudry, the head of Tzomet[2] Division, answered. "We have such a senior agent in Azerbaijan. We call him 'Georgi'. He's in contact with the Mujahideen. They even gave us an advance in the form of a slightly disturbing intelligence message." Jonathan looked at those sitting around him, lingered on the expressionless face of the director, then read from a page he was holding. "An assassin for the Hezbollah is somewhere in the world, perhaps even on his way to Israel, and plans to kill a high-ranking official in Mossad in retaliation for the death of one of their own."

"I have a theory about who the arrows are pointing at," said Alex as he turned to Fischer. "I've already told you they'd be looking for revenge. But that's just a theory. A mere speculation…"

They all knew perfectly well who the theory focused on: the head of the Caesarea Division, the one responsible for operations and assassinations worldwide. But Arik didn't

---

[2]A division in Mossad that operates agents and informants across the globe, according to foreign publications.

seem concerned in the least. He appeared as if he hadn't even heard what was said.

His two vacation days had ended. His mother was in the care of a nurse, and the prime minister had passed him an unequivocal message through his military secretary, Major General Amishav: "Expect retaliation. You know he doesn't like being stood up. He's the only one allowed not to show up."

Now Arik just stared back at everyone and asked indifferently, "What? Sorry, did I miss something?"

"We're concerned for your health," said Fischer with typical sarcasm. "You haven't been paying close attention to what has been said here, have you?"

"Yes, well, I… My mother's very sick, and I must—"

"Let me repeat," Alex cut him off in a matter-of-fact tone. "The Hezbollah has sent an assassin to avenge the assassination of a senior in their organization. He intends to take out one of our own. As you're responsible for assassinations, we're afraid that—"

"No one will get close to me." Arik was washed with the feeling of over-confidence that always took over him in moments of danger. Suddenly, he felt the absence of the gun he had deposited before entering the conference room. "I'd shoot him first."

"I'm not sure you'll have the chance," Fischer said calmly. "You know better than anyone else here that there are many ways to kill a person. Not only by shooting." He began to collect his papers. "I don't intend to convince you to take precautions or set you up with a bodyguard. That will be a job for the next director of Mossad." He smiled. "Perhaps this is the right moment to let you know his identity." He waited a moment, relishing the tension he had created. "Major General Ben-Ami Cornfield," Fischer announced ceremoniously.

For a moment, an expression of concern darkened the faces of some of those seated around the table. The rest visibly demonstrated their contempt.

"Good day, gentlemen!" said Fischer, and he left the room, abandoning them to their fates.

Chapter 7

On Tuesday afternoon, a small convoy of vehicles swerved from Road No. 5 and drove up a road marked by a sign reading: *Private Road—No Trespassing!* Beyond the bend, in a spot hidden from the sight of the thousands of drivers passing through on the highway, a sophisticated roadblock obstructed the convoy's way. Beside it stood Mossad's chief security officer. He had been standing there for over an hour, exposed to the midday sun and waiting for his new boss: Major General Ben-Ami Cornfield. The security officer, a tall, grim-faced redhead, hated tardiness even more than he hated the scorching sun.

He approached the first vehicle and motioned for the driver to open the dark-tinted window. Surprisingly, the rear window that slid open instead. A large, curly head peeked out and said in a low bass voice, "I'm Cornfield. I think you're waiting for me."

"Yes, sir. I'm Dov Shapir, head security officer. I'll just ask my men to write the details of your driver and the people sitting in the other car. This will only take a minute. I need you to prepare your ID's or your official certificate."

"Hurry up. We haven't got all day!" Cornfield growled as the window slid back up.

A few minutes later, the cars followed a white SUV marked "Security" to the top of a hill, upon which stood a five-sided building, modernly designed and overlooking the coastal highway. The security officer got out of the SUV and rushed to open the door of the vehicle behind it. The tall figure of a man sighing with effort emerged. In spite of his advanced age and missing leg, Major General Cornfield appeared as tall, muscular, and slim as a professional basketball player. He climbed the stairs quickly, leaning on a mahogany walking cane with a carved head shaped like the head of an eagle.

"The director of Mossad is waiting for you in his office," said the security officer and pressed the elevator button. When they reached the fifth floor, he slid a magnetic strip card in the slot beside a wide door, and it opened with a quiet *whoosh*. At the other end stood two young, handsome men dressed in suits whose waistcoats bulged due to the concealed weapons beneath. "Welcome," said one of them in an official tone. "Please take out all metal personal objects and place them in the plastic basket. Additionally, you'll need to deposit your personal weapons, cell phones, watches, and beepers as well as belts with a metal buckle."

"Then you'll go through the metal detector," said the second one with a grim face.

"Are you serious?" Cornfield snarled. "I have a metal prosthetic leg—do you expect me to place it in the basket as well? Open the goddamn door right now!" The anger distorted the right side of his face and exposed the fact that his evil expression partly resulted because of his glass eye, which was barely noticeable when his face was relaxed.

"I'm sorry, sir," said the security officer. "Those are the security regulations. One cannot enter the director's office with weapons or devices with transmission capability." He spoke with the peace resulting from the knowledge that he represented good order and routine. "Once you're Director, we can continue to discuss changing the security regulations," he added, then paused and changed his mind. "You can come with me this one time, but your assistant will need to go through the procedure," he said and motioned for the guard to open the electric door.

"Join me when you're done," said Cornfield to his assistant with resignation and followed the security officer, indicating his displeasure by huffing and puffing angrily.

The heavy glass door revealed a large room, its large windows overlooking the Herzliya shore. A handsome, middle-aged woman approached them. "Please, come with me, Major General Cornfield. The director is waiting for you." She pressed a concealed buzzer, and another door opened. At a large table, carved in its entirety from Carrara marble, sat the outgoing director of Mossad, Dr. David Fischer, who rose with a bitter smile on his lips to shake the hand of his successor.

Cornfield ignored Fischer's extended hand and walked about the room. He examined, with visible distaste, the alabaster marble floor covered with expensive Persian rugs and the walls plated with reddish cherry wood on which hung original paintings of famous Israeli artists. He raised his eyes above the table. The emblem of Israel, a brass *menorah* surrounded by the portraits of the president and the prime minister, hung right behind the director's head. Books of poetry, philosophy, reference, art, history and military strategy rested on the bookcases. The photo of an elderly woman, surrounded by her children and grandchildren, rested on one of the shelves. "My family." Fischer chuckled shyly. Cornfield didn't respond. Still looking about with authority, he went and opened a side door, which led to a small restroom with a shower. "Is this where you screw?" He chuckled while winking with his healthy eye and making an obscene gesture with his hand.

Fischer was amazed even though he didn't expect refined manners from someone who was close to Prime Minister Lolik Kenan, a ruthless politician who betrayed everyone who helped him climb the ladder. The latter had been complaining for quite some time about Mossad turning into a weak organization devoid of any fighting spirit under Fischer's leadership. He called Fischer a second-rate foreign minister behind his back. No one in the prime minister's office recognized Fischer's longstanding contribution, and no one recalled the fact he had acted as the special emissary for three former Prime Ministers and set the stage for the peace agreements. The way he dressed, like a British gentleman, and the way he spoke with a slight British accent made him appear as a recent immigrant in their eyes. His age transformed him into a dinosaur whose expiration date had long been past due. The prime minister's people used to mock him when they met at The Farm, the prime minister's house in the south, and imitated his speech while sitting around tables laden with whiskey and roasted lamb.

Cornfield wasn't too fond of Fischer either. Having lost his leg and eye because of a grenade tossed at him by a double agent, he simply couldn't understand how a man heading the Mossad, the major security organization, a man whose only weapon was a Montblanc fountain pen, had never seen combat or participated in a war. He examined Fischer with his one healthy eye with demonstrated contempt. Fischer gave him back a worried look, deeply concerned. "I prepared a detailed file for you with all the information you'll need to settle in," he said and presented Major General Cornfield with a thick, leather file folder. "I know you army people don't have a lot of patience for reading, so I tried to focus on the important things."

Cornfield wordlessly took the file folder, measured its weight and thickness, then slammed it on the large marble table.

"When would you like to start?" Fischer asked with tired acceptance.

"How about right now?" Cornfield barked, went around the table, and dropped into Fischer's chair. "You got a problem with that?" he asked, making himself comfortable. He sent his massive hand below the large chair to adjust the lifting lever.

Fischer looked at him, slightly amused. "Why not?" he said in agreement. "Sometimes it's best to simply cut to the chase." He opened a closet door and collected some personal belongings into a battered leather bag. "I'll send someone to collect the rest of my things early tomorrow morning," he said when he reached the door.

"Don't worry," Cornfield growled. "No one will touch your junk."

As soon as Fischer had left, Cornfield hurried to open the file folder. For a long time he busied himself with reading one document after another. Suddenly, he stopped and lifted the telephone receiver.

"Yes, sir," the voice of a young secretary soldier was heard.

"Where the hell is my assistant, Zimmer?" he screamed.

"He's right here, getting briefed by Fischer's assistant."

"Send him in right away!" Cornfield slammed the phone down.

The door buzzed, and Shlomo Zimmer, who had been Cornfield's loyal personal assistant for many years, entered the room. Cornfield waved a document at him.

"There's something surreal here," he said. "An assassin for Hezbollah wants to assassinate the head of the Caesarea Division to avenge his father's death. Sounds like a load of crap. I know this Arik too well. He's nothing but a paper tiger. This entire organization is rotten from the core. They hear a little gossip and start pissing in their pants. Anyway, I want you to check the source for this one."

The assistant looked at the document, raised his eyes to his commander, and said, "There's an order here, signed by Fischer, to assign him a personal bodyguard."

Cornfield slammed the table with his fist. The metal spheres of a Newton's Cradle placed on the large table came to life and began to swing and tick. "Never! Write on that shitty document that I'm annulling it. This is my first order as the new director of Mossad, and I don't care what anybody says. Is that clear?"

Chapter 8

Kfar HaNagid Village

Cornfield woke at dawn in his house and went down to the ground floor, dressed in shorts and a tank top and leaned on crutches. He loved the house his father had built after emigrating from Bulgaria during the fifties. He enjoyed sitting beneath the *pergola* every morning and drinking Turkish coffee simmered in a pot. Intentionally, he turned his back to the large living room, crowded with modernist sculptures and paintings his wife, Amira, collected. He hated the artwork she liked and much and preferred to look at the blooming garden and the cactus rockery where the first flowers of summer began to blossom. The smell of hay rose from the neighboring cowsheds. He took a deep breath, inhaling that rich smell and the morning tranquility.

Amira came down to the ground level as well, dressed in a flowered nightgown. They had met forty years before when she had been his secretary in the Mista'arvim, the undercover counterterrorism unit of the Israel Defense Forces. They'd been together ever since. They'd lived parallel lives and slept in separate rooms for years. The intimacy they had once known had been replaced with a life of comfort each lived by themselves. Cornfield was busy with his military affairs in the

Israel Security Agency or the prime minister's office. Amira, on the other hand, spent her days in the company of her grandchildren and friends. She also volunteered for various organizations and regularly went to sing-along evenings or folk dancing in the nearby town.

During the weekends, he cooperated with all her requests and demands: dishwashing, grocery shopping at the supermarket in the nearby city of Yavne, patiently listening to the stories she felt compelled to tell him about a book she had read or the exploits of one of their grandchildren. She served as the anchor that connected him to reality, his children and grandchildren, and always made excuses for his frequent absence from family events and glorified his dedication to his work. It was also convenient for her to be left on her own. "Ben-Ami is keeping our country safe," she would confide with her children.

She looked at him sipping his coffee. He looked very serious and distant. She could feel his discomfort. "What's up?" she asked. "Is Lolik bothering you again?"

Cornfield looked at his wife. She had done something to herself. Some sort of cosmetic surgery, perhaps a breast or facial lift? Her visage had become different, glowing. He decided it was best not to ask. Secretly, he had always suspected she was having an affair with the man who was their neighbor in the Palmachim Military Air Base. "Arik the Smiling Bastard" as his detractors called him. Cornfield was definitely one of them, and his suspicions only served to strengthen the resentment he felt toward the handsome officer. And yet he never dared to confront his wife about the subject. Mainly because he had been neglecting his duties as a husband for many years.

"There's still some coffee left in the pot. Let me warm it up for you," he said and rose on his one leg, supporting himself with his crutches.

"Ben-Ami, I'm not drinking Turkish coffee anymore. I drink herbal tea. With your diabetes, you should consider cutting down on coffee and sweets as well," she called after him.

"How do you take your tea?" he shouted from the kitchen.

"Pick some lemon verbena, a handful of mint, and lemongrass from the herb garden. Wash them with cold water, cut them with the little scissors in the drawer under the gas stove and pour some boiling water. No sugar, please."

"Where is your herb garden, and since when do we have one?" he asked with embarrassment as he limped back to the *pergola*.

"Just sit down. I'll make my own tea," said Amira impatiently and headed to the kitchen.

When she came back, carrying a pitcher of greenish tea, Cornfield clenched his lips and hissed, "I've got news."

Amira froze. Every time Cornfield gave her 'news' it meant there would be more burdens for her to bear.

"The prime minister asked me to accept the role of the director of Mossad."

Amira chuckled. "Are you asking for my opinion or simply informing me?"

"I went there yesterday afternoon. I'm starting on Sunday. This is going to be the job of a lifetime!"

"When are you finally going to retire?"

"Five minutes before I die," Cornfield recited his regular mantra. "I'm sure you already know that."

As always, she found him predictable. She swallowed her anger along with all the things she had wanted to say to him when she was younger during the long nights she spent by herself in bed. Now, in her advanced age, she spent those nights watching stupid television shows and reading romance novels. She told him nothing of her yearning to be touched, to have someone caress her and speak words of love in her ears. Instead, she just said, "In that case, I insist that you clear your head a little before you begin. Esther and Joe Amar have a vacation house in Taormina on the coast of Sicily. It is a historic, reconstructed dream house in the old city. I showed you some photos, remember?"

Cornfield didn't. He shrugged. "Who took the photos, Esther?"

"I took them! Don't you remember? A coastline full of inlets and bays, a deep blue sea and on the other side, the smoking Mount Etna... I was there with them last year, while you were roaming Europe with your boss. You really don't remember?"

Cornfield didn't remember and wasn't listening. "I need to go to the Jerusalem today. I've got a lot of things to discuss with the prime minister and the rest of the gang before I officially take office."

"Ben-Ami, you're just like a little kid. I need to protect you from yourself. You'll end up collapsing! That's how you became diabetic in the first place! Besides, you're so busy with your top-secret nonsense, you don't even have time to listen to the news on the radio. Just so you know, the prime minister flew to Washington last night to attend the Jewish Congress Annual Conference. Then he's flying to Miami to attend the Israel Bonds conference. He won't be back in the country before next Monday. The weekly cabinet meeting on Sunday has been cancelled as well, in case you're wondering."

Cornfield cursed in his heart. His wife was right. Now he would need to think of a good excuse not to stay home so he won't start climbing the walls with boredom. He needed to be active, to be constantly challenged. The trouble was, he was temporarily unemployed. He was no longer the prime minister's advisor and, at least officially, not the director of Mossad yet. Under the circumstances, even going on a trip with Amira seemed like a good idea.

"All right, then. We'll go to… Where did you say it was? Sicily? All right. But I'll still need to go to Jerusalem this morning for some arrangements. I'll meet you at the airport later. Update Eve, my secretary, about all the details. Tell her to send my diplomatic passport here and pack some clothes for me. All right?"

"All right," called Amira, already on her way to the kitchen, carrying the empty pitcher and glasses.

"And pack my new prosthetic leg as well," he shouted after her. "This one's starting to bother me. Bring some painkillers too. The weather's still cold, and my broken ribs are starting to say hello again."

Chapter 9

Israel Intelligence Heritage & Commemoration Center—
Tel Aviv

Six in the morning. A short, stout, and muscular man with Caucasian features parked a rented dirt bike in the shrubs next to the fence of the Israel Intelligence Heritage and Commemoration Center. He climbed up the nearby hill and hunched over with his head low, so the spotters patrolling the roof of Mossad Headquarters on the other side of the hill wouldn't notice him. He wore a camouflage suit with a hood. In his pocket rested an international ornithologist certificate, specializing in bird migration. It was issued by the University of Omsk, located in southwestern Siberia. In his backpack, he carried a camera with a telescopic lens, powerful binoculars, and a can of red spray paint and two bottles of pure benzene disguised as mini bar vodka bottles.

The abundant rain that had fallen in the winter made the vegetation on the hill grow tall. But now, it was dry due to the heat of the summer. He felt secure. He settled in a small clearing overlooking a curve in the road outside the roadblock guards' field of vision. From among the dry thorny bushes, he watched the vehicles entering Mossad Headquarters with his binoculars. He knew that the division heads drove a BMW

X5 SUV, so he focused his attention every time such a vehicle stopped in front of the roadblock. He wrote the license plate numbers and sought one with a bent front bumper.

At seven fifteen, the vehicle he had expected arrived. He leaned forward and focused the binoculars on the right spot. The car passed in front of his eyes, slowly moving up the sharp curve. He followed it until it disappeared. Then he took out the red spray paint from his backpack and marked the underbrush around him with color. After that, he crawled very slowly down the 300 yards of thorny bushes that separated him from the sharp curve. It took almost an hour before he finally reached it and hid the two small bottles of pure benzene that would explode and cause a fire. He had to keep low as a patrol car passed by. Then he carefully crept down the hill heading west, still hidden by the bushes.

The dirt bike awaited him like a trusted steed. He mounted it with a jump and took off to seek an escape route that would take him from the hill back to his hotel by the Herzeliya Shore north of Tel Aviv just five miles away. On the way, he stopped at a payphone, the last one remaining in the neighborhood, and quickly dialed.

"Armenian Patriarchate of Jerusalem," a voice said from the other end of the line.

"Brother Vasili, please," he asked in Russian.

The receiver was placed down, and a few seconds later a heavy bass voice was heard. "Vasili speaking."

"This is Ruslan. I need to collect the holy vessels you've prepared for me."

"Come after the morning prayer," said Vasili. "I'll meet you in the Cathedral of St. James. Then we'll go to the Seminary School, where your package awaits you."

At the appointed time, in the Armenian quarter at the old city of Jerusalem, Ruslan waited in the cathedral. Vasili passed him by without saying a word, and Ruslan followed him to the other side of the road. There was a small sign on the door, written in Armenian: *Seminary*. They went into a chilly entrance hall and turned to a side room stacked with boxes of candles, candlesticks, and folded robes. A large, elongated bag rested on the table, closed with wax strings and lead seals. The initials "DIP" were imprinted on its side.

"This is the first time we've received a diplomatic pouch straight to the seminary," said the priest. "Don't you think it might arouse suspicion?"

"It won't be here in a minute," Ruslan said emphatically, then slung the bag over his shoulder and left.

The bike sped down Mount Herzl toward Ein Karem Canyon, passing by the Hadassah Medical Center and disappearing between the trees of the John F. Kennedy Forest next to Eshtaol Village. The parking lots, packed during the weekends, were now completely deserted. Ruslan sat next to one of the many wooden picnic tables scattered in the park, cut the strings and wax seals with a sharp knife, and opened the bag. His hand sought and felt the oiled parts of a sniper rifle wrapped in black burlap. He fished them out carefully, peeled off the cloth, and expertly put them together. Then he added a silencer and a dimmer tailcap. Finally, he slid the telescopic sight and sought a target for practice.

Looking at the *wadi* facing him through his long-range sight he noticed an old Chevy vehicle parked between the bushes with a couple making love inside. Over half a mile separated him and the vehicle with the lovers. He lay on the ground and watched, generously allowing them to climax.

The head of the man filled the lens and the crosshair was placed on his forehead. Ruslan held his breath for a moment and gently squeezed the trigger. A light crack was heard as the bullet sped to find its target at 4,000 feet per second. The man's skull burst like a ripe watermelon dropping off the back of a truck. The woman opened her mouth and emitted a scream that immediately turned to silence as the fragments of her head mixed with those of the man. Ruslan mounted the dirt bike and headed back to the his hotel at Herzliya shore. He felt the same sense of elation he always felt after a kill.

After midnight, Ruslan left his hotel room and drove to the hill next to Mossad Headquarters. He hid the bike between the bushes and started his climb . He took the binoculars out of his backpack, and set them to night mode. The starlight night vision came on, and he saw his own footsteps from that morning between the thorn bushes, as well as the spot he had painted, glowing red. He put the sniper rifle together, opened the bipod, and prepared two cartridges. Then he cut an opening in the bushes and wore a multispectral camouflage ghillie suit that would prevent anyone using night vision from spotting him. Now all he had to do was wait for morning.

He planned to shoot tracer rounds up the hill, ignite a fire in the thorn field next to the road, and create a smoke screen that would stop anyone who arrived at the sharp curve in the road. He needed a few seconds of delay to make the target slow down and allow him to hit it with precision.

Dawn arrived, and vehicles began to move up the road. He paid them no mind. At ten past seven, he noticed the BMW with the bent front fender turning into the private road leading to the top of the hill. He was already filled with elation, just a portion of the happiness he'd feel after pulling the trigger. Another minute or two and he would shoot a bullet straight into the forehead of the son of a bitch who killed his father and injured his younger brother in Paraguay. He watched Arik with hatred as he stopped at the roadblock, lingered for a moment, then advanced toward the curve.

Ruslan fired two tracer rounds at the benzene bottled he had hidden early in the morning and set the thorn bushes around the curve on fire. The driver, who had not yet noticed the fire, continued to drive the vehicle up the road. The morning breeze was stronger than usual, and the road filled with smoke within seconds. Ruslan hurried to place the crosshair on the driver's head, but it disappeared within the smoke. He decided to fire a shot at its estimated location.

The bullet fired out of the long rifle put a hole in Arik's car, just a few centimeters above his head. Arik instinctively hit the gas pedal, and the car sped forward while the assassin, with the eagerness of a predator, followed with a quick volley of three additional bullets to the spot he fired before .

Then everything turned upside-down.

Someone, perhaps a resourceful guard or his intended victim, ran toward Ruslan, fully exposed and firing regular shots from pistol as he ran. The two roadblock guards ran after him and opened automatic fire into the bushes. The wind changed its direction and returned the smoke straight into Ruslan's lungs. He hoped to retreat, but feared getting up now would expose him. The fire advanced toward him, threatening to trap him in the burning field.

He started crawling backward across the scorching earth, shouldering the rifle and the equipment-filled backpack. The smoke that almost suffocated him protected him from those seeking to kill him until he disappeared from their field of vision. Then he stood up and frantically ran down the hill. A few bullets whistled close to him as he started the motorcycle's engine and sped down the dirt road into a nearby orange orchard. The howl of sirens cut through the air. Ruslan didn't know whether they belonged to the fire engines coming to take care of the fire or to a police patrol car that had somehow managed to locate him. He hid the bike, the rifle, and the equipment between some bushes, returned to the coastal highway on foot and flagged a taxi to get back to his hotel room. This time, he had failed.

There was an old Chechen saying: "He who lives by the river knows where the animals come to drink." Ruslan had studied the course of the river, familiarized himself with the place the animal drank from, and simply needed to wait for its return.

Chapter 10

Taormina, Sicily

The old village at the top of the hill proved to be a real jewel.
Far more beautiful than Cornfield had anticipated. The small
cafes, seafood restaurants, *piazzas*, and churches wrapped
him with a pleasant sense of comfort. The house they stayed
at was spacious, yet inviting. *Where did that great bastard Joe
Amar get the money to buy such a house from? It must be worth
millions*, he wondered with admiration as he walked between
the large rooms stacked with antique, rustic furniture.

"While you and your friends were lying in ambushes,
playing boy's games, he studied at the Massachusetts Institute
of Technology, created a high-tech company from scratch,
along with a few friends, mortgaged his parents' house,
and employed Esther as a free secretary until some giant
American corporation bought them for a lot of money. Now
he's working there as the R&D vice president. He's spending
six months in San Francisco and six months in Israel."

Cornfield whistled in mock enthusiasm. "Well, I'm going
to rest. Wake me up in an hour, and we'll go and have dinner.
You feel like fish or meat?"

Amira didn't answer. She froze, charmed by the island
views. Cornfield shrugged and limped to the bedroom where
he threw himself on the bed and fell asleep immediately.

Dinner was marvelously delicious. They finished their meal with glasses of chilled Sicilian Regaleali Bianco wine, which had a wonderful aroma. Cornfield leaned back, looked at Amira, who was dressed in a red evening dress which made her look charming, and for the first time in quite a while, felt at peace. A large, reddish moon hovered above the restaurant porch. "*Luna rosso*," called the waiter and pointed at the moon as if it were his own creation.

That night, Ben-Ami and Amira slept together in a large, soft four-poster bed. Perhaps it was the wine that dulled Cornfield's constant desire for control. The couple ended up cuddling and kissing passionately until their passion dwindled, and they both fell asleep in each other's arms.

At five o'clock in the morning, Ben-Ami's cell phone rang, shattering the peace. Amira woke up with fright and saw an Israeli number on the screen and the name "David Fischer" above it.

"Hello?" she answered in a whisper. "Ben-Ami's sleeping. Can he get back to you later, please?"

"I'm sorry for the inconvenience and the early hour, but there's simply no choice. Please wake him up. It's urgent."

Amira sighed and placed the phone between the pillow and her husband's ear.

Fischer, sharper and more vigorous than usual, opened without introductions, "Wake up, Cornfield. Things are happening."

"How come you're running things? I've been away for a day, and you've already managed to crawl back into my seat?"

"Your seat is empty. Strictly speaking, you don't have the cabinet's official appointment yet. That is why they turned to me."

Cornfield couldn't stand the thought the information he needed was at the hands of another person. "What happened? Explai—"

"You'll need to come here if you want explanations." Fischer cut him short. All his European manners disappeared, and it seemed he enjoyed scolding Cornfield. "Aren't you supposed to be the director of Mossad? Where have you disappeared to?"

"Sicily," Cornfield mumbled in a voice hoarse with sleep.

"Which side of the island?"

"How should I know? I got here yesterday afternoon. The place is called Taormina."

"I know where it is. We'll send one of our own to take you to the airport. I'm arranging a private jet to bring you here within three hours. Keep your phone on."

"What time is it in Israel?" Cornfield asked with a heavy voice.

"It's already six AM here. Our man will hand you an envelope with background information for your eyes only. Please burn it before boarding the plane."

"All right, all right, Fischer. Don't fret. I got it." Cornfield returned to his usual rough tone of voice. "Do I at least have time for breakfast?"

Fischer hung up. Cornfield sat in the middle of the bed, his graying hair disheveled, and his one healthy eye rolling in its socket.

"What's going on Ben-Ami? The honeymoon's over? You've had too much quality time with me?" asked Amira with open disappointment.

Cornfield answered her with a childish tone: "Enough, Amira. Come here and give me a good morning kiss. You think there's something to eat around here? After last night, I'm as starved as a donkey in heat." He flashed her the same smile that made magic forty years back. Before the injury that had distorted his face and made him lose his eye and right foot.

"Let's have coffee first."

They sat on the villa's porch, which was surrounded by fragrant jasmine bushes, and drank from small, porcelain cups. A strong espresso for him and herbal tea for her. The first sunbeams broke through the eastern skies. Huge tourist boats docked in the bay.

Amira couldn't conceal her sadness. "What did he want from you?"

"I don't know," Cornfield answered.

Amira glanced at him suspiciously. "You're cutting our vacation short, stopping a wonderful process that could revive our relationship, and you're not even willing to tell me why?"

"Because I don't know!" Cornfield shouted. "Someone is coming to give me classified material, so even after I'll read it I won't be allowed to tell you anything. After all these years with me, you suddenly want to be in on the secrets?"

Amira rose and said with an expressionless face, "Go shower and prepare, I'll go down to the bakery to get some bread and prepare us a light breakfast."

When he came out of the shower, the familiar smell of Israeli food welcomed him. "Are you preparing *shakshuka*?" he asked with wonder while buckling his new prosthetic leg above a special sock. Amira didn't reply.

Cornfield leaned on the kitchen table and watched her as she filled a frying pan with fresh garlic, eggplant cubes, tomatoes and capers. She fried the vegetables in olive oil, then carefully placed on them fillet slices of fresh sardines, a few canned anchovies, and some eggs. She sprinkled coarse salt and black pepper on everything and closed the lid.

"Now we just need to dig into that fresh bread you've brought," said Cornfield with a wide smile. Amira continued to be quiet.

Cornfield dipped his finger and tasted the dish. His healthy eye widened and his smile widened even more. The food was incredibly tasty. "What's it called?" he asked.

"*Caponata,*" she answered briefly.

The sound of the doorbell made them both jump. Cornfield looked at Amira. Uncharacteristically, she didn't react. He wobbled to the entrance and opened the heavy wooden door. At the entrance stood a crop-haired woman. She looked about thirty-five, wore a close-fitting green leather suit and had a Bluetooth headphone in her ear. She spoke to him in Hebrew with a heavy Italian accent. "Hello, I'm Iris Fortisini. I'm from the 'office'. I came especially for you." Then she handed Cornfield a sealed brown envelope.

"How'd you know what house we're at?" Cornfield was surprised.

"The moment you answered your cell phone, our satellite located you. I just put the information into my navigation software, and it brought me straight here. Simple, isn't it?" She chortled.

Cornfield took the envelope and went into the bedroom. He heard his wife speaking to their guest in fluent Italian. "Would you like some coffee, *signorina*?"

"She's so polite, it's annoying," he said to himself.

He tore the envelope open and quickly studied its content: assessments made by Dr. Alex Abramovich, head of the Research and Intelligence Division, regarding an assassin roaming the country with the intention of assassinating the division heads, possibly the director of Mossad himself. It also included a report about the assassin's first operation: an attempt to assassinate Arik Bar-Nathan that had taken place at the entrance of Mossad's headquarters this morning. "That son of a bitch," Cornfield shouted angrily. "He's always getting all the attention!"

"Did you need something?" Cornfield heard Amira's voice from beyond the door.

He didn't reply and turned to the restroom. The smell of fresh lemon coming from the scrubbed toilet was replaced by that of smoke as he burned paperwork. Cornfield allowed the ash to drop into the toilet bowl and flushed several times.

"Is something burning?" asked Amira as he returned to the porch.

"Just my heart," Cornfield answered angrily.

The guest blurted a few words in Italian. Amira answered her, and they both burst out laughing. Cornfield was amazed. Since when did Amira speak such fluent Italian? How little did he know about his wife?

"*Andiamo*?" asked Fortisini and stepped outside, collecting Cornfield's small trolley bag. Ben-Ami located his cane and, a moment before walking out the door, gave Amira an apologetic look. Amira returned a slight nod and approached the door to close it.

"How long will you stay here?" he asked while placing his arm on her shoulder affectionately.

She released herself from his grip, demonstrating her insult. Iris turned her face from both of them, so as not to embarrass her superior, and opened the passenger door of a red Alpha Romeo Giulietta. Cornfield hissed a nasty curse. The sports car was too low and narrow for a man his size and with his handicap. He bent and forced himself inside with loud groans, humiliated. He felt a need to get back in control.

"How long have you been working for the office?" he asked in the lowest, most authoritative voice he could muster.

Iris remained silent and concentrated on driving down the winding road, shifting gears expertly. Her phone rang, and she answered in Italian. It sounded to Cornfield like she was instructing someone.

"What division are you in?" Cornfield moved on to the next question.

She still didn't answer, and Cornfield stopped pressuring her. They both knew she wasn't allowed to answer the questions of a stranger she had just met. All she was asked to do was to bring him to the airport. But he wasn't "just a stranger" and felt a desperate need to prove it to her.

After about twenty minutes of fast driving the Alpha Romeo went into the airport through a back gate. A small private jet already started its engines at the end of the runway, ready for takeoff. The car slowly drove all the way to the plane's passenger door. In Sicily, just like everywhere else in Italy, a few Euros allowed Cornfield to avoid going through the terminal and the usual security procedures.

"Have a good flight, sir. You'll find a small cooler with some fresh *cannolis* from the finest bakery in the area. They told me you like Arabica coffee, so I've prepared a thermos as well. You'll be in Tel Aviv two and a half hours from now. Have a good flight and say 'hi' to the homeland for me. Or, as we say in Italy, *complimenti a casa.*" She gave him a handshake, as firm as a tennis player's, then turned to go back to her car.

"Hold on," Cornfield called after her. "The name's Iris, right?"

"Iris." She nodded.

"And do you know who I am?"

"Yes, but only by word of mouth. As far as I'm concerned, you haven't been identified."

"All right, all right," said Cornfield in a fatherly tone. "Can I ask you for something?"

"That depends," she said with a smile.

"I don't know where you're normally stationed, but I'd like you to stay in the area and keep an eye out for Amira, my wife, so nothing happens to her. I don't need a close surveillance. Just tail her from afar, all right?"

"I'll let my station manager in Rome know. I don't think there'll be a problem with that. Have a good flight, boss."

Cornfield smiled. That last word made him feel much more confident.

In the late afternoon hours, Amira came out of the villa and strolled toward the beach. She walked alone on the deserted beach, bending from time to time to collect odd-shaped and colored seashells for her grandchildren. The sun slowly set, coloring the sea and sky with gold and red.

When she turned to return to the vacation apartment, she noticed someone watching her from inside a red sports car. Much to Amira's surprise, that someone waved hello to her, Amira hesitantly waved back. The vehicle door opened, and whoever was inside got out and walked toward her. Within seconds, the mystery was solved. Amira recognized the woman who had visited them in the morning.

"*Buonasera*," Iris greeted her kindly. She wore a tight pair of jeans and white t-shirt that emphasized her slender, stalk-like figure.

"What are you doing here?" asked Amira in Italian.

"Oh, I decided I needed a little vacation too." Iris smiled. "Feel like a swim? The water's warm this time of year."

"But I don't have a bathing suit; I just came down for a stroll."

"There's no one for miles around, loosen up."

Iris took off her clothes and placed them in a little pile on the sand. Amira, mesmerized, looked at her small breasts, her pubic hair, shaved into a narrow strip, and her tanned body.

"Are you coming or what?" asked Iris and began to walk toward the water.

Amira looked around with embarrassment. She felt both dread and excitement. She had not undressed in front of another woman since her days as a young soldier. Iris was nothing like her old army friends. She oozed carefree sexuality. When she laughed and hurled her body against the waves, her firm, tiny buttocks awoke new and unfamiliar sensations in Amira.

After she had made sure no one else was around, she took off her shoes and her clothes. She placed them on the sand, next to Iris's clothes and walked to the waterline, covering her breasts with one hand and her crotch with the other.

Iris burst out laughing. "Are you ashamed?"

"I… How do I say it…" Suddenly all her Italian disappeared. "I'm not your age, I've had three pregnancies, and my chest…" She removed her hand from her breasts. "See for yourself. Besides, I haven't even shaved my legs."

"That's just the way I want you," Iris called and took her into her firm arms in a tight embrace.

Two hours later, the two lay naked and exhausted from pleasuring each other in the four-poster bed.

Iris lay in the same exact spot Cornfield's heavy body had been just hours before. "If he knew you're here..." Amira whispered.

"But he does," answered Iris in a whisper. "He was the one who sent me."

Amira straightened up, leaning on her elbow and giving Iris a penetrating glance.

"To keep you safe!" Iris completed her sentence and erupted into a loud, infectious laughter.

Chapter 11

Arik drove down the well-kept streets lined with Islamic style mansions with *arabesques* decorating their walls, tall *mashrabiya* windows, and large inner balconies concealing gardens or orchards. Arik allowed his navigation system to direct him to the Van Leer Institute. When he arrived, he saw that there was no parking available, so he simply parked on the sidewalk and placed the blue-red strobe on the dashboard. Then he checked the message he had received from Eva, which contained the full program of the convention at the Spinoza Center. The lecture series was open for the general public and focused on the subject of guilt, compassion and forgiveness, concentrating on the works of Friedrich Nietzsche. The convention was scheduled to start at seven PM. His watch indicated ten past seven.

He ran down the corridors of the modern building, hoping that, just like any other event in Israel, this one would be slightly late to begin as well. And so it was. When he reached the right lecture hall, he saw that the lecture had not yet started, but Eva was already up on the stage, dressed in a gray, tailored suit, her hair tied into a golden knot behind her head. Her large eyes brushed the audience, and Arik hoped she was seeking him. He sat at the end of the lecture hall and unsuccessfully tried to catch her eye.

Eva began her lecture in English: "Tonight, I don't want to talk about guilt. It is a burden for us Germans to bear in the most obvious and noticeable way. When World War II ended, the German government took full responsibility and admitted to the mass murder of Jews. Since then, it has constantly sought to secure the position of Israel in both the financial and the military aspects. Tonight, I'd like to speak from my viewpoint as a young German about something much more difficult. I'd like to speak about compassion and forgiveness. The process of forgiving requires the active participation of both the seeker of forgiveness and the one who needs to forgive."

Arik's thoughts carried him far from there. When was the last time he had asked anyone for forgiveness? He apologized now and then, mainly to Claire, but almost never felt a real need to be pardoned. Who could he ask forgiveness from? His subordinates, from whom he constantly demanded perfection? The enemies he'd killed?

"So forgiveness is an interpersonal activity, but it is also a personal, reflective process. Sometimes it is an ongoing process, and other times it is done because of inner resistance. That is why, even when we know we ought to forgive someone, we find the act of forgiveness to be so difficult. Paradoxically, the more hurt we are, the more we need to forgive, but in such cases it is also much more difficult for the hurt party to forgive. A minor slight, such as pushing while standing in line, is easy to forgive, but the need for forgiveness isn't very pressing. It is much more difficult to forgive something terrible, but the need for forgiveness is vast and critical. How can we solve such a paradox? Will the two parties ever be able to build a bridge that will connect the offenders and the ones who need to forgive?"

Arik's thoughts now wandered to his parents. Did they ever find it in their hearts to forgive the ones who had tried to murder them? He never thought of asking them, and now there wasn't really anyone to ask.

"Forgiveness doesn't allow you to close the wounds of the past and open a new page; it only covers the events that had happened. It is more difficult, perhaps even impossible, for people who went through the Holocaust. Hence the origin of the forgiveness paradox. When I demand an apology, I force the offender to take part in a sort of humiliation ceremony which allows the creation of balance between the offender and the offended. This is why forgiveness allows a common life and eventually reflects the good character of the one who is forgiving."

An uneasy murmur, mixed with restrained anger, passed through the crowd. Arik shifted uneasily in his chair as well because of Eva's last statement. He wasn't convinced by the concept of forgiveness as expressed by Eva. At heart, he was an avenger.

"I know what I'm saying may be difficult for some of you to hear, and I apologize for it. Forgiveness means the ability to overcome the feelings of humiliation and hostility. The emotional protest following forgiveness is not about restraining your grudge, but about overcoming it. Maimonides said that a wise man who knows God is immune to hurt from other people and, therefore, doesn't feel like a victim. Hence, a person who holds himself in high esteem won't feel hurt upon becoming a victim, as he is aware of his own worth. Based on such concepts, we need to correct ourselves before we can correct the world."

The creaking sound of chairs being pulled back filled the lecture hall. The implications of Eva's words—that Holocaust victims who demand forgiveness suffered from a low self esteem— caused a group of elderly people to leave the lecture hall in protest. Eva ignored it.

The lecture hall emptied a bit, and Arik noticed the presence of a dark-haired, muscular man with extraordinary features, dressed in a leather jacket. He leaned on the wall not too far from where Arik was sitting and looked tense, as if expecting something to happen. Arik noticed his fingers. Each had a different tattoo, and he vaguely recalled they had something to do with Russian mob hierarchy. The man snuck a glance at Arik, but his slanted eyes immediately returned to focus on Eva, who continued. "In my opinion, one can forgive while still feeling a sense of moral hatred. Forgiveness doesn't necessarily mean reconciliation. It doesn't justify the act or ask one to forget it; it only assists in overcoming difficult thoughts and emotions, in overcoming the desire for vengeance."

Another dissenting murmur rose through the audience. The conference's moderator struck the table with his wooden hammer, trying to call the audience to order.

Arik was no longer listening. He concentrated on the dark-haired man who didn't appear to belong in the conference or the lecture but didn't seem embarrassed in the least.

"Many people want to forgive, but are unwilling to forget. Which means they would like to let go of their difficult emotions, but their ego is unwilling to let go of the sense of strength that resentment offers them. So now I'll say something that may anger a few members of the audience even more, but I'm still going to say it as a true friend of the Jewish nation: for the past sixty years, you Israelis have built your national ethos as one that depends upon the Holocaust. You've developed a nationalistic, messianic, victimized perception which, in my opinion, only serves to hurt second- and third-generation Israelis."

Arik barely heard Eva's last few sentences. He closely examined the dark-haired man and hardly heard the protests of the audience members.

"Using the memory of the Holocaust to justify the occupation or other acts of war is unacceptable to me and to growing parts of the western world. The inability to forgive has become a burden for the victims themselves, a factor that hinders the way you Israelis conduct yourselves and see the world. Today, the state of Israel is strong enough as an independent entity and is accepted by the entire international community. Remembering the Holocaust is a historic duty, both for us Germans and you, the sons and daughters of the victims. Nevertheless, this memory cannot be a factor in the making of political or military decisions, especially when considering the complicated reality with which your politicians need to cope."

The audience was now furious. Difficult words were said. A number of people waves clenched fists at the stage.

The man with the tattooed fingers continued to watch, and a thin smile rose to his lips. Arik was willing to bet he hadn't understood a single word of what was said.

"Thank you," said Eva and nodded—a slight gesture which enchanted Arik. "I'm done."

Eva's words finally sank in, and Arik, still looking at the tattooed-fingered man, felt the rage bubbling within him.

He wasn't angry at Eva because of her words but because of the memory of the Holocaust embedded in his soul, the price he had paid when losing his own childhood in order to parent his sister, Naomi, because of the mental and physical injuries inflicted upon his parents and the price he needed to pay because of his mother's anxiety to lose another child, an anxiety because of which he had never learned to ride a bicycle, skate or swim. He was angry for never having grandparents to spoil him, for the demeaning treatment he had had to suffer at the hands of native-born Israelis who claimed the victims were led like lambs to the slaughter.

"Does anyone want to respond? Any questions?" asked the mediator.

Arik immediately rose and went to the microphone at the front of the lecture hall. Eva was surprised to see him, but attempted to hide her emotions. Arik spoke in Hebrew and Eva hurried to put on the simultaneous translation headphones.

"Professor Von-Kesselring," he began, sensing the eyes of the dark-haired man scorching his back. "In your lecture, you addressed the logical, philosophical and psychological aspects of forgiveness. I'd like to speak of the emotional aspect as viewed from my own, personal perspective. If I understood you correctly, no wrong should be unpardoned because, by lacking the ability to forgive, we simply harm ourselves, and there is nothing worth harming ourselves for. Am I right?"

Eva approved with a nod.

Arik continued excitedly, forgetting all about the mystery man for a moment. "In 1989, the year that marked the two hundredth anniversary of the French Revolution, the Chinese General Secretary was asked to sum up the influence of that revolution. His surprising answer was that it was too early to make an assessment. You, madam, are speaking of forgiveness, compassion, and forgetfulness a mere sixty years after the Holocaust, the worst industrialized massacre in history, a massacre whose initiators had regarded their victims as mere objects, lacking any soul or identity. As a second-generation Holocaust survivor and an Israeli, I cannot forget and am not allowed to forgive. On whose behalf would you like me to forgive and absolve? On behalf of my grandfather, who was murdered in Treblinka while only fifty years old along with most of my large family—a family I have never known? On behalf of my grandmother, who survived Dr. Mengele's despicable experiments in Auschwitz only to die of typhus and weakness just days after the camp was liberated by the Red Army? On behalf of my older brother, who I never knew because he was shot to death by SS officers who wanted to know how many bullets they could put in the body of a Jewish baby tossed into the air like a clay pigeon before it landed on the floor? On behalf of my father, Leibish Rechtman, may he rest in peace, who managed to escape a prison camp for Polish soldiers captured by the Nazis and took two bullets to his tailbone and pelvis—bullets that remained embedded in his body to the day he died? On behalf of my mother, Ethel Rechtman from the house of Beiman, who was left scarred and mentally hurt after losing her son and husband who had been killed as a Polish soldier when she was only nineteen? My sister and I, second children to bereaved and hurting parents, served as a kind of correction for them, an attempt to heal a deep wound in their hearts. But their hearts constantly bled with painful memories. As children, we unwillingly took upon ourselves the role of replacing the dead of our own people." A shiver passed through Arik's hands and his hand clenched the microphone until the knuckles turned white. "This is why, madam, when I am asked about forgiveness, I reply with questions of my own: On whose behalf? Am I even allowed to forgive? Do I have a mandate to do that? Did they ever permit me to serve as their representative in your forgiveness project?" Tears filled his throat and made him choke.

Eva's eyes shone. She identified with his plight.

"Sir, with all due respect," said the moderator, "unless you have an actual question to ask the lecturer, I must ask you to finish."

"I don't have any questions. I'm finished," Arik said and was rewarded by applause from the audience.

He was embarrassed by the applause and quickly retreated back to his seat at the end of the lecture hall.

A few others of the people present stepped to the microphone to ask their questions. Arik stopped listening. Later on, they all went out for a coffee break in the main lobby. Journalists flocked around Eva. Cameras clicked and flashlights illuminated her beautiful face again and again.

The sound of a bell announced the beginning of the next session. The audience returned to the lecture hall, and Arik motioned the smiling Eva to follow him to the nearby corridor. All the office doors in the corridor were closed, and Arik wrapped his arms around Eva's body. They both clung to each other without words, connected by a silent embrace. Arik wondered what she felt about the difficult words he had hurled at her, but avoided asking so as not to spoil the sweetness of the moment. She spoke first, and her words surprised Arik, who was still very emotional. "Why didn't you call me? I haven't heard from you since Sunday. I received a lot of tempting offers for dates and dinners, but I waited just for you." She stroked his face, looking around her with concern. "Can I invite you to dinner at my hotel? The conference ends at nine. They'll be raising a celebratory toast to mark the end of the conference, but I'll try to escape."

The sense of unease he created by her lecture and the presence of the slanted-eyed man suddenly merged with the sense of suffocation that overtook him whenever a woman tried to establish their relationship.

She brought her mouth to his ear and the scent of her breath filled him with pleasure. "I decided to stay here in Israel," she whispered. "A few months ago I asked for a sabbatical at the Hebrew University, and today they let me know it has all been arranged."

Arik disentangled himself from her with a sharp movement.

"Aren't you happy?"

"I'm sorry, Eva, I'm overworked right now. I told you I'd find you, and here I am. I'll find you again." He turned and disappeared escaped to the far end of the corridor.

A chilly Jerusalem night welcomed him outside. When Arik got close to his car, he noticed the street lamp before it, as well as the one behind it, were both broken. He stopped and tried to recall if that had been their condition when he had arrived but wasn't successful. The days were long that time of year, and when had parked his car, the streetlights had not yet been turned on. He was suddenly filled with a sense of apprehension. He thought about leaving the car and taking a taxi but feared what the new director of Mossad,

Cornfield, would say when he found out the head of the Caesarea Division was afraid to approach his own car just because it was parked between two broken streetlamps. Arik walked up the sidewalk on the other end of the street, parallel to his car, and bent to check the lower part of the vehicle. The guard standing on the other side, at the entrance of the President's House, looked at him with careful interest. Arik took out his ID and called him. "I work for the prime minister's office. Did you see anyone walking about this car?"

The guard came to him and examined the vehicle with its government license plate ending with the digits 77. "No, I haven't, and there's not much traffic in the street this time of night."

"When did you start your shift?"

"Six PM."

"And the streetlights weren't working at the beginning of the evening?"

"They haven't been working since the beginning of the week."

Arik followed him when he returned to the guard station and hissed a curse. That baseless fear, along with the words he had said in the conference, took him back to his childhood and the rule he had set for himself never to be frightened or think of retreat. He took one step down the road, followed by another, and crossed toward his vehicle.

And then it happened.

A heavy dirt bike with a dark figure riding it emerged from nowhere with a deafening sound, racing toward him and blinding him with its headlight. Arik tried to retreat to the sidewalk, but the biker aimed for the exact spot he would occupy a few seconds from then. Arik tried to change directions and cross the street running, but the biker adjusted his course as well. Arik noticed a pile of trimmed foliage that blocked the sidewalk and thought about picking up one of the branches to jump back and hit the biker once he would reach him. Then it occurred to him the biker might be armed. He sent a hand to his pistol holster, rolled on the asphalt, and crouched in a firing position, thinking that the entire defense staff of the President's House would show up within seconds of hearing the sound of gunfire.

His prediction proved wrong. Two powerful beams of light flashed from the end of the street. They blinded both Arik and the biker. A large vehicle that emerged from the Van Leer Institute raced straight toward the biker while sounding ear-piercing honks. The biker tried to avoid it, but the vehicle hunted him in the same way he had tried to hunt Arik just moments before. A loud thud was heard, followed by a scream and the screech of brakes. The vehicle continued its wild ride and disappeared beyond the curve of the road. Arik didn't get a clear view, but he thought he saw the symbol of a leasing company and the shadow of a woman behind the wheel.

Arik ran, pistol in his hand, toward the biker who lay on the road, illuminated by the headlights of the upturned motorcycle. His motorcycle jacket sleeve had been torn, exposing a brown shoulder bearing a tattoo of a sword embedded in a skull with a crowned snake wrapped around it. Arik knew that any member of the former Soviet Union bearing such a tattoo could only be a gang leader, or "*vor v zakone*" in Russian.

When the biker saw Arik approaching him with a pistol in his hand, he rose to his feet with the nimbleness of a cat, picked up the bike from the road and raced on it against traffic. Arik tried to chase him, considering whether or not he should open fire in the middle of a residential neighborhood, but the assassin already disappeared down the street, scorching the air with fumes from his bike's exhaust.

Chapter 12

During his brief stay in Sicily, Cornfield's had men transformed Fischer's luxurious bureau into a spartan military office. The gleaming alabaster floor was covered with pale white ceramic tiles, the carved Carrara marble was replaced by a large wooden desk, the priceless Persian rugs were stored somewhere, and the cherry wood paneling was removed from the walls, now painted white. A large photograph hung on one of them: the proud image of three Israeli F-15 fighter jets flying above a snowy Auschwitz concentration camp in Poland. Another photo hung behind the chair of the new Mossad director, one that has always moved him: the image of a Jewish boy in the Warsaw Ghetto raising his hands above his head, surrendering to a German soldier threatening him with a gun. A small bronze plaque beneath the photo declared, "Never Again."

Other walls in the office were covered with photographs documenting Cornfield's military roles as well as his meetings with various public figures. The poetry and philosophy books on the shelves had been replaced by golden swords whose hilts and scabbards were encrusted with jewels, souvenirs given to Cornfield by kings and heads of state, trophies, and plaques commemorating his distinguished military career. There was no trace of Amira or any other member of his family.

Cornfield was pleased both by the results of the renovation and the quick pace with which his men had acted. "From now on, this is going to be the pace in this office," he said during the first morning meeting with the division heads. "And unless you stop gossiping and badmouthing me, you'll find yourselves cleaning the sculpture garden outside." They all just sat and listened with expressionless faces.

Two days after taking office, Cornfield summoned all Mossad employees from the rank of department head and up, to an urgent introductory meeting. On the way to the main lecture hall, his veteran personal aid, Shlomo Zimmer, pleaded with him. "Please go easy on them, boss. You can be quite blunt when you're using your military language. Remember, you're talking to civilians. You need to earn their trust and respect."

Cornfield said nothing and just winked at him with his good eye and motioned for him to open the meeting.

Zimmer went up on stage, introduced himself, and immediately invited Retired Major General Ben-Ami Cornfield to speak. Cornfield went to the podium and looked about the lecture hall. Some of the men he recognized from his army service or from meetings at the Ministry of Defense office.

"Good morning, my fellow Institute for Intelligence and Special Operations employees of Mossad, which some of you call 'the office' for some reason. It is a great privilege to stand here before you and accept one of the most sensitive positions in the country, the position of Mossad Director. I'd like to speak about my vision for the organization and how I envision it ten years from now. To be honest, I find today's Mossad to be too fat, too heavy, and crawling with people who saw the enemy only behind the safety of a television screen."

None of the people present protested, but a cloud of discomfort visibly began to hover in the air of the spacious lecture hall.

Cornfield continued and detailed the prime minister's expectations from Mossad in the face of the numerous threats Israel was faced with. "We need a Mossad comprised of soldiers, not pen pushers. The most important war is the one that's prevented. We will use all the courage, professionalism and aggressiveness, which many of you have unfortunately lost."

The hushed voices of protest gradually turned louder, interrupting the flow of his speech, and Cornfield became furious.

"You are all state employees," he shouted at them. "If the elected prime minister wants to bring a certain policy to fruition, you have no right to counter him. You are a part of the executive branch, and you need to follow orders!"

"We are a professional organization whose role is to both to consult and make decisions," a voice called from the end of the lecture hall.

Cornfield strained his single eye to identify the speaker. He felt he was losing control. His famous "alligator smile" rose to his lips, exposing his glass eye. He raised his voice. "Gentlemen, anyone who doesn't want to be here is more than welcome to leave. Your non-operational staff has grown by almost fifty percent in the past few years! You've become a second-rate foreign ministry and a third-rate intelligence agency," he shouted at the men sitting in the lecture hall. Their protestations merely served to strengthen his conviction. "Yes, yes, you can all write nice reports, using elaborate words, some of which I don't even understand, but that's not what Mossad is about!"

His audience's disgruntlement merely served to infuriate him. Zimmer, who knew exactly what was about to happen, jumped up on the stage and tried to have Cornfield finish his speech, but Cornfield didn't even notice him. He surveyed the lecture hall with a baleful gaze, leaned back on the podium and said with characteristic bluntness: "Gentlemen, it's time for you to get your thumbs out of your asses and pull yourselves together."

"You're not in boot camp here; you need to show us a little respect!" A voice was heard from one of the front rows and Cornfield, half blind, was unable to recognize the speaker again. He took a mental note to ask Zimmer to identify those who had spoken against him. Dissent among the employees grew, and they gradually rose to their feet and left the lecture hall. Cornfield, who was used to absolute obedience from his underlings, was shocked by their behavior.

"Just a minute!" he shouted at the emptying lecture hall. "Don't leave yet. I'd like to introduce you to the most decorated major general in IDF history, Mot'ke Hassin, the man who served as the commander of the General Staff Reconnaissance Unit and the head of General Staff. He will help me undertake the necessary organizational changes in Mossad and bring back some fighting spirit to this office. It is my intention to appoint him as Deputy Director and head of the Special Operations Division."

In the front row, the row intended for department heads, Arik sat by himself. He felt so frustrated that he couldn't even bring himself to get up and leave. The appointment of Major General Mot'ke "Steak Face" Hassin was a terrible blow for Arik. He absolutely detested Mot'ke. Now, that terrible man was about to be his new superior.

Cornfield's eye singled out Arik's face. "Bar-Nathan," he called him, "get up and come with me to my office. I need to talk to you right now."

Chapter 13

Mossad Director's Office—Much Ado About Nothing

Cornfield examined Arik who was looking at the photo of the Warsaw Ghetto child. "Powerful image, isn't it?"

Arik couldn't help himself. "Were you, yourself, in the ghetto?"

"Were you?" Cornfield fired back.

"All my life," replied Arik.

Cornfield was surprised by his answer and hurried to change the subject. "Let's begin. I want some explanations about the mess you've been causing throughout the country. First, there was a fire right here next to Mossad Headquarters. We're still unsure about who started it. Maybe it was you. Then there was an accident next to the President's House, in which all parties involved disappeared, leaving you the only one on the road. You don't miss out on any strategic site, do you? What's next? A mess right next to the Dimona nuclear reactor?"

"What are you trying to say?"

"Look," an evil gaze and a sly smile stretched the corners of Cornfield's lips, "we all know you screw anyone who has two legs and a pair of tits. Do I really need to spell it out for you?"

"Yes, you do," Arik said coolly.

"Just try to think, which of the ones you screwed lately has a jealous husband?"

Arik smiled.

"That's not funny!" Cornfield rumbled.

Arik thought it was very funny and even ironic. The one husband who really fit the profile was Cornfield himself, Amira's husband.

"And what's worse, your adventures made that dork, Doctor Alex-something, think someone is trying to hunt down our division heads. That's why I was urgently called back in the middle of a vacation in Sicily. First time after years that I get a chance to spend some quiet time with my wife…"

It's about time, Arik thought and smiled again.

"What's so funny? Stop smiling all the time!" Sparks of anger rose in Cornfield's single eye. "Start explaining. What in God's name is going on here?"

"Director, sir, there's no jealous husband. Alex received information from a confirmed source that a Chechen assassin is roaming the country with the intention of killing the person responsible for the murder of his father and the injury of his brother during an operation we conducted in the borders of Argentine, Brazil and Paraguay. As the head of the Caesarea Division, I am his number one target, and Fischer suggested that I be assigned a bodyguard."

"I didn't agree to that," Cornfield hissed.

"You'll be surprised. Neither did I. And yet…"

"And yet what?"

"I can't prove anything, of course, but I have a feeling someone was there during the last assassination attempt. Someone saved my life."

"An angel?" Cornfield mocked him.

"Something like that. An angel with a big car. A female angel, actually."

"You see? She found out about her husband's plan to kill you and tried to prevent it. She must love you very much. Think hard, there must be one husband who'd be willing to—"

"I suggest we stop right here," Arik interrupted him. "If you don't trust Alex's sources, either fire him or seek verification from other sources."

"Are you crazy? You want me to risk other agents and send them to collect nonexistent information? Then pay more staff workers to analyze it and Alex to write an unfounded report? Let me tell you something." Cornfield went around the table and stood in front of Arik. Arik, a full head shorter than Cornfield, could feel the breath of his new boss as if his face.

"Alex is going to go home real soon. I'm going to keep two, maybe three departments from his entire division open. The Soviet Union is gone, so I don't need any Russian Bolshevik bullshit here. I won't have any Potemkin villages built on my shift."

"Alex is *really* not like that—"

"Forget about him now. It's more important that we talk about your division," Cornfield examined the paperwork on his desk, which had rows and data highlighted with a yellow marker. "I'd like to know why your division headcount has risen by forty-seven percent in the past three years. I'd like to know how many of your men are soldiers and how many are actually out in the field."

"Is this now a work meeting?" Arik asked.

Cornfield replied by waving his hand dismissively, and Arik gave up and cooperated. "The increase in manpower was necessary," he said, speaking slowly, like a therapist explaining something to his patient. "The world's changing, and the classic definitions differentiating field men and office employees have changed with it. A large part of the operations we conduct have to do with cyber warfare and financial threats."

Cornfield snorted with contempt. "I've run operations. Major coordinated operations that involved commando and ground troops. I can't be fooled by your bullshit. I still don't understand why you needed to add hundreds of pen pushers to your roster."

"Sir, you commanded a special forces unit about thirty years ago, right?" Arik prepared a counter-blow. "The only unit you consider to be a fighting unit in Mossad is the Kidon Task Force, which is a part of my division, right?"

Cornfield approved with a nod and waited.

"Well, with all due respect, the Kidon is the not the sharpest pencil in the box under my command. Nowadays, people sitting in air-conditioned rooms in front of plasma screens can cause much more strategic damage to an enemy state than an entire tank division."

Cornfield's expression demonstrated his doubt and distrust.

Arik smiled. "Let me tell you about our Cyber Warfare unit, which we call by the codename 'Digital Fortress.' It is headed by Dr. Maayan Dermer, a former mathematician for the Weizmann Institute, specializing in cryptography. This is a unit we've labored very hard to prepare by stealing top high-tech personnel and approving the payment of high salaries.

If we pay them a crummy government salary, they wouldn't stay here a single day. These people are using a mouse and a keyboard as weapons rather than guns and tanks. Currently, they are planning, in cooperation with the NSA, a cyber-attack against strategic centers in Iran and Syria using Stuxnet worms and Flame worms we've developed here. They've managed to program the worms into the assembly lines of Taiwanese computer manufacturers. Unknowingly, the computer manufacturers we've infiltrated sold such worm-infested computers to the Iranian companies."

"What are these worms?" asked Cornfield.

"A type of malware," Arik explained patiently. "In order to create them, you need a lot of knowledge and creative thinking. Let me give you an example. We've developed a system that allows us to infiltrate the enemy's encrypted communication systems. Our system sees the enemy's radar sensors and allows us to take them over. If any of our planes infiltrate enemy airspace, our men here can simply reprogram their radar system to monitor unrelated areas, far from our airplanes. The enemy won't even know its systems were compromised, so everything is in order, as far as they are concerned."

"And this was all developed by your cyber people?" said Cornfield with disbelief.

"This system is so new and original that we needed to draft young hackers, some of them sociopaths with criminal records, teenagers who hacked into the computers of large companies. We even have two employees on the autism spectrum with Asperger's Syndrome."

Cornfield erupted. "You mean to tell me you're paying such high salaries to criminals and retards?"

"These 'criminals and retards' can attack and delay the systems in charge of developing nuclear weapons while significantly damaging the enemy's centrifuges and nuclear reactors. They are able to harm command and control centers of enemy countries, such as major power stations and other strategic facilities, and they are able to take over vehicle navigational computer systems and cause a multi-vehicle accident on a major highway."

"And this is all called 'cyber,' right?" asked Cornfield, trying to hide the fact that he had never been exposed to the world of Internet and computers.

"Sort of. 'Cyber' is a term referring to the entire cybernetic space. Six billion interconnected devices worldwide."

Cornfield didn't know anything about computers and actually hated technology. He believed in field soldiers, tanks, and cannons. He had some vague knowledge about the abilities of sophisticated fighter jets , submarine or battleships, but regarded all the rest as a type of computer game. "All right, so let's suppose for a minute, we need the cyber criminals like we need collaborators. What about the office employees not working with computers?"

"That's the unit I take most pride in. The Backdoor Unit, which specializes in economic warfare against terrorism, is headed by Mrs. Sarah Haji-Yaakob, a brilliant economist with a PhD, a Harvard Law School graduate. We snatched her from the corridors of the New York Deutsche Bank's research department. All the people in her department are economy and finance experts. Some are veterans of local and international banks, specializing in clearing systems. They were able to achieve some great results. Our 'finint'—financial intelligence department—has recently sent the CIA's financial department a list containing information about financial assets belonging to Iranian, Libyan and Syrian heads of state. The Americans suspect those men of committing war crimes and financing terror organizations. Since they cannot be taken out of their countries, the American president has decided to punish them in a different way and issued a presidential decree freezing their assets in American banks. He was able to do it thanks to the information we've provided."

Cornfield finally smiled. Victory was something he could always appreciate.

Arik cheered up. "Sir, nowadays, the smart way to go is to allow all of our various divisions and departments to work in harmony and cooperation. That way, every bit of information that comes in from the intelligence-gathering department is immediately classified by automatic computers, analysts, distributed by distribution algorithm and keyword tools and immediately brought to the attention of all field and office departments. We also have excellent cooperation with the Military Intelligence Directorate, Israel Secret Service, police, and all the national security and intelligence agencies in Europe and all United States agencies. All this information is filtered by Dr. Alex Abramovich, head of the Intelligence and Research Division and goes into a database called The 'Pool', which accumulates all the information. Access to this database is determined according to the security clearance and position of the asking party. Dr. Abramovich received the Israel Defense Prize for initiating this project."

A thin and focused smile rose on Cornfield's face. "What I still don't get, is why all these departments need to be in your division of all places? Why not transfer the financial warfare department to the National Security Advisor's department and the cyber unit to the Military Intelligence Directorate's Unit 8200, which is responsible for collecting signal intelligence and code decryption?"

Arik was beginning to lose his patience. "Look, Cornfield," he said angrily. "These are all operational divisions. Our vast advantage lies in the painstaking work invested by the people that preceded us and created The Pool. It served as the foundation upon which we've been able to build layer upon layer of knowledge. Such a collection of information can be created only in a place in which a flow of information is constantly collected and analyzed in perfect coordination. If you separate departments and divisions, a lot of information will simply slip through the cracks due to a lack of proper perspective."

Cornfield's face demonstrated his doubt.

"You must have heard about 9/11, the collapse of the Twin Towers and the World Trade Center two years ago and the attack on the Pentagon," Arik said fervently. "Did you know that the CIA had concrete advance intelligence about the terrorist attack but did not share it with the FBI, which, in turn, was following those same Saudi students who carried out the attacks? This all happened because the organizations weren't working in coordination and were busy fighting various battles of ego," Arik concluded

"I've already heard all that from David Fischer." Cornfield spat the name of his predecessor as if it were a curse. "So what is Kidon doing in the meanwhile? Playing computer games?"

Arik did the best he could to maintain a relaxed expression. "Kidon is doing what it does best, and you know exactly what I mean. But it can't operate in a vacuum. I send the agents of Kidon to carry out assassinations with surgical precision only when I have a reliable and clear picture of the situation in the field based on solid intelligence. Without proper intelligence we might end up leaving a trail of dead soldiers behind us."

A low beeping sound rose from the telephone lying on the new wooden desk. Cornfield pressed a button, and the door of the room opened. Shlomo Zimmer, the new bureau chief came in and placed a note on the table between the thick arms of Cornfield, who glanced at it and said, "All right."

Zimmer saw it as a sign for him to leave. After Zimmer had left, Cornfield swayed back and forth on his large chair, pensive. A minute or two later, he said, "As you probably heard in the lecture I gave regarding my vision of the organization's future, I've asked Major General Hassin to join us and serve as Deputy Director. He will take care of all operational activities and initiate an all-encompassing organizational change. Anything that doesn't belong to the core of Mossad—to its DNA, as I see it—will need to go. And I say that with all due respect to your geniuses from The Pool."

"What about Gideon Perry, the current deputy director?"

"He asked to retire, and I approved. He wants to talk to the prime minister. I agreed to that as well. I hope you know it won't really help, right?" Cornfield laughed. "The prime minister wants the same thing I do: to instill some order here after too many years of David Fischer."

"Sir," Arik spoke in a formal tone again, "with all due respect, I don't like this aggressive approach and the way you look down on everything that had taken place before your appointment. Perhaps it's time for me to ask for an early retirement as well. All my army friends retired when they were forty five."

"And who's going to protect you from the crazed husband that wants to kill you?" Cornfield shouted, holding the note he'd received and waving it about. "When you got here, I asked our redheaded security officer to carefully check your SUV, just in case someone placed a bomb to blow you up within the complex. Would you like to hear what he found?" Arik waited.

"A satellite tracking device, attached to the inner side of your fuel tank. A place that's normally left unchecked. They smeared it with black grease, just to be on the safe side. That husband sure wants to know where you're having a good time with his wife."

The conversation had become too tiresome for Arik. "Like I already said, I'm resigning my post," he insisted. "I'll place my official discharge request with your secretary first thing tomorrow."

"Don't make a scene here. I'm not going to beg you to stay." Arik approved with a nod.

"But I need you here!" Cornfield surprised him with a shout. "Israel needs you here!"

Arik tilted his head back. All the tension, the resentment he felt toward Cornfield, the fear he felt about the possible ruin of the amazing organization he had inherited and cultivated, they all burst out of him in the form of a bitter fit of laughter.

"What's so funny?"

"You haven't changed. All those years have passed, yet you, like some sort of withered tree, stayed the same old Ben-Ami Cornfield. 'The Butcher' who believes acting like a bully and using force can solve just about anything. And now, you're bringing Steak Face Mot'ke to back you up."

"I won't allow you to call him that!" Cornfield raged. "The man lost his face and hands for the sake of this country, and I won't have him ridiculed." He stood up and turned his back on Arik, looking through the window at the vehicles passing down the coastal highway. When he finally turned around, the anger was gone from his voice. "Give Mot'ke Hassin a chance. He's a good man."

"He's a mad dog. I've seen him slaughter collaborators he no longer deemed necessary with his own hands. I've also heard everything about his misdeeds in the previous roles he'd filled. I don't want to serve in a Mossad he is a part of. I don't even want to be in the same room with him."

"Watch your mouth and your back!" Cornfield hissed. "You're like a suitcase without a handle. You can't be carried but unfortunately can't be tossed away just yet."

"Don't make too much of an effort to carry me. I don't want to be here with you. As far as I'm concerned, I'm already out."

"And what would you do out there?" Cornfield asked. "Sit in the park and play chess with senile old men? Take care of the grandchildren you don't have? Mr. Bar-Nathan, you're going to wither out there like a water lily in the middle of the Gobi Desert. You need the adrenaline rush this job offers even more than I do. You're an addict; it takes one to know one."

Arik began to lose his fighting spirit, and the look in his eyes betrayed that fact.

"I'm an emotional man in a cynical world. I believe in the need to always take the initiative and be daring. I can't stand people who stick to the status quo. I despise men who shirk responsibility, and therefore, just like me, you can't quit." Cornfield surprised Arik. "Besides, Fischer left some unfinished business for you to take care of."

"Fischer left a lot of unfinished business."

"The Mujahideen al-Islamiyya," said Cornfield in a low voice, as if he feared someone was eavesdropping.

"What do they have to do with me?"

Cornfield shrugged. "I don't know. Look at it as Fischer's inheritance to you." He erupted into a hollow laughter and presented Arik with an envelope sealed with wax and bearing the words: 'Operation Flower Bud'.

"You'll find precise instructions inside. As soon as you get the code words 'The flower bud has opened,' you must act upon them immediately."

Arik slid the envelope back between Cornfield's thick arms.

"What is it exactly that you want from me?" Cornfield shouted. "A raise? You know I can't do that. A new car, a bodyguard? Why won't you tell me what you want from me, goddamn it!"

Arik sought traces of irony in Cornfield's single eye but could only see what appeared to be genuine honesty. The more he thought he knew the man, the more he discovered he doesn't really know him at all. Arik thought of him as an uninhibited maniac who was lacking any inner truth. Could it be that his brain had been damaged along with his eye and leg?

"I don't want a bodyguard. I've never asked for one." An idea flashed through his mind, "But what I do want and need is some time off. My mother is sick, and I haven't seen my children in a long time. I need to think about my future in this organization, in light of your new vision for it."

"You forgot to mention your new German girlfriend."
Arik twisted his face with distaste. "If you're going to run Mossad the way you want to, I guess that's going to be your new intelligence source now: cheap gossip."

"I can approve a two day vacation, no more than that." The tone of a military commander overseeing new recruits returned to Cornfield's voice. "Come back here on Wednesday, and take the envelope. I know you don't give a fuck about me, so just do it for your own sake. Do it for Fischer, who counted on you for some reason."

Arik rose, took the envelope, placed it in his bag, and made his way outside.

"Wednesday, you hear me?"

"Loud and clear," Arik said and closed the door after him. The eyes of the soldier secretaries sitting behind their desks in the lobby were all fixed on him.

"My condolences," he muttered at them and took off to his office for some final arrangements.

Chapter 14

Arik watched the factory chimneys in the bay of Haifa industrial zone emit bluish vapors, buying himself a few more seconds of respite before he went into the dark stairwell leading to his mother's apartment in the old block.

As always, the sour smell of the enclosed space hit his nostrils, mixed with the scents of cooking and the sharp aroma of detergents. He climbed the battered staircase to the second floor and rang the doorbell.

No answer.

He rang again. From beyond the door, he heard the five o'clock news television broadcast in a deafening volume. He banged on the door with an open palm, trying to overcome the deafening sound of the newscaster, and called his mother. "*Momme, Momme!*" Finally, he tried to unlock the door with his own apartment key, but it stopped midway. His mother had left her key in the keyhole.

For lack of any other choice, he pounded the door. Neighbors peeked into the stairwell and gave him curious glances mixed with pity. The few who remembered him nodded a silent greeting.

Arik was surprised the nurse didn't open the door for him. He immediately assumed she must have gone to the store and would come back in a minute or two. After several minutes had passed without any trace of her, he continued to pound the door with his fist. The door remained closed.

Desperate, Arik began to look for a locksmith on his cell phone. Then, finally, his mother's raspy and fear-filled voice sounded from beyond the door. "*Wer ist das?*"[3]

"*Das bin ich, Momme,*"[4] Arik answered in Yiddish and immediately continued in Hebrew, "Open the door, please."

He heard the sound of the lock being opened, then immediately closed again. His mother pulled the door and shouted, "It's closed."

"*Mamele,* turn off the television and take the key out of the lock," he said loud and clear.

She understood. He heard the creaking sound of the key being removed from the lock and hurried to insert his own and open the door. Nothing could have prepared him for the sight that awaited him behind it. His mother stood in front of him, wearing nothing but her underwear, her heavy breasts drooping on her bulging belly and the curious, uninhibited look of a little child in her eyes, completely unaware of her nakedness. Her full hair was disheveled, swirls of white spreading through the reddish color. "Are you hungry, *Leibele*?" she asked.

He concealed the sight of his mother's nakedness by filling the entrance with his body, then quickly slipped inside and shut the door behind him, careful not to touch her and closing his eyes so as not to look at her naked body. The revulsion he felt was mixed with compassion. "Yes, *Momme,* I'm hungry. Go change, and I'll see what's in the fridge."

---

[3] Who is this?
[4] It's me, Mother.

She just stood there, looking at him in confusion. Arik hurried to the bedroom, took a colorful silk dressing gown he had bought her on one of his trips, and covered her. Then he walked her to the living room.

"*Momme*, where's the television remote?"

She pointed at a cordless phone placed on a small coffee table next to the armchair.

"The *farkakta* thing is broken," she said and tried to turn down the volume with the buttons.

Arik knew there wasn't any point in arguing. "I'll fix it." He found the remote behind the armchair backrest pillow. "Sit here, I'll warm us something to eat."

"No, no, I'm the *balabuste*[5] here. I'll prepare something for us to eat."

Arik followed her to the kitchen and watched her take a small pot containing a thin soup with some chicken, potatoes and carrots. She placed the pot on the kitchen table, went to the stove and turned one of the gas knobs. The sharp smell of gas spread in the air. She looked at the pot, as if trying to recall something, then distractedly went back to the living room and sat in front of the television.

Arik was filled with sadness and desperation. All at once, he was overwhelmed by the understanding his mother's life was in real danger and that she mustn't remain by herself even for a single moment. He hurried to turn the gas knob shut, opened the window to air the room, and called his sister.

"Naomi, you said mother has a nurse, right? Where is she? I need to go somewhere, and I can't leave her by herself, even for a minute."

---

[5]Mistress of the house.

"I thought you've taken a vacation just to spend some time with Mom," she said in a defiant tone that filled him with discomfort.

"I've got some other things in my life. My children, for example."

"Yes, it's about time. Anyway, I'm sure you don't remember, but I've told you a long time ago that Sunday is the nurse's day off. She's going to St. Peter's Church in Jaffa and will be back at nine. Please stay with Mom until she gets back."

He glanced at his watch. He was faced with three and a half hours of depression and boredom. "I'll wait," he said resignedly.

He cut some vegetables and sprinkled them with lemon and olive oil, warmed the soup, cut some old bread he found, and placed the slices in the toaster. He set the table and went to the living room to bring his mother. She walked beside him heavily, shuffling her tired feet. Only the happy smile stretched on her lips and her green eyes remained as silent witnesses of the mother and woman she had used to be.

She ate with great relish, and Arik assumed she hadn't eaten anything since morning. He asked her whether she had taken her medicine and immediately realized just how silly his question was. Obviously, she had no idea.

After the meal, he returned her to the living room and sat her in the comfortable armchair he and Naomi had bought her for her eightieth birthday. He turned off the television and sat in front of her.

"You know your dad came to visit me last night?" she said with a smile.

"*Momme*, Dad passed away almost thirteen years ago," he gently chided her.

She looked at him as if he were still her little boy and said something extremely silly. "You think I don't know that? But lately, he comes to visit me almost every night. He comes into my bedroom, sits on the edge of the bed and strokes my head. He told me not to let any strangers into the house."

Arik didn't know how to react. He caressed her kind, comforting, shivering hands. Now he noticed just how emaciated they were, strewn with wrinkles and liver spots.

"*Momme*, you can't stay here by yourself. You have a nurse. She'll be back here soon and—" Her smiling, tranquil expression suddenly turned into threatening anger and he stopped in mid-sentence.

"You get out of here right now!" his mother shouted in fury. "I'm the lady of the house. You hear me? I own this place! No one, not the nurse, or anyone else, can tell me what to do with my life, do you hear me?"

Arik tried to hug her, but she forcefully pushed him away. "Go to hell! You're never around when I need you!" Her screams became a heart-wrenching whimper. Then she regained her composure and shouted at him angrily, "I'll give all my inheritance to Naomi and her kids, you hear me? As far as I'm concerned, you don't exist anymore. You're not in my will!"

Arik wasn't surprised by her outburst. Crying fits and emotional blackmail had been her secret weapon since he was a child. Back then, he had been angry at her. Now, she simply seemed miserable and fragile in his eyes. Paternal feelings rose in him, and he got up and took her in his arms. This time, she yielded to his embrace.

"*Mamele*, there's nothing to do about it. The doctor said unless you agree to a nurse, you'll need to go to a retirement home." He responded by using her own weapon.

"No, not the retirement home! Not the retirement home. I only want to stay here in my house!" She wept again, and Arik regretted his words. He knew how much his mother dreaded the retirement home. He and Naomi had promised her they'd never place her in such an institute, not even if it looked like a luxury hotel.

"There's no choice, *Mamele*. You need help. Your nurse is a very good woman." He recalled with regret, that he hadn't even asked Naomi for the nurse's name. "You're the lady of the house, the *balabuste*. She does only what you tell her to do."

"But she's a thief! She steals money from me. She even steals my braziers," the elderly woman complained.

"*Mamele*, maybe I'll make us some tea with lemon and honey?"

His mother didn't reply. Arik looked at her and saw that her eyes were closing as she drifted in and out of sleep. He gently picked her up in his arms and carried her to the bedroom. He covered her with her favorite down comforter, kissed her forehead, and went to clean the kitchen.

As he washed the dishes, he looked out the narrow window facing the street. His car was parked there, two of its wheels up on the sidewalk. A boy slowly rode his bicycle down the street, and a truck honked for him to get out of the way. After the truck passed, he saw the sidewalk across the building. A tall, skinny, feminine figure stood there, dressed in a pantsuit. The color of her hair and its abundance left no room for doubt, in spite of the baseball cap and dark sunglasses she was wearing.

Eva.

He closed the tap and observed her as she leaned against the fence, looking forward. Was she looking at his window?

He tried to catch her eyes, but immediately realized the distance was too far, and there was no way she could see him through the narrow kitchen window. He headed out to the porch, planning to lean across the rail and call her name. Most people, he knew, weren't able to resist the instinctive reaction of turning their heads when their name was called. But by the time he looked at the street again, she was gone.

From behind him, he heard the voice of his waking mother. "*Leibele*, when did you get here?" she asked with surprise.

He was still shocked by the mirage he had seen. "I just got here," he lied without blinking, while trying to recreate what he had just seen in his mind. He was convinced it wasn't a mistake. He has actually seen Eva.

"Are you here by yourself?" his mother asked and examined the large living room suspiciously.

He chuckled. That was exactly what he was asking himself. "Yes, *Mamele*, I'm here by myself."

"Are you sure there's no one else here?" She went to look through the various rooms of the apartment, and Arik followed her.

After she had been convinced there was no one else in the apartment, she ordered him to take down the restroom door and bring it to the living room.

He started to get used to her oddities, but that last request was too strange even for her. "I don't understand. You actually want me to take the door off its hinges and bring it to the living room?"

"What's there to understand?" his mother yelled. "Just take down the *farkakta*[6] door and bring it here."

---

[6]Shitty, lousy

The door was easily pulled off its hinges. He carried it to the living room and placed it on the floor. "Now what?"

"Turn it around and lean it against the dining table," she ordered with determination. Her green eyes were focused, clear and penetrating. The urgency in her voice had made him forget Eva or her mysterious lookalike he had seen in the street. He turned the door so that its lower part now faced up. He noticed a wooden ruler with a small depression stretched across the bottom of the door. "Do you remember what I told you about the Jewish carpenter who had saved my life in the camps?" his mother asked with a mysterious smile. "He built this safe in the door for me. Press the ruler."

Arik hesitated. She didn't wait and pushed a fingernail into the depression. A dark and narrow hidden compartment was revealed. She went to the kitchen, and when she returned, held a long wooden spoon in her hand, which she inserted into the compartment. Flat packages wrapped with the yellow pages of a Yiddish newspaper fell out of there one after the other. When she finished, fifty small packages rested on the table.

"Make sure it's empty," she ordered Arik. He lit a match and peeked inside. The compartment was empty.

"There are fifty packages here, each with a thousand dollars. This money is for you. Buy houses for your children with it," she said with excitement.

"I can't take this money," said Arik. "Who else knows about this?"

"Only me and your late father, God rest his soul. We've saved it for times of war or, God forbid, another Holocaust. It's always good to have money so you could bribe the guards and escape. Now you're alone, you've no wife, and you have little children, so I thought to myself, 'I'm too old to run away.'"

"*Mamele*, my children are all grown up. They're your grandchildren, Michael and Nathalie, and they're doing well financially. I need to tell Naomi about the money and share it with her."

"There's no need! Naomi gets the apartment here, in Neve Sha'anan. It's a nice apartment right next to the Institute of Technology," she added like a seasoned real estate agent.

Arik didn't answer. He went to the kitchen and returned, carrying a tray with a pitcher of tea and lemon, thin Polish porcelain cups, a set his mother reserved for important guests, and a plate of *rugelach* cookies.

His mother smiled appreciatively. She began drinking and immediately faded back to old age, the lost and distant look returning to her eyes.

He collected the newspaper-wrapped bills, placed them back into the secret compartment, and put the door back on its hinges. Then he sat in the living room and watched the evening news, waiting for the nurse.

His mother slept beside him with her head on his shoulder. When the nurse returned, dripping with sweat and reeking of cheap perfume, he told her everything that had happened that afternoon with the key . "I know everything," she said in broken English. "Just give me Mom's key so Mom not lock door."

He took out his mother's key and handed it to her, feeling as if he had just placed his mother's life in the nurse's hands.

"You need find someone when I'm on vacation," she added. "Tell Naomi we can't leave Mom all alone."

When he went down the staircase, repulsion and guilt mixing in his heart, he wondered if the nurse had said that last sentence to scold him or simply to give him the information. He peeled a traffic ticket of his car's windowpane and got inside. Suddenly, the memory flashed in his mind. What were the chances a woman looking just like Eva would just happen to be in that particular street, in a city dozens of miles from Jerusalem, just when he was visiting his mother? He dialed Eva's cell number. "Arik!" she called happily.

"Where are you?" he demanded.

"Why are you asking?" she replied with amazement.

"Where are you?"

"In Jerusalem, of course. Where else could I be?"

She sounded sincere enough, but Arik remained suspicious. "Where in Jerusalem? Do you have a landline?"

"What's going on with you?"

"Give me a number."

She dictated him a number and added, "Room two hundred and two, if you'll ever have time to finally come over." He wrote the number on the traffic ticket and dialed.

"American Colony Hotel. How can I help you?" he was immediately answered. He asked to be transferred to Eva's room.

"Now will you tell me what's going on with you?"

"My mom's sick," he said in a defeated voice. "I guess I'm a little unsettled. I thought I saw you in Haifa."

"Well, you could have just asked me instead of playing games."

"You're right. I'm sorry."

"Do you want to tell me about your mom?" she asked carefully.

"No, it's… It's still too fresh in my mind. And too painful. I'll talk to you once I get to Jerusalem. I'll call you."

"All right," she said, and he thought he detected a hint of suspiciousness beneath her seemingly soft-spoken tone. "I'll be waiting."

The suspicious agent in him just wouldn't calm down. He redialed the number she had given him.

"American Colony Hotel, good evening, how may I help—" He heard the voice of the receptionist again and immediately hung up.

Chapter 15

Hezbollah Headquarters, Dahieh Suburb, Beirut— Lebanon

Three black Land Cruisers emerged from a side gate in Rafic Hariri International Airport and sped their way to the Dahieh suburb. They didn't obey the red traffic lights and crossed the Lebanese Army checkpoints manned with Shiite soldiers without stopping. In fifteen minutes, the convoy reached its destination.

In Dahieh, the Shiite suburb of Beirut, the cosmopolitan atmosphere of the city known as "Paris of the Middle East" had transformed to hostile suspiciousness. Iranian and Hezbollah flags fluttered on the rooftops. Giant portraits of Iran's spiritual leader, Ali Khamenei, were displayed on the walls of public buildings beside the portrait of Hezbollah's Secretary General, Hassan Nasrallah. The two bridges, bombed and demolished by IDF airplanes during the last war, were in final reconstruction stages. Cranes and construction scaffolding belonging to Jihad al-Bina, a company owned by Hezbollah, could be seen everywhere.

The three SUVs stopped in front of the entrance of a large building on whose façade numerous flags hung along with a sign that declared: "Welcome to Hezbollah Headquarters."

The distinguished guests were welcomed by Imad Husniyah, Hezbollah's chief of operations, dressed in a dappled khaki uniform and wearing a baseball cap and tall Palladium boots.

General Mazen Suleimani, head of Iran's Revolutionary Guards' Al-Quds Force, emerged from the first SUV, his hands extended and a wide smile on his face. The two embraced amicably. Suleimani's staff officers came out the other SUVs, carrying briefcases with paperwork they had prepared for the work meeting awaiting them. On the way to the conference room, the smile evaporated from Suleimani's face.

When they all sat in their chairs, staring at the smiling portrait of their leader, Nasrallah, Suleimani immediately began to speak. "By Allah's name, my brothers, you leak like an old sieve. This week, the Jews took over a boat loaded with weapons that was supposed to reach you. It contained dozens of Fajr-Five missiles as well as raw chemical materials for the production of drugs, which were supposed to help you make millions. The Zionists' audacity is more than we can tolerate. They intercepted the ship right next to the Islamic Republic's territorial waters in the Strait of Hormuz. How do they know about our every plan?"

Husniyah and his aides were silent.

"My brothers, soldiers of the *mukawama*,"[7] continued Suleimani, "the commander of the Revolutionary Guard, General Ali Jafari, has requested me to ask you directly, as is customary among friends, if it is possible the Jews have a mole hidden deep in your ranks?"

---

[7]Resistance.

Imad Husniyah swallowed in fear. "Gentlemen, honorable guests coming from our eldest sister, the Islamic Republic of Iran..." He opened with flattery. "...in the name of our great leader, Sheikh Nasrallah, I bid you welcome and thank you from the bottom of my heart for your support of the Lebanese resistance movement for the liberation of Palestine from the hands of the Zionist conqueror. It is no secret that the Zionists have been trying to infiltrate our ranks with their spies. Our counterintelligence unit has captured a few of them. We've also found some surveillance and listening devices that the Zionist army has hidden in the field, but with all due respect, General, sir, the big secrets do not leak from us. I'm not implying the leaks come from your end, of course, but..."

"But what?" asked Suleimani.

"Brothers," Husniyah tried to change the course of the conversation, "the Israelis will be thrilled to learn about our differences and that we are busy in exchanging false accusations."

"All right," Suleimani said, certain that the dissatisfaction he had demonstrated would be enough to cause his Lebanese colleagues to initiate a thorough investigation among their ranks. "We must deter the Zionists from performing preventative strikes close to the shores of the Islamic Republic. We must demonstrate our strength. Therefore, I ask that your 1800 Unit carry out attacks in Europe, in the Middle East, South America, and the Far East. I want to hear about Jewish diplomats being blown up, Chabad Jewish Centers, which are actually undercover Mossad branches, burned down, and Jewish schools and community centers destroyed. As far as I'm concerned, they are all soldiers in the service of the Zionist devil."

"They will respond by bombing us," Husniyah said with concern.

"We've thought about that," said Suleimani. "We will strengthen you, militarily, in a way that will deter the Zionists from attacking you. We will provide you with long-range missiles capable of hitting any target within the Zionist entity. In return, you must commit to harm Jews and Zionists anywhere you possibly can. They need to realize our long arm will reach and annihilate them everywhere. We will also provide weapons and war materials to the Hamas and Islamic Jihad in Gaza. That way we will be able to attack the northern and southern borders of the Zionist entity simultaneously."

"But," Husniyah replied hesitantly, "they will simply intercept the ships and bomb your truck convoys in Sudan, Eritrea, and other African smuggling routes."

"After you carry out two or three attacks, they'll think twice before doing that. Besides, in the future, we will transfer you Syrian knowledge, technology, and raw materials that will allow you to develop nuclear warheads. In return, we want to see some major achievements!" Suleimani finished his speech by lightly tapping the table.

Husniyah felt the need to point out at least one accomplishment. "You know, our plan to flood the Zionist country with drugs is working well. We continue to damage the social structure of that spiderweb country," he reported with pride.

"Well done!" said Suleimani. "But we expect more than that."

"We are honored to accept your plan, General," said Husniyah. "And I personally commit to meet all the objectives. I only request one more thing. I need the means to carry out the attacks to wait for our squads at the Iranian embassies of all target countries."

"Agreed. Our diplomatic mail services will transport the weapons and explosives to the destinations of your choosing. Now, let us pray for the success of our plan."

The company exited the room and moved to a small mosque situated in one of the rooms in the building. At the end of the prayer, while they were all still kneeling, Suleimani said, "Only the nation of Allah will end up gaining the upper hand." He touched the carpet with his head, stretched up, raised his hands high and cried, "*Takbir!*" and everyone echoed him by calling three times, "*Allahu Akbar!*"

An hour later, when he was sitting in the plane headed back to Tehran, Suleimani relayed a three word message to his commanders, via a secure satellite phone line: "It has begun."

Chapter 16

The Prime Minister's Office—Heads of Intelligence and Security Services Meeting

"I want you to bring me the head of that son of a bitch on a stick," the prime minister looked straight into the eyes of the new Mossad director. "Is that clear? In the past few months, the Iranians have raised their heads again. But that was only to be expected." He took a thick booklet into his hands, a report prepared by Alex. "The Israeli embassy in Baku has been attacked." He read aloud the details Cornfield was only too familiar with.

"In Egypt, a terrorist cell has been exposed. The cell intended to carry out an attack on the Suez Canal and the Israeli embassy in Cairo. The Turkish authorities have exposed a terrorist cell that attempted to carry out an attack against the Ahrida Synagogue of Istanbul. In Thailand, Hezbollah operatives have been arrested while trying to attack the local Chabad Jewish Center. In Spain, Hezbollah operatives, riding a motorcycle, opened fire on the wife of an Israeli diplomat and severely injured her. On the Paraná River…" He raised a warning finger. "…at the border of Paraguay and Brazil, a Hezbollah squad, carrying forty-five pounds of explosives hidden within the lining of a suitcase, has been captured on its way to Argentine to carry out a terrorist attack against the local Jewish community center. In New Delhi, a Chabad envoy and his wife have been killed by terrorists who opened fire on them. Only their baby and his nurse have survived." He placed down the booklet. "This represents a major escalation. I also think this is only the beginning. Can I count on you to take him out?"

"It's not that easy," said Cornfield. "The Kidon have been unsuccessfully trying for several years. He is a very cautious man, a real chameleon, constantly changing identities and locations. We know he is carrying a diplomatic Syrian passport under the false name Jawad Nur a-Din. We're not the only ones looking for him. The Americans and several European intelligence agencies whose agents or soldiers he had taken out are looking for him as well."

Alex joined the conversation. "He's up there on the list of terrorists most wanted by the American government, right next to the heads of Al-Qaeda. There's a five-million dollar reward on his head. Recently, following a request by the Argentine government, Interpol issued an international arrest warrant against him and five Iranian senior officials who are suspected of being involved in the planning of the Buenos Aires AMIA bombing in 1994. In 1995, we wiped out his brother in Beirut, hoping he'd come out of hiding to attend the funeral. He didn't show up. We tried to assassinate him last February in a major operation at the border junction of Paraguay, Argentina, and Brazil. We killed a lot of men involved in the funding of terrorist attacks against us, but he managed to slip away."

The phone on the prime minister's table buzzed. "The Defense Minister asks to join you," announced the secretary.

"All right," the prime minister growled. "We're talking about Husniyah," he said with frustration as the minister came into the room.

"Yes, a real saint." The Defense Minister chuckled. "No doubt the world would be a much better place without him. It's also going to send a clear message to Iran and Hezbollah."

"You need to take into account that each attack immediately brings about a counterattack. We hurt them and are being hit back immediately," Alex pointed out.

"We've been hit without taking out Husniyah," the prime minister reminded him, using his usual sarcastic tone. "This is why I ask— No, I demand that you do it. I don't care how difficult it is. I know you can carry out anything if you really want to. The only question is when?" He passed his cold, blue eyes across the other men's faces in careful expectation.

"I can't give you a timetable," said Cornfield carefully, "but we do have a lead."

"Stay here a moment," the prime minister said and motioned to the others that the meeting was adjourned. "What did you mean?" he asked when they sat by themselves.

"Tevel[8] received information from the Americans about a mistress Imad Husniyah keeps. Her name is Layla al Tirawi. She's Shiite and manages an Iranian school in a suburb of southern Damascus. He goes to visit her for a few hours once a week. Tzomet already has the place under surveillance using agents and local operators."

"Don't screw this one up," the prime minister said eagerly. "Do whatever it takes to nail the bastard. You don't need to run this by the Security Cabinet. The fewer people know

---

[8]Mossad department responsible for liaisons with allied governments.

about it, the better. I want Arik, head of Caesarea Division, to personally command the attack and make sure everything goes smoothly."

Cornfield protested: "I thought about assigning Mot'ke Hassin as the commander in charge. We've had some problems with Arik lately."

The prime minister's expression became aggressive and determined. "Take Arik! He has a personal interest in being successful after his previous failures in South America and Beirut."

"All right." Cornfield gave in. "Arik Bar-Nathan will command the operation." A defiant expression of loathing settled on his face.

Chapter 17

Mediterranean Chess

A reminder popped up in Arik's digital diary: "Operation plan approval meeting." He went into Cornfield's office, tired from a day of preparations with his men and a sleepless night during which he had considered the various options of carrying out the attack.

"I've seen the suggestion of the Caesarea Division's chief for Operation Elusive Shadow Two." Mot'ke Hassin opened the meeting.

"Hold on, there was an Elusive Shadow One?" Cornfield asked Arik.

"Yes. That was in February, at the border junction of Paraguay, Argentina, and Brazil, but he managed to slip away."

Hassin continued. "I have to say, I don't like Caesarea's plan at all."

Arik exchanged looks with his division manager associates: Alex; Jonathan Souderi, head of Tzomet; head of Neviot;[9] and the head of Tevel, It was apparent they were all on his side.

---

[9] The division in charge of infiltrating stationary structures (such as buildings), obtaining information, and obtaining intelligence by using electronic means, such as the planting of listening and surveillance devices.

"There could be lot of possible complications involving the use of disparate forces: Arab collaborators that are not a hundred percent reliable; men of the General Staff Reconnaissance Unit, who are excellent soldiers; members of Kidon, whose high level of skill has already been demonstrated during the 'Koresh' Operation during the failed assassination of Khaled Mashal in Jordan; as well as Air Force rescue units. In short, too many parties are involved; too many things can go wrong. It's just too complicated." He finished his short speech and sent Arik a mocking smile.

"What do you suggest as an alternative?" Arik interrupted him.

"I suggest having the Air Force drop a precise, one-ton bomb on the house Imad Husniyah will be at. We take down the entire house and end the problem. Nice and clean. Why do we need to take the risks involved with the logistics of coordinating so many forces and endanger our men?" Hassin wondered aloud and was rewarded with a satisfied smile from Cornfield.

"And you think the Syrian president will just sit quietly after you take down an entire house right in the middle of Damascus, killing hundreds of innocent civilians in the process?" asked Alex.

All the operation divisions heads nodded in agreement.

"Don't start acting like bleeding hearts," Hassin answered angrily. "'When you cut down a tree, chips will fly.'"

"With all due respect," Arik replied, raising his voice a little, betraying his tired and stress-filled state, "what you suggest in an amateurish and superficial attack. I suggest an entirely different plan. A surgically precise operation that will harm Husniyah alone. That way, we do not commit a *casus belli.*[10] I don't think the Syrian president will mourn for this man."

Cornfield looked at him curiously, yet there was still doubt in his eyes.

"When I sat with my men to plan this assassination, I knew we are faced with an enemy who is a terrorist mastermind. When faced with a mastermind, what you need is a sophisticated master plan," Arik said. "He's already slipped right between our hands twice. A few months ago in South America and in 1995, when we took out his brother in Beirut. He had guessed our intentions and didn't show up for the funeral. He's also managed to slip away from the Americans and Europeans easily."

"What are you getting at, then?" Cornfield hissed like a cobra about to bite its victim.

"In the real world of special operations, you need to connect the few dots your information offers you and try to guess your rival's behavior pattern from a practical point of view."

"Get to the point."

"I know the plan I've presented you with is based on hazardous guesses of the enemies' actions, but this only means we need to be careful of the dangers of logical thinking or the tendency to react in a predictable way different scenarios."

"Come on already." Hassin spurred him on. "I'm tired of listening to your fancy philosophical bullshit. What do you suggest we do?"

"A plan with three levels of security that will cover every option. A powerful explosive charge in his car seat headrest, poison on the steering wheel, and another option…"

---

[10] An act that provokes war.

"All right, I approve the explosive charge in the headrest thing, as well as the poison, but what is your third option, and why isn't it in the paper you've prepared?" Cornfield demanded.

Arik answered slowly, selecting his words carefully. "It has to do with one of our collaborators. We've been suspecting him of switching sides for a long time. Should both stages of the plan go wrong, he will follow Husniyah in a bomb-rigged car. Of course, he won't know his car has been rigged, only that he needs to take Husniyah off the road. At a certain point of time, once they're out of Damascus and heading to Beirut, I'll give the order. He will bypass Husniyah, and his vehicle will blow up. We kill two birds with one stone."

"You said you suspect him of switching sides. How can you be sure he won't give the details of your plan to the Hezbollah?" Cornfield was interested to know.

"He won't know a thing. All he'll know is that he needs to wait at a certain place and at a certain time, and if he receives an order, he must get into his car, follow a particular vehicle, and cause it to go off the road."

Jonathan Souderi, the head of Tzomet, spoke up. "You're taking too many chances. Why not simply blow up his lover's apartment and disguise it as a gas cylinder explosion?"

"We've thought about that and checked the destructive effect of such an explosion. We're afraid it might bring down the entire building," said Arik.

Cornfield looked at him thoughtfully. The more he thought of the plan, the more he liked it. Should it succeed, he could take credit for it as the only Mossad figure the public was familiar with. Should it fail, he could get rid of Arik permanently. Two birds with one stone indeed. "All right, I approve the plan," he said. "When are we going out there?"

Chapter 18

Operation "Elusive Shadow Two"—Damascus, Syria

The night skies filled with lightning, and the Mediterranean stormed. Heavy clouds obscured the moon, and visibility on the Syrian shore, south of Tartus Port was minimal. Arik stood on the deck of a navy landing craft. Two reconnaissance unit teams squatted beside him, wearing Russian army combat uniforms and holding short-barreled Kalashnikov rifles with foldable stocks and silencers, normally used by the Spetsnaz.[11]

The glare of a green laser flashlight emerged from the shore. That was the signal. The landing craft approached the barren sand strip, a door opened, and five Russian SUVs, bearing the insignia of the Russian navy, emerged from it. They descended to the shallow water and effortlessly continued to the rock-strewn beach. A Mossad operative replaced the driver in the first SUV. He was going to be their navigator for the drive to Damascus.

High above the soldiers flew an airplane stacked with sophisticated equipment for electronic warfare. While the ship had still been at sea, all radar and communication

---

[11]"Special unit taskforce"–an elite Russian army unit.

systems belonging to the Syrian and Russian naval bases in Tartus had been tampered with. Mossad operatives cut off the power lines providing electricity to the local military bases. The Syrian and Russian soldiers cursed their misfortune and the bad weather, which they blamed for yet another power outage.

At Tartus Port, about 120 miles northwest of Damascus, Russian soldiers were permanently stationed, so there was nothing new or surprising about the small convoy of Russian vehicles driving toward Damascus. The Syrian soldiers who manned the roadblock at the exit from Tartus Port didn't even bother to get out of their booth because of the heavy rain. They simply opened the electric gate for the SUVs and shouted "*Spasiba!*" from a safe distance.

After three hours of driving through the pouring rain, the forces reached the gathering point: a large hangar situated in an industrial zone on the outskirts of western Damascus. The doors closed behind them. The head of Mossad's Tzomet Division was already waiting for them there along with his local operatives.

A light meal had been prepared for the soldiers and placed on tables lined across the walls. After they ate, they each found their own corner in the hangar and fell asleep on straw mattresses prepared in advance. Twenty-four hours remained before zero-hour.

In the morning, Kidon soldiers landed at the Damascus International Airport disguised as businessmen, tourists, and members of a Dutch archeological expedition. They all settled in hotels or pilgrim hostels throughout the city. Support teams crossed the southern Jordanian border, disguised as truck drivers transporting sheep and cattle. Inside the trucks, concealed in hidden compartments beneath the floor, were weapons and medical and electronic equipment the soldiers might need. At one PM, pairs of soldiers waited at different points for a small tourist bus to pick them up. On its windshield, a sign was hung with the words, both in Arabic and English: Tour of the Citadel of Damascus and the Army Museum.

Following a thirty-minute drive toward the northwestern side of the city, accompanied by a fast Honda motorcycle making sure no one followed, the minibus turned to the industrial zone and entered straight into the hangar in which the reconnaissance unit soldiers were already waiting.

"I want everyone to gather around me," called Arik. During the night, he had glued a thick Arabic mustache above his upper lip, dyed his hair black, and dressed in a gray safari suit, making him look like a local businessman. "Welcome to Damascus. I'm the commander of the operation you've been training for by using simulations and models. The objective of this operation is to take out Imad Husniyah, the man responsible for numerous terrorist attacks against Jewish institutes abroad, as well as the kidnapping and killing of Israeli and American soldiers. We have some solid intelligence that this afternoon, Husniyah is intending to pay a visit to a certain lady residing in a high-rise building in southern Damascus. The man is a mastermind escape artist and has slipped through our fingers several times, causing the death of many of our men in the process. I have no intention of letting him get away this time."

A large aerial photo was spread on the floor. Arik approached it and pointed at a map on which several streets appeared. One of them was surrounded by a red circle. "Our men have been surveilling this building for quite some time. An American satellite is providing us information as well. The Americans will let us know when Husniyah gets out of Beirut and begins the drive up the Beirut-Damascus highway. It's a two hour drive, give or take. We've placed operatives across the road to make sure he doesn't linger or decide to go elsewhere."

Arik walked away from the aerial photo and stood at the center of the circle of soldiers, passing his eyes from one to the other. "The objective given us by the government is to make sure that man doesn't get out of here alive. Nevertheless, we don't want innocent casualties or an armed conflict with the local police or the Syrian army. That is why I want you to open fire only as a last resort and only if your life or the lives of others depends on it. The building and its surroundings will be sterile. You are not going to enter it. The only ones operating inside will be members of a reinforced Kidon team. I don't want to see improvisations or personal initiatives that were not part of your original assignments, is that clear?"

The commander of the General Staff Reconnaissance Unit nodded reluctantly.

Arik distributed the scene maps among the team commanders and briefed them. "Team One will be positioned at the end of the street and will block it under the pretense of a vehicle mechanical dysfunction. Team Two will block the exit from the neighborhood using the same pretext. In case of any contact with the local police or any other hostile element, you will pretend to speak Russian only. You will have our local drivers who speak the native dialect. Let them do all the talking. Let me repeat this one more time: you do not open fire unless your life or the lives of others are under immediate danger. Is that clear?" Arik looked at the commander of the military force, who appeared to be craving some action. "We're not going to have another Entebbe Operation here, are we?"[12] The officer nodded with embarrassment.

"The moment the street is blocked," Arik continued, "Kidon teams will go into action. The first team will open Husniyah's vehicle, using a remote we've decoded, and replace the headrest of the driver's seat with an identical headrest filled with explosives. You have one minute to get the job done and take cover. Wait for my call before remotely detonating the charge. This will happen only after the target enters his vehicle and starts the engine and only following my direct instruction. Are we clear?"

The commander of team one blurted a quick, "Yes."

"Team Two will serve as a backup for the first team. While the first team replaces the headrest, the second team will get into the vehicle and place a deadly poison on the steering wheel. The poison, neurotoxin forte, is tasteless and odorless. A single touch with an uncovered hand causes the toxin to be absorbed into the body. Within minutes, his red blood cell will explode and he will die in agony, completely paralyzed and lacking the ability to call for help."

The men of the various teams stirred impatiently. They'd already heard the briefing a number of times during their training in Israel. Arik noticed their growing impatience. "I know you've heard it all before, but in my experience, the final briefing always reveals something you've missed. Let's move on. Team Three will serve as backup. It will be parked

---

[12]https://en.wikipedia.org/wiki/Operation_Entebbe, accessed 24 September 2016.

right outside the parking lot where Husniyah is supposed to park his vehicle. The team will arrive in a gray Mitsubishi Pajero, very similar to one owned by one of the neighbors who will be at work. The vehicle will be loaded with over two hundred pounds of explosives. The explosives in the SUV will be used only if the booby-trapped headrest or the poison don't work as planned. Exploding the SUV next to the building would demolish it and cause the death of dozens of innocent civilians. Therefore, the explosion is planned to take place only next to Husniyah's car and only while he is on the road back to Beirut. The team will exit of the vehicle after it is parked, then go up to one of the roofs in the area to surveil the situation. A local operator will be stationed next to the vehicle and keep watch. Is everything clear so far?"

Once more, the team members responded by nodding.

"Team Four will operate as a cleanup team and will also be in charge of securing the scene against any possible interruptions. If Husniyah arrives with a bodyguard remains behind to guard the vehicle, he must either be distracted or quietly annihilated and disposed of before teams One and Two get into action. My radio code is Assad Wahid. Each of you will receive his own code name and needs to memorize it. All communication between us will be in Arabic only. In the beginning of the operation, I will say, *basal*, and at its end, I will say *asal*. The minute you hear the code word 'asal,' you all clear the area quickly and, with the aid of our local operatives, get to the evacuation area, south of the gathering point. The minibus, the five Russian SUVs, the equipment truck, and an evacuation vehicle disguised as an ambulance will be waiting for you. Each team will head out in a different vehicle and take a different route. You each have a cover story you've been memorizing. At the end of the operation, all routes will meet at the evacuation point close to the border between the Golan Heights and Jordan. There, we will be picked up by helicopters. It should take you about an hour and a quarter to get there." He glanced at his watch. "It is now two PM. Get a move on, and start taking your positions. I'll be positioned in a location which will allow me to overview the entire operation. Questions?"

No one raised his hand, and Arik rushed outside the hangar to empty his tormented bladder in a quiet corner.

At five PM, they all heard Arik's baritone voice on the radio: "*Basal.*" Imad Husniyah was on his way to the neighborhood. A gray Mitsubishi SUV was parked in the predetermined spot by two soldiers, a man and a woman, from Team Three. The two of them then left the scene with the woman pushing a baby carriage with a doll inside. The SUV's intended driver waited close by in the company of a local agent. The men of teams One and Two sat in a coffee shop and watched a black Mercedes SUV enter the parking area of the building complex. A chubby man in his mid-forties exited the vehicle. His silver beard was carefully trimmed, a baseball cap rested on his head, and his eyes were concealed by sunglasses. Arik sat in an apartment that had been rented in advance, situated right in front of Husniyah's lover's apartment, and watched the intended victim through a pair of binoculars. He looked for a bodyguard or an escort, but couldn't see one. "Teams One and Two, hold your positions and wait," he whispered in Arabic into the microphone and looked at the large screen which broadcast, through a tiny camera hidden in a fan above Layla Tarawa's bedroom, watching everything that took place in her bedroom. Thirty minutes had passed before he saw the chubby man entering the bedroom, and the two of them began to make love. "Teams One and Two, go," Arik whispered in Arabic.

The electronic device with the vehicle's remote code was activated, and its door opened. The driver's seat headrest was replaced. At the same time, a soldier from team two entered the SUV, wearing a gas mask and double-layer rubber gloves. He smeared the deadly poison on the vehicle's steering wheel with a special brush he unscrewed from a tiny flask. A minute later, the vehicle's alarm system kicked in, and its doors relocked. The beeping sound marking the alarm system's activation was swallowed by the noise of children playing soccer in the parking lot.

A police car drove slowly down the street. Arik watched it with concern. The police car stopped next to the coffee shop where the Kidon teams were sitting and waiting, and two cops came out of it. One headed to the restroom while the other took a pita with spicy tuna salad from the counter, then got back to the police car without paying.

Arik held his breath. The team members at the coffee shop grabbed the butts of their guns under the *jellabiyas* they wore. One of them slowly pushed the headrest under his chair. Five tense minutes passed before the policeman came out of the restroom. On his way out, he went to the refrigerator and offhandedly took a bottle of Coke. The police car slowly moved away. Everyone emitted a sigh of relief.

Two hours later, Imad Husniyah went down to the parking lot, wrapped in a warm coat. He circled his car, bent, and peeked underneath. Nothing aroused his suspicion. Mothers called their children, who were playing in the parking lot, to come up for dinner. Fathers came back from work. Everything looked normal.

"Team Three, stand by," Arik whispered.

Imad Husniyah went into his vehicle. He punched the activation code and inserted the key into the ignition switch. The car began to move. The deadly poison on the steering wheel began to be absorbed into the skin of his fingers.

"Team One, now!" Arik called.

The explosion in the driver's seat headrest severed Imad Husniyah's head from his body, which slumped forward. The armored windows absorbed the sound of the blast. The SUV kept moving slowly down the road, until it collided into the booby-trapped Mitsubishi parked at the parking lot entrance.

Arik's blood froze in his veins. He feared the collision might activate the explosive mechanism. Nothing happened. Suddenly, an idea flashed through his mind. He instructed the local operative watching over the rigged SUV to drive it to the Mukhabarat[13] Headquarters in central Damascus. *If does as he's told, then he probably didn't switch sides.* If he handed the SUV over to the Mukhabarat, they could still explode it in order to create a diversion.

"*Asal!*" he ordered, then immediately repeated the command. He abandoned his observation point on the roof and ran down the stairs to verify the kill, his hand deep in his gray safari suit, clutching his loyal Glock pistol.

Neighbors and curious onlookers gathered to stare at the surreal scene of a headless man's body leaning against the dashboard. Inside the vehicle, blood and brain fragments were splattered all over the armored windows. A brief glance was enough for Arik. He knew that within minutes, the neighbors would alert the police, which would be followed

---

[13]The Syrian secret police, known for its ruthless methods.

by the men of the Mukhabarat, who would block all the exits from the neighborhood.

The local operator went into the SUV, sat beside the wheel, and headed north to central Damascus, ignoring the curious eyes of the neighbors. He parked the SUV in front of the Mukhabarat building's entrance as he had been ordered, then quickly took off. Another local operator followed him in his car and sent a radio signal that caused the SUV to shatter in a mighty explosion that wreaked havoc in the Mukhabarat Headquarters. The attention of the Syrian intelligence people was diverted, and no one noticed Mossad teams that slipped south toward safety.

Arik walked calmly toward his escape vehicle: an ambulance parked at the end of the neighborhood. He sat beside the driver, dressed in the white gown of a 'Red Crescent' paramedic, and hung a stethoscope on his neck. The ambulance went on its way, sirens wailing. Following a short drive, it stopped to pick up Team Three, a pair of soldiers, a man and a woman. The woman wore an inflated rubber belt beneath her dress that made her appear like a woman in the last months of her pregnancy. A white headscarf, just like the ones worn by local Druze women, was wrapped around her head. She lay in a stretcher, and her 'husband' sat by her side, wearing the clothes of a Druze farmer, a round mustache proudly glued above his upper lip. They all held Micro-Tavor rifles with silencers within arm's reach. The rest of the teams drove down rural roads and trails, parallel to the main road leading south. The soldiers of the Reconnaissance Unit, still disguised as Russian commando soldiers, moved down the fields, away from the main roads, navigating via night vision augmented equipment.

Arik took a tiny radio from his pocket, placed it against his lips and whispered, "Almagor, this is Assad Wahid requesting the evacuation of Asal within one hour."

In the air, above the border of the Golan Heights, an Israeli Air Force plane circled, operating as a flying headquarters. Cornfield sat inside, surrounded by communication and Air Force intelligence officers. That was the company he liked to keep and the environment he felt most comfortable in. "This is Almagor One. Roger that!" he replied, then added, laughingly, "Nice work! *Ya Assad.*"

Chapter 19

Beehive on the Cliff Neighborhood in Palmachim Air Force Base

Arik hated the hours that followed an assassination, even if it had been a justified one. He was driven by a military SUV from the helipad to his house in the Beehive on the Cliff neighborhood. The hour was late and the weather dreary. Arik stood in his bedroom, wondering what he might do in an evening in which both the house and his heart felt so empty. The operation debriefing was scheduled for the following day at the Defense Minister's office.

Finally, he decided to go running to relieve some of his stress. Hopefully, some physical exercise would allow him a good night's sleep. He dressed in a warm sweat suit, went down to the stormy beach, and began running south. The lights of Ashdod twinkled from afar, and the waves of the sea, noisily breaking against the limestone cliffs, washed the sand strip under his running feet.

A few hundred yards later, his body filled with tiredness. He panted, coughed, and slowed his pace to a quick walk. Sharp pangs between his ribs forced him to sit down on one of the rocks. Cold sweat washed his body. He could barely breathe. He forced himself up, wobbling on unsteady feet as he walked back home, feeling dizzy and sick to his stomach. Black spots appeared in front of his eyes, and he was barely able to climb the stairs cut in the cliff.

When he got back home, he got straight into the bathroom and took a warm shower. It was difficult for him to breathe regularly, or even to remain steady on his feet beneath the stream of hot water. Finally, his legs buckled, and he dropped to the shower floor, hot water still pouring from above.

After long minutes, he heaved himself up, went out of the shower and put on a bathrobe. In the living room, he activated the hearth with a click of a button. A few minutes later, warmth spread through the house. The logs crackled happily, and a pleasant scent of eucalyptus oil filled the air. Arik collapsed on his large leather armchair and snuggled in his warm bathrobe.

He was filled with fear. The breakdown of his body took him years back, to the uncomfortable territory of his childhood. With a shivering hand, he poured himself a glass of Rémy Martin cognac and added some sweet Cointreau, a mix he had learned from a French friend. The alcohol spread through his body, offering him comforting pleasure and relaxing the dread that held him. His thoughts became sharp and clear. *There's no choice*, he decided, *I'll go and see a doctor tomorrow.*

On the following morning, while he was driving to the clinic, his car phone rang. He looked at the screen. "Mossad Director's Office," the digital letters blinked.

"Yes!" he spoke into the mouthpiece above his head.

"Listen," said Shlomo Zimmer, Cornfield's bureau chief.

Arik detested the use of that military word at the opening of a sentence.

"Yes, what do you want?" he asked angrily.

"It's not about what I want. It's about what Cornfield wants. He asked me to tell you, 'The flower bud has opened.' He said you'd know what to do."

"Of course I know what to do," Arik lied, "I'll get on it right away."

He drove a few more miles until he reached a gas station. In an enclosed tire shed was a clandestine safe. There, Arik took out of the safe the envelope Cornfield had handed him a few weeks before and opened it. He went over the instructions of the operation and got back to the road, calculating the shortest route to the nearest airport.

He called Cornfield's bureau chief on his phone. "Zimmer, I need you to arrange a plane to take me to Baku, capital of Azerbaijan. I'm on my way to the Air Force military base at the Ben-Gurion Airport right now. Let me know when the plane's ready for takeoff."

Chapter 20

Heydar Babayev International Airport—Baku, Azerbaijan

Arik looked at the luxurious and spacious terminal named after the former

president's father and predecessor. He was experienced enough not to look down on the country's form of government. Western democracy, he knew, was not suitable for every country. There were societies in which a presidential dynasty, or even a dictatorship, was conceived to be the better way.

He stood in line for the passport control, and as always, memorized his false name, as it appeared on the Canadian passport he was holding.

Two police officers came out a side office, approached him and silently beckoned him to join them. He left the line and walked between the two of them to a wide door that silently opened, then closed behind him. He found himself in a large and carpeted VIP lounge. The numerous sofas lined against the walls indicated it was used for hosting important guests. A tall, lanky man walked toward him with his hand extended.

"Georgi," Arik said happily, using the predetermined code name.

"Raymundo," the man replied.

They shook hands warmly. "Would you care for a drink after your flight?"

The man didn't wait for an answer, quickly pulled aside a curtain, and exposed a bar laden with alcoholic beverages. Arik smiled. He should have guessed Georgi, who was actually Dato Zerekidaze, the president's bureau chief, would keep the finest alcoholic beverages at hand. Dato took a bottle of local vodka from the freezer and a plate of herring from the refrigerator. "It's shitty vodka," said Dato. "The state of vodka can always tell you how well we are doing with the Russians, diplomatically speaking. When things are good, there's a steady supply of good vodka. When the Russians are angry, we need to settle for this shitty local vodka. Personally, I prefer our local Chacha brandy."

Arik took a small sip and coughed. Dato laughed. "I see you still haven't learned how to drink," he chided Arik. He tilted his head back and emptied his frosty glass with a single gulp. His face reddened, and the hairs of his mustache stood on end. He took a piece of herring and swallowed it while biting a slice of black bread, which he generously buttered. Then he poured himself another glass and smiled at Arik, who patiently waited for the ceremony to end.

"Now, tell me…" He placed his hand on Arik's arm. "Are you sure you'd like to meet that witch? I'm not even sure she's in Baku. I think she might be in Paris now."

"I know she's here now. Ask your people. I need her for her abilities, and she could use my help to advance her business. Just set up a meeting, and I'm sure we could come to a mutual understanding."

Dato shrugged. "I'll try, but there's something else I need you to help me with as well. Something very important."

Arik listened.

"Our president, Nur Sultan Babayev, is unwell. He underwent a certain surgery in Paris, which wasn't successful. He's extremely concerned. His father had passed from the same illness when he was thirty-eight. The Parisian doctor recommended Dr. Jackie Maman, an Israeli urologist from the Hadassah Medical Center in Jerusalem who has already saved many patients by using brachytherapy."

"What is the president suffering from?"

Dato squirmed uneasily. "I'm not authorized to discuss it. As you know, the president cannot openly visit Israel. He is the chairman of the Organization of Islamic Cooperation."

"Don't worry." Arik smiled. "We know how to handle such obstacles."

Arik considered all developments, both positive and negative, that might result from such an operation: the president might die on the operating table, someone might recognize him, one of his own men might take over the country in his absence and claim he had always been a traitor and a Zionist spy... On the other hand, he had to consider the enormous benefits gaining such a friend could bring, a friend with strategic assets right at the northern border of Iran.

Dato guessed what was in his mind. "Just give us a list of things you need, and I'll do anything in my power for it to be accepted, for a suitable price, of course."

Arik thought of Cornfield. Would that rough man be able to be involved in such a delicate, eastern style give and take negotiation?

"And the appointment with Mariam?"

"Consider it a gift demonstrating the respect I have for you. I checked. You were right. The witch is indeed here in Baku. You'll be able to meet her as soon as possible."

"Thank you," said Arik. As always, he felt overwhelmed by how flexible the truth was in those parts of the world and by the ability of the people of the east to lie and immediately retract their claims without any sense of unease. "It's important that she doesn't know who I am until the very last moment. Just tell her I'm your friend, an international businessman who will be able to aid her business in France, both politically and financially."

"All right, I recommend that you do your homework on her. She's a tough lady who leads a group of terrorists. She's seen it all. Nothing scares her anymore. Do you know that the Iranian Islamic Revolutionary Guard Corps murdered part of her family to avenge her organization's support of Saddam Hussein?"

"Yes," said Arik. He had learned everything there was to know about Mariam on the flight to Baku, from her family's history to her sexual habits.

Dato took a cell phone from his pocket, dialed, exchanged a few sentences in Azeri and returned he phone to his pocket. "The presidential chopper will be ready in an hour. If you're tired, we could take you to a hotel, or you can wait in our VIP lobby while I make the proper arrangements."

Arik knew that time was just as flexible as truth in those parts of the world. An hour could often stretch into four, which meant going to a hotel and back could postpone his appointment for many hours. "Thank you, I'll wait here."

Dato extended his hand for a handshake again, and immediately moved to a series of hugs and wet kisses on both cheeks. "Good to see you here," he said a moment before stepping out the wide door. "The president and I are convinced we have great things ahead of us." He winked to Arik.

Chapter 21

The Presidential Palace—Baku, Azerbaijan

Much to Arik's surprise, Dato returned to the VIP lobby in less than an hour. "The helicopter is ready," he said with sparkling eyes, and Arik could only assume President Nur Sultan Babayev really needed his operation urgently. When they walked on the runway, Dato added, "I did some checking. Mariam Halachi was deported from France after her organization had been declared a terrorist organization. She has sought asylum from our country and is now in our debt."

Arik looked at the Caspian Sea through the window of the presidential chopper. It was strewn with gas rigs spitting tongues of fire. Across the beach strip, the chimneys of refineries spat smoke. Thousands of oil pumps rose and fell as if in mock prayer. Beside them, across the horizon, stretched the miserable shanty towns of foreign laborers.

"Which means what, exactly?"

"Which means she will do anything we tell her to do."

Arik nodded in satisfaction. That was the answer he had hoped for.

"You will meet the lady in a private conference room inside the Presidential Palace. As you've requested, we haven't told her anything about you, but she's not stupid."

Dato wasn't wrong. In a room with a wood parquet floor laid with beautiful Azeri carpets, a woman waited for Arik on a red leather sofa. She looked fortyish and wore a dark blue, tailored suit that fit the bright gray shade of her eyes. Her white skin, her manicured nails, hair, and black eyelashes all spoke of a well-groomed woman. Her body language indicated her sense of self-importance. She rose to greet Arik and shook his hand. The two inspected each other like two carpet merchants in a Persian bazaar. "Thank you for coming to see me," Arik said in fluent French, a language he had mastered years before while serving as Mossad's station commander in Paris.

"Am I correct in assuming I'm speaking with a representative of the Israeli Mossad?" she answered in French with a thick Iranian accent and met his gaze.

Arik was surprised by her direct approach, but was careful not to betray his emotions. "At this stage, let's just assume I represent an international organization with similar interests to your own. I think we could greatly benefit each other."

She smiled with demonstrated skepticism. "Are you sure?"

Arik knew the game well enough not to be worried by her cynical reaction. What he needed could be obtained by other means; what she and her organization needed was a matter of life and death.

"We know," he said, "that you are currently at the top of the American State Department's list of terrorist organizations. We also know that it is important for you, personally, to be regarded by the western world as a pioneer of advanced Islamic politics and a freedom fighter."

Her face remained expressionless.

"We can help you. Perhaps we can ask our friends in Paris

to allow you reopen your Paris headquarters and offer you a special status as political refugee. Maybe even provide you with a VIP diplomatic passport."

She continued to examine him with her beautiful eyes, still saying nothing.

Arik continued. "We admire the fact the members of your People's Army are dedicated to the organization's cause and vision. I even heard a few of them had burned themselves to death in Paris last year to protest your arrest by the French government. We are also aware of the fact a large part of your organization members have divorced their wives, according to your instructions, to demonstrate their loyalty to the organization."

A crack finally appeared on her armor of indifference. "We are not Muslim fanatics, and they weren't asked to demonstrate their loyalty to the organization or to me personally. Under the circumstances, the members of my organization cannot enjoy the comforts of marriage. We are confronted with a ruthless enemy and mustn't be diverted. I, too, have divorced my husband. Each of our organization members believes in the cause of bringing democracy to Iran and is willing to sacrifice himself for it."

Arik wasn't impressed. He had read all the details about Mariam's divorce, which involved a young lover, a soldier in her organization, and money. Lots of it.

Even though it was Ramadan, a servant wearing a colorful Azeri garment silently entered the room, holding a tray laden with dry fruits, nuts, and a teapot of herbal tea, which emitted a wonderful aroma. He placed the tray on a table carved with beautiful damask patterns and left the room. Arik was hungry and thirsty. He took a handful of dried fruit and filled them with nuts and began to chew with great relish. She examined him, and he lifted the teapot from the tray and gave her a questioning look. She approved with a nod, and he poured tea for the both of them. She took a sugar cube, placed it in her mouth, and sipped the tea with open pleasure. He could not remove his eyes from her face, which suddenly wore a sensual expression. They sat quietly for long minutes, drinking tea and continuing their negotiation with their eyes.

"What else can your organization offer me?" she suddenly asked.

"What else do you need?" Arik replied with a question of his own.

"I need money, arms, communication and explosives training, optical equipment and advanced communication equipment, encryption means and computers, powerful dirt bikes, and perhaps fast race-boats as well."

"Would you like to work with us directly or through the Kurds?"

"So you admit to being a Mossad agent. By the way, you still haven't told me your name, although I'm sure you're going to lie to me anyway.

"Just call me Raymundo."

"Raymundo." She chuckled. "The name of a Latin lover. You look like a Norseman but have Mediterranean table manners. She extended her hand, "My name is Mariam Halachi, and I'm the elected president of the Iranian National Council of Resistance. I'm the leader of our exile organization abroad, but I assume you already know all that."

"Yes," Arik admitted.

"The organization's boss is my brother, Professor Massoud Halachi. He is still in Iran, hiding from the revolutionary guard's hit squads who've been looking for him since he was deported from France in 1986..." She sipped the remaining tea from the bottom of her cup. "What do you need from me?"

"We want a group of your organization's soldiers, say about three hundred men, to arrive at the city of Kirkuk, at the heart of the independent Kurdish controlled area of Iraq. There, they will practice in mining activity, sabotage, communication, encryption, collecting tactical intelligence, and riding dirt bikes..."

"And who would train them?" asked Mariam. "Not the men of your organization, I hope?"

"As far as you're concerned, they'll be trained by US Special Forces personnel."

"The Americans have allowed you to use their services?"

"You shouldn't worry about that. We'll take care of everything."

She paused for a moment. "You're asking for a lot," she finally said. "In addition to settling the question of my status in Paris, you will also need to open a bank account in my name and deposit a million Euros in it for initial expenses."

"I'll check," Arik promised.

"And one more thing. Paris is a dangerous city. I'll need an armored car, preferably a Mercedes-Maybach."

Arik suppressed a smile. He knew all about the "spy syndrome." The office had given him all the in-depth psychological knowledge he needed. He knew that in order to make someone do something, he needed to find their emotional weakness. He also knew all about common weaknesses: sex, money, ego, and rancor.

He was experienced enough to understand Mariam's personal demands would come at the end of the list. They'd reached the point of no return—the point that represented Mariam's emotional needs. Thus, it was the right moment to add another demand to his shopping list. "There's something else that we want, something that would benefit your organization as much as it would benefit ours." She tightened her lips in discomfort, and Arik ignored it. "We need twenty-five outstanding students, graduates of Tabriz University's computer science department in Iran, all Azeri in origin. We want them to take a cyber warfare course in military base near Baku. This will allow them to work as cyber spies for both our organizations as early as three months from now—"

"We've talked enough for now." She cut him short and rose from her seat. "Let me check with the proper parties and do some thinking. I suggest we meet here tomorrow to coordinate our mutual interests as well as discuss the technical details." She offered Arik a firm handshake and a smile that revealed two rows of pearly white teeth and left the room, tapping the floor rhythmically with her high heels, well aware of the fact he was following her with his eyes.

Dato came inside before the door even closed. "Don't worry," he told Arik, without trying to hide the fact he had eavesdropped on the conversation. "She'll give you everything you've asked for. Let's go to town. I'm inviting you to dinner in a nice restaurant. Have you ever eaten Azeri food?"

At the heart of the old city of Baku, next to the souvenir stalls and a short distance from the Maiden's Tower, inside a stone cellar, a beautiful oriental restaurant was hidden: The'

Firuza ' Restaurant. The floor was covered by Azeri carpets and colorful, embroidered tablecloths were spread on the tables. The place was teeming with life because of the end of the Ramadan fast. The delicious food reminded Arik of the Ottoman restaurants in Istanbul: *taboon* bread; lamb chops grilled over charcoal; kebabs on a bed of yogurt sauce; *tara* dishes—green mallow plant leaves—with small dumplings and green pickled plums; a bowl of rice pilaf with meat; carrot sticks with cumin seeds; and fresh salads sprinkled with nuts and pomegranate seeds.

"Now, let's discuss the preparations needed for the president's operation," said Dato after gulping several glasses of frozen Polish vodka.

On the following day, Arik met Mariam for lunch at the same conference room in the Presidential Palace. This time, she arrived wearing a green suit and matching shoes. She was much more relaxed and smiled often.

A servant wearing traditional garments entered the room and served the guests fresh breads stuffed with meat, sheep cheese, and fresh pomegranate juice.

"I've discussed your offer with my brother, and we've decided to accept it. As an advance, I am willing to share everything we know about Ahmadinejad's nuclear plan with you. We call him 'the dwarf' by the way. That man is a kind of modern Napoleon who wants to return Iran to the glory days of the great Persian Empire. In order to achieve that, he wastes my country's resources on the huge Islamic Revolutionary Guard, supporting Shiite terrorist organizations all over the world and developing an ambitious program for transforming Iran into a nuclear superpower, thus dragging all the other Gulf states into an insane nuclear arms race. We simply won't have that. I think your organization should know we've determined to assassinate the scientist involved with this insane plan."

"That is your decision to make," said Arik, suppressing a smile. He knew Cornfield would be delighted with this news and would happily take credit when revealing the information to the prime minister.

Chapter 22

Mossad Headquarters

Early in the morning, Arik landed at the military section of the Ben-Gurion Airport. His car was already waiting for him there with one of Mossad's drivers. "Go straight to the office, please," Arik instructed him, feeling elated.

The two men waiting for him at the office weren't as cheerful. Major General Mot'ke "Steak Face" Hassin was sitting next to Cornfield. "What's up, Arik?" asked Hassin. Arik immediately realized Cornfield had instructed Steak Face to manage the debriefing and assumed it was just one more of his control games.

"I met Mariam Halachi in Baku," he said calmly, careful to conceal his emotions. "I assume you know who she is from reading Alex's reports."

"And?" Hassin urged him on.

"She will make a force the size of a brigade available to us which we will train in Kirkuk, in the Kurdish controlled area of north east Iraq. I have a list of equipment, arms and money she's requested from us."

"And what is she offering in return?" asked Hassin.

"Hold on, I'm not finished yet." Arik ignored him and continued to address Cornfield directly. "The training must be coordinated with 'ELGA.'"

"Who the hell is 'ELGA' and why should we coordinate anything with her?" Hassin wondered, exposing his ignorance.

Arik did his best not to chuckle. "ELGA is the codename we use for CIA forces." Arik turned his eyes to Cornfield. "I suggest you finalize the details with your friend, Admiral Jack Derby. Fischer used to meet with him twice a year to tie up loose ends and coordinate our operations. I think as the new Mossad director, you should also maintain such a relationship with the director of the CIA."

The two generals snorted in contempt at the sound of Fischer's name.

"We're walking on eggshells here," Arik explained. "We can't leave any fingerprints when it comes to our relationship with Mariam. Her men will be willing to cooperate only as long as they believe they are working with the western superpowers against the Ayatollah's regime. If they discover Israel is involved, the entire operation would probably fall apart. Some of them have been hunted by the Savak, the Shah's secret police, whose men we helped train in the past."

"But what can she offer us in return?" Hassin demanded to know.

"She still has many connections inside Iran. She has people everywhere, especially in the northern part of the country where there's a population of thirty million Azeri. She will give me a few dozen outstanding students from the Tabriz University, who will be trained by my Digital Fortress Team to become 'keyboard spies.'"

"What in God's name are 'keyboard spies'?"

"Cyber soldiers." Cornfield silenced him. "Good guys. They know how to do some serious damage with computers and worms, right?"

Arik smiled. Cornfield was definitely a quick learner.

"And how much money does she want?" asked Cornfield. "How much is this going cost me?"

"I suggest that we take a look at the cost-benefit analysis before we discuss the actual—" Arik answered.

"How much?" Cornfield demanded and slammed the table with his fist.

"In addition to weapons and equipment, she's asking for a million Euros and help with convincing the French DGS to offer her a diplomat's status. She also needs arms licenses for her bodyguards and an armored Mercedes." Arik left out the Maybach part of the vehicle description, as it almost doubled the price.

"That's a lot of money," said Cornfield. "I'll need to discuss this with the prime minister." He thought for a moment. "As for the weapons, I approve. Doing what we can with the French… Maybe. But I'm not authorizing that Mercedes nonsense!" he said decisively.

Hassin nodded in agreement, and Arik looked at them both with mocking eyes. *Rosencrantz and Guildenstern*, he thought. *And I'm stuck here like some kind of Hamlet.* He tried to summon all his powers of persuasion. "Cornfield, the Mercedes represents her emotional attachment to the deal. We're talking about small change. Especially when compared to the enormous benefits such a deal could offer us. Let me handle this directly with our finance division."

"I won't approve it, do you hear me?" Cornfield barked.

"My mother once taught me something that may sound stupid to you: every agreement is sacred and must be honored, even if it was done with scumbags. I gave Mariam my word we'd honor the agreement."

"Then take it to the finance division yourself as you've suggested!" Cornfield rose from his seat, indicating the meeting was adjourned.

"Hold on. There's something even more important to discuss," said Arik. "A matter that came up during my meeting with Georgi in Azerbaijan."

"Who's Georgi?" Hassin wondered aloud.

Cornfield placed a large hand on Steak Face's shoulder. "I'll explain later." He dropped back in his large chair and sighed. The phantom pains he was suffering from gave him no rest. Arik looked at him curiously; the new Mossad director reeked of alcohol.

"Hold on a minute. I need something to drink. My leg is killing me." Cornfield took two Tylenol, opened the large wooden globe placed on the side of his table, and took out a bottle of Glenfiddich 21. He poured himself half a glass and swallowed the pills in a single gulp.

"Medicinal alcohol, of course," he said jokingly, and Hassin echoed his bitter laughter, having been maimed in battle himself.

Arik got back to the subject at hand. "I've received a request from the president of Azerbaijan, Nur Sultan Babayev, involving a sensitive matter."

"What does he want?" Cornfield interrupted him impatiently.

"To come here incognito and undergo an operation at the Hadassah Medical Center. I think he has prostate cancer, and the operation he underwent at the Percy Military Hospital in Paris did not go well."

"Since when does Mossad care about healing some Kurd's dick?" asked Hassin.

"First of all, he's Caucasian." Arik now spoke with authority. "Secondly, his country is located in a highly sensitive geostrategic location between Russia, Iran, and Armenia—a location they all would love to annex because of its vast gas and oil reserves. Thirdly, Azerbaijan and Iran have been in conflict for decades; the Iranians claim the region was stolen from them by the Russians at the beginning of the twentieth century."

"I still don't understand," Cornfield admitted.

"Nur Sultan Babayev is in distress. His father had died from prostate cancer and he's afraid of suffering the same fate. He needs us. During the war in Afghanistan, he allowed the Americans to use former Soviet bases for logistical purposes. He would be willing to do the same for us."

"I'm still waiting for you to get to the goddamn point," said Cornfield, who had reached the limits of his patience.

"I think if we saved his life here in the Hadassah Medical Center, offered him aid, and sold him surveillance equipment and weapons, he'd agree to let us have a signals intelligence base right on the border of Iran. Perhaps he would even lease us one of their military's inactive Air Force bases. This means we could have a fighter squadron right in the Iranian's backdoor."

"Now you're talking!" Cornfield laughed with the joy of a child who had just received a desirable toy.

"Anything else?" Cornfield asked, "I need to take a leak. My diabetes is killing me."

"Mariam Halachi has told me her organization is interested in sabotaging the Iranian nuclear program. I think they'll wait for us to give them the proper equipment and training before actually starting to assassinate Iran's nuclear scientists."

"Excellent, the prime minister is going to love this. All right, get this Kurd here to Israel and fix his pecker. Yes, it's a great idea. Go for it. Try to convince them."

Arik suppressed another smile. He had already gotten the Azeri's principal agreement to the idea. At least that had been his impression following his conversations with Georgi. Still, he wanted Cornfield to be able and take credit for the achievement. "I think you need to close the details with him face-to-face once he's in Israel," he suggested. "This is above my level of authority. Perhaps we would even need to arrange for him to meet the prime minister."

Cornfield felt another stab of fear. Should the visit be marked a success, he'd be able to take credit for it, but should it fail… "All right," he said and rose to go to the restroom. "But I want you to be his escort officer for the visit."

Arik emitted a sigh of relief. That was exactly the offer he had hoped for.

Chapter 23

Hotel Burj Al Arab—Dubai, United Arab Emirates

From the windows of the congress hall, on the 117th floor of the hotel, the skyline of the United Arab Emirates stretched to infinity. High-rises were carefully lined across the shore beside low houses like a mouth with broken teeth, their windows gleaming in the afternoon sun. Fifty-seven men sat around the huge wooden table, some wearing *keffiyehs* and robes strewn with gold threads, others wearing elegant suits. All were Muslim leaders of the member-countries of the Organization of Islamic Cooperation.

Nur Sultan Babayev, President of the Republic of Azerbaijan and the organization's acting Chairman, opened the convention, trying hard to look at his fellow leaders' faces instead of the lenses of the television cameras. Behind him and all other leaders in the room sat each country's dignitaries and their entourages.

Nur Sultan examined his surroundings with a forced smile that concealed the fact he suffered a searing pain down the lower part of his body. He hit the table with the wooden hammer he was holding and began. "*Bismillah al-Rahman al-Rahim*… There is no God but Allah, and Muhammad is the Messenger of Allah. Your eminences, kings, presidents, and heads of states, thank you for coming to this important convention of the Heads of State Committee, which leads the Organization of Islamic Cooperation."

His private cell phone rang in his pocket. Nur Sultan took advantage of the temporary interval created by the applause and stole a look at the screen. "They've agreed. I got a green light. When can you take off?" A text message winked at him. The tension did not show on Nur Sultan's face. He looked straight at the floral arrangements, flown from Amsterdam that morning, and continued. "I ask the organization's general secretary, Professor Ahmet Aydin Ishangulo of the Turkish Republic, to give us an overview of the organization's activity in the past year and its financial status."

The moment the general secretary's raspy voice rose from the speakers, Nur Sultan shook his head apologetically and rose from his chair. His pelvis burned with pain. He knew the television cameras were following him and wore an expression of urgency on his face as if he had just been called to attend to a matter of great importance. He left the room with measured steps and, the moment the door closed behind him, moaned to his bodyguard. "Tell Dato Zerekidaze to get here urgently."

The bodyguard hesitated, not wanting to abandon the leader he had sworn to protect. He knew the hotel was guarded by the best security forces the small kingdom had to offer, but Azerbaijan and President Babayev had many powerful enemies.

"Go already!" the president commanded and dropped into one of the armchairs. The bodyguard, a former Olympic wrestler, moved with surprising nimbleness for a man his size. He went back to the conference hall and quickly returned with the bureau chief. Babayev motioned for him to sit beside him and then waved his hand at the bodyguard, who hurried to take his distance and keep an eye out from the other end of the hall. Babayev covered his mouth with the palm of his hand.

"Do you think it's safe to travel to the Jewish country?" he whispered, leaning toward Dato.

"Yes. I've spoken with one of their Mossad officers. He promised no one would know who you are."

"That's not enough!" hissed Nur Sultan, "I want complete medical confidentiality. If someone ends up identifying me, they can't know I'm sick or, God forbid, dying. The moment word of this gets out, all my remaining loyal subjects will abandon me."

"Sir, the lives of many people depend on you."

"You are Georgian, so you are not entirely familiar with our culture." The president sighed. "Our people are like a pack of wolves. The moment the pack senses a weakness with the alpha wolf, all its members unite to attack and bite it to death."

"Don't worry, Mr. President. I trust the Jews. They have an interest to buy oil and gas from us at bargain prices and sell us weapons and equipment. This is a win-win situation, a safe deal for us."

"Allah will help us." Nur Sultan sighed again. His pains gradually worsened, and he longed to have the treatment over with. "Prepare the plane. Instruct the pilot to present a flight plan to Amman. I have connections there who will allow me to continue to Israel without leaving any footprints. You're going to fly with me as well, and so will he." He pointed his finger at the bodyguard, who gave him a blank stare. "Send out a press release stating I was urgently recalled home to handle security issues at the Nagorno-Karabakh region. Back home, release an announcement stating I flew directly to hold talks with the Russians at the Sochi beach resort. This way, no one will notice I'm missing. How many days do we need for the operation?"

"Two or three days, including recuperation."

"I want to pray at the Al-Aqsa Mosque in Jerusalem."

"I'll see to it."

An hour later, Nur Sultan lay on a narrow bed in the presidential plane headed northwest. His bodyguard and Dato silently looked at him. Nur Sultan sighed and said, "Don't worry, we'll get through this." In his heart, he asked himself how their lives would look without him. He wasn't worried about the bodyguard, who would simply protect his successor. But Dato's life, should he stay alive, would not be easy at all. He examined him with fatherly affection, recalling the day he had discovered him during a graduation ceremony at Baku Polytechnicum. Dato had come from the neighboring country of Georgia to study oil and gas engineering, sponsored by a generous scholarship awarded to gifted students from all over the Soviet Union, and finished first in his class. Nur Sultan often thought he would marry his daughter to Dato if the latter weren't a Christian and of Georgian origins.

The plane suddenly shook. Nur Sultan felt a sharp pain piercing his groin. Dato held his hand. "Dato," Babayev whispered, "should anything happen to me, everything will collapse. Our chief of staff is a veteran of the Moscow Military Academy, and I doubt his loyalty. The prime minister is a religious Shiite and has excellent relations with Tehran. The

Armenians will try to raise their heads and conquer more parts of the country just like they did in the Nagorno-Karabakh region. The Russians will back them up to get to our gas and oil."

"Don't worry, Mr. President," said Dato. "You're a very strong man, and you'll survive."

Nur Sultan beckoned him to get closer and whispered in his ear. "I have a bank account in Hong Kong I've set aside for a rainy day. In the Presidential Palace, you will find a secret safe beneath the carpet on which my table is placed. Only Esmeralda, my secretary, knows about it." He took off a thin necklace from his neck on which a key was hanging. "The safe contains a secret escape plan, which includes a map leading to a hiding place in the village. There is also a villa on the shores of the Caspian Sea. There's a fast boat hidden there in a boat house. It will take you and my family across the Caspian Sea to Kazakhstan. Please take care of Esmeralda as well; she doesn't have a family. She has dedicated her life to me."

"Please don't worry, Mr. President," said Dato and placed a comforting hand on his president's shoulder. "For the past five years, I've created, within the government, army and security forces, a network of people who are loyal to us, people I completely trust. They have all been rewarded for their loyalty in various ways, each according to his needs, and operate as a kind of government within the government. They are loyal only to us. Now please allow me to give you a pain relief injection."

"You are also relieving the pains of my heart and my concerns," Nur Sultan smiled at him before falling asleep.

After midnight, the plane landed at the Amman airport. A sedan transferred its passengers to a parking area reserved for King Abdullah's private jet. An hour later, the plane landed at the military section of the Ben-Gurion Airport, where it was directed to Runway Three. An airport navigator waited for him there in a yellow vehicle with a sign saying: "Follow Me." The plane kept rolling for long minutes until it reached a secret hangar. The moment it stopped, it was surrounded by a company of armed soldiers wearing gray uniforms and green *berets*. A ramp was attached to the front side of the plane and its door opened.

A tall, handsome man in his fifties came inside and said in English, "Welcome to Israel, Mr. President. My name is Arik Bar-Nathan, and I'm in charge of the operations division in the Israeli Mossad. I am honored to serve as the escort officer for your visit. The prime minister relays his warmest regards and wishes you a speedy recovery. He also wanted to thank you for placing your faith in our country's medical services."

"Thank you," said Nur Sultan in English with a thick Russian accent. He shook Arik's hand with some hesitation. "Please relay to your prime minister my deep appreciation and gratitude. I am completely in your hands."

"Don't worry, sir," Arik said in an assured voice.

When they exited the air-conditioned plane, sweat immediately covered Babayev's face. The weather wasn't so warm and damp in his own country.

A black Mercedes limousine slid toward the foot of the ramp, and the president entered it and filled his lungs with cool, air-conditioned air. Dato sat to one side of him, and the Mossad officer, whose name he had already forgotten, sat on the other. The bodyguard took his place beside the driver, and the vehicle went on its way, two police motorcyclists racing ahead of it. Nur Sultan took a look at the changing views across the highway leading to the Israeli capital. In spite of the late hour, the road was illuminated, and the traffic was heavy.

Dato remained silent throughout the drive and so did the Mossad officer. The president trusted Dato, and now he had deposited his very life in the man's hands. And yet, somewhere at the back of his mind, a suspicion arose. His instincts had saved him numerous times in the past. Now they were telling him there was a secret connection between the men sitting on both his sides.

For the first time in his life, Nur Sultan felt helpless.

Chapter 24

The VIP protection unit transformed the urology ward of the Hadassah Medical Center into a sterile area. The president was taken to the examination room, and his groin was shaved. He lay, drifting in and out of sleep, and waited for the operation. Dato sat in an armchair close to the president, while the bodyguard waited outside with Arik and did his best not to fall asleep. Suddenly, the bodyguard erupted into a series of sneezes, not bothering to cover his nose.

"Bless you," Arik said in English. The bodyguard didn't reply. Arik examined the bodyguard's heavy chin and huge body. He wondered if the bodyguard was smart enough to share the president's secret or even knew where he was. Then his thoughts drifted to Eva. He had almost forgotten her at the moment he started taking care of "Operation Flower Bud." He took his personal cell phone from his pocket, wondering whether he should call her, and at that same moment, his work phone rang.

"What's happening?" Cornfield asked.

"Are we on a secure line?" Arik replied.

He heard Cornfield echoing the question to his driver, who curtly replied, "No."

"Please place your cell phone in the scrambler, and use the red receiver in front of you to talk to me," Arik explained patiently.

After a minute or two of rattling sounds and angry curses, Cornfield told his driver, "Do me a favor and connect the darned thing."

"It's connected," the driver finally said, and Cornfield returned to speak with Arik.

"Well, how did it go? The…operation in the president's balls?" Cornfield erupted into laughter.

"They've just started," Arik said in a reserved tone. "The procedure is brief. They'll be finishing in an hour. Then they'll take him to the recovery room. After that, he asked to be taken to pray at the Al-Aqsa Mosque."

"Did anyone recognize him in the hospital? Did anyone get suspicious?"

"Not at all. We registered him under a false name. The medical team thinks he's an oligarch from an East Asian country. They've already learned not to ask too many questions, so we won't need to lie to them."

"All right, keep me posted," Cornfield hung up without saying good-bye.

At nine AM, Dr. Jackie Maman, a silver-haired surgeon, came out of the operating room. "The operation has been completed successfully," he said in a tranquil voice. "The patient was transferred to the recovery room for a few hours of rest and monitoring."

Arik thanked him and called Cornfield again. "The operation was a success," he said briefly.

Cornfield, as usual, became impatient. "So what do you think he'd feel about what I want to offer him?"

"I think he'll agree. He's going to be discharged in a few hours and then we'll have two days to work him up to it, including the visit to al-Aqsa. I suggest that you talk to him in the presence of his bureau chief. If you recall, we gave you an update about him. He's Georgian and has been a very important source for us in the Caucasus area for quite some time. We've invested a lot of resources on him."

Cornfield muttered. "All right."

Arik repeated everything he and Dato had agreed on during their meeting in Baku. "I assume he would agree to a deal that will include building a signals intelligence base in a location we've located in the southern part of his country, including leasing an Air Force base for our activities. To start with, we may need to operate through an English or an American shell company. That's going to be his condition: that we leave no traceable fingerprints."

"All right, we have such companies."

"And another thing, he's going to want an arms deal as well. They need UAVs and high-precision guided weapons to use against the Armenians. Finally, we'll need to deposit something into his Swiss bank account, and, of course, bribe his bureau chief as well. His boss obviously doesn't suspect he's our man."

"Great. In principle, the prime minister has already approved everything. Have him stay in the Presidential Suite at the King David Hotel, our treat. I'll wait for you in the hotel's lobby at fourteen hundred hours. Once he's ready, I'll go up to the suite. You'll introduce me and then leave us to conduct a private conversation," Cornfield instructed.

Arik was pleased and worried at the same time. So far, the plan had worked just as he'd hoped it would. Still, he feared Cornfield wasn't sophisticated enough to handle the negotiations ahead.

Chapter 25

The British Military Cemetery—Mount Scopus,
Jerusalem

As the doors of the recovery room closed behind Nur Sultan, a sense of restlessness overtook Arik. He had always been frustrated inactivity. Now he had a few hours to kill and wondered whether he should go home or head to the office. Then he recalled Eva once again.

Eva was hidden in a dark corner at the back of his mind, a corner he tried to erase so as not to expose his growing need of her. He hesitated a minute or two before actually taking courage and calling her.

She answered immediately and whispered, "I'm in the middle of a lecture. Can I call you back?"

"Are you the lecturer or the audience?"

She suppressed a chuckle. "The audience this time."

"I'm in Jerusalem. I'll be with you in thirty minutes."

"All right. I'll come out to meet you. You don't have an entry permit, but I'll get one for you by the time you get here."

"I don't need entry permits."

"Oh, yes. How could I forget?" Eva reacted sarcastically. In the background, Arik could heard the creaking of an opening door, the sounds of conversation, and music. "I'm in the corridor. There are a lot of people and much noise out here. How about meeting someplace quiet where we could actually talk? My hotel room, for example?"

Arik thought that was exactly the one place he was trying to avoid. There were many things he still needed to learn about Eva. "How about a special place, peaceful and secluded?"

"I'm open to suggestions."

"Go on foot to the street that comes down from the campus, past the Hadassah Medical Center. To your right, you'll see the British Military Cemetery for fallen servicemen in World War I. You'd be able to recognize it from afar because of the massive cross-shaped monument."

"A cemetery?" She emitted a nervous laugh. "*That's* where you bring all the women you meet?"

He ignored the jibe. "I'll wait for you in half an hour on the stone bench at the footsteps of the chapel."

"Sounds frightening, but actually, maybe it's better this way. No one will be able to eavesdrop on our conversation."

Arik stopped his car next to the open gate and sat at the rendezvous point. His suspicions grew. What secrets could she possibly have? Why didn't she want anyone to eavesdrop on their conversation? He noticed her shapely profile coming down the road. Down in the valley, a view of the ancient city of Jerusalem spread before his eyes. On top of the mountain facing the cemetery, the dome of the Mosque of Omar twinkled with sunlight. He rose toward Eva and waved to her.

When she had reached him, she placed her lips against his in expectation. He turned her face gently, kissed her cheek, and invited her to sit beside him. She sat and placed her hand on his knee and then on the palm of his hand. He remained unmoving. "Are you angry at me? Your hand feels like a corpse's. Cold and distant."

He remained silent a few more seconds, then blurted, "Who are you, Eva?"

"What do you mean?" she asked with surprise.

"Exactly what I asked. Who are you?"

"After everything you and I shared and everything I've told you about myself, now you need to ask who I am? You know everything about me. I'm the one who knows nothing about you. Where exactly you work, why you keep popping in and out of my life…"

Arik interrupted her. "I have a feeling you're not who you say you are."

She removed her hand from his. "What makes you think that?"

"I have my reasons."

"You think I'm a spy?" she asked and followed her question with what sounded like forced laughter to Arik's ears.

"I don't know," said Arik. "Something about you makes me suspicious. Why did you say no one will be able to eavesdrop on our conversation here? Why would you care about that?"

"Because it's true. Sometimes, a cigar is just a cigar."

The warm sun flooded the bench. They retreated into the chapel, which enclosed and shaded them. "I feel like I can't believe you," said Arik.

"I think you're nurturing your suspicions because you don't want our relationship to develop. You're afraid of intimacy. Perhaps even afraid of yourself?"

"Don't change the subject. We're talking about you, not about me."

"We're talking about both of us. About you interrogating me like I'm some sort of suspect and about me not understanding why. You keep rejecting all my attempts to get closer. You ran away from me in the Van Leer Institute, and now you can't even bring yourself to kiss me. What happened? You don't feel like sleeping with me anymore?"

"This has nothing to do with it."

"So what is this all about?"

"I can't quite figure you out. I can't understand what you're doing here and where you came from. And, worst of all, I keep seeing you every place I go, in places you can't possibly be in, like a kind of paranoia."

"This isn't paranoia." She placed her lips against his ear, filling it with her sweet breath. A shiver passed down Arik's back.

"It's called love, Arik."

Arik looked deep into her eyes and found only softness and honesty there.

"So what's next?" she asked.

"You're still staying at the American Colony Hotel?"

"Yes."

She looked into his face. Cracks showed in the mask of his tough demeanor. Suddenly, he appeared to her like a hunger-filled sparrow fluttering its wings against the bars of a cage containing a bowl of seeds, yearning for freedom yet terrified of it. "Do you have your car here?" she asked.

Arik took her hand and started walking.

Chapter 26

The American Colony Hotel—East Jerusalem

The American Colony Hotel's parking lot was full. Arik reversed from its entrance and drove to the nearby Salah Eddin Street. He stopped right behind a "No Stopping" sign. Eva looked at him curiously. "I don't pay parking tickets," he stated, and her eyes silently scolded him.

A few minutes later, Eva stopped next to the gate leading to the hotel's garden. "Wait five minutes, then come up to room two hundred and two."

"Are you ashamed of me?"

"I'm concerned for you. All the foreign correspondents in Jerusalem live here. My guess is that you're an important government official, and some of them might recognize you. If they see you coming into the hotel with a woman, they'll try to find out who I am and discern the nature of our relationship."

"All right." Arik gave up. In his heart, he knew she was right. Another minute or two and the Mossad officer in him would probably have warned him about the unnecessary exposure. Still, was she thinking only about his benefit? Perhaps she had her own concerns.

He waited, leaning against the gate pillar. A tourist couple gave him suspicious glances, or at least that's what he thought. He looked at his watch one last time and went inside.

A group of noisy, possibly drunk, UN officers sat in the middle of a manicured garden with a stone fountain at its center. He went inside the lobby and stopped for a moment to read the signs. As expected, Room 202 was located on the second floor. Arik used the stairs, walked down the carpeted floor with little footsteps, and lightly tapped Eva's door.

Eva opened immediately, hiding behind the door. When she closed it, he saw she was completely naked. She clung to him and kissed his lips. He pulled her lower lip into his mouth. The softness he loved so much about women's lips did not arouse him this time, and Eva noticed that.

"You look tired. Would you like to freshen up and take a shower?"

"Maybe…" he started, then immediately said with determination, "Yes." The usual thought passed through his mind, *One mustn't demonstrate emotions or give himself completely to another. If I yield to her, I'd be lost.* True, he was definitely attracted to her. He liked her smell, her taste, the intellect that made her think and form original ideas, but she demanded his independence as a price. He felt that without him noticing, or even wanting it, their relationship had drifted from an easygoing affair to uncharted territories. He had lost control.

When Arik stood under the stream of water, he heard the shower door open, then felt a hand covered in soap caressing his back. Eva went inside, shut off the water and pressed against his back, her erect nipples rubbing against him, lubricated by the soap. He felt her pubic hair tickling his buttocks, but still did not feel any arousal.

"Turn around," she whispered, and he obeyed. She continued to rub against his body, trying to wake his limp member. "Come to bed," she whispered and washed them both.

He followed her, feeling the coming retreat in his bones. The mattress was hard, just the way he liked it, and the sheet was cool and ironed. He lay on his back and allowed her to take care of him. Her tongue travelled along his member, and her warm mouth closed on it.

Nothing happened.

"It's all right..." She traced a path of soft kisses to his face. "You must be tired."

Her sympathy simply served to heighten his anxiety. Eva loved him, understood his failings, and accepted the odd hours he had to work. She had already prepared breakfast for them when they had been in his house. She had asked why he didn't call her, and so, without even noticing, he was already in a relationship with her!

Eva placed her head on his shoulder and snuggled against his body. "That's all we need in order to be together," she said.

He closed his eyes and fell asleep almost immediately, dreaming of the both of them sitting in the kitchen of his house and watching television. It wouldn't be such a bad dream if he hadn't happened to catch a glimpse of their faces, reflected in the glass surface of the table. They were both old. Ancient.

The phone rang and Arik woke up with a start. "Your guest just woke up and asked about you."

"I'm on my way!" said Arik and jumped up from bed.

Chapter 27

The Al-Aqsa Mosque, Temple Mount—East Jerusalem

"How do you feel, Mr. President? I have to say, you look much better." Arik praised the president of Azerbaijan's recovery process.

"Thank you," Nur Sultan answered and immediately added excitedly, "Shall we go?"

"Go where?"

"To al-Masjid al-Aqsa al-Mubarak," answered Nur Sultan as if it were the most natural thing in the world.

"Shouldn't you rest a little? You've just undergone an operation…"

"No, I feel great. I must go to al-Aqsa this very day."

"Only if the doctor approves it."

Dr. Jackie Maman, the surgeon, nodded in affirmation.

"All right, sir. On our way, we'll stop at the Jerusalem Theatre. We'll have a professional makeup artist change your appearance in such a way that not even Dato would be able to recognize you."

"Dato will always be able to recognize me," Nur Sultan said cynically. "We have a saying: a dog will always recognize his master's hand so long as it feeds him."

Arik looked with embarrassment at Dato, who was sitting beside the president. Dato's face was sealed.

A short drive later, the car slid into the Jerusalem Theatre's back entrance. The makeup artist, a smiling, portly woman, waited for them in one of the dressing rooms. Makeup tubes, vials, and powders were placed on the table. "Hello, everyone," she said amicably.

Nur Sultan gave Arik a worried look, and the latter nodded reassuringly.

Half an hour later, a dwarfish man wearing a coal-black wig exited the theatre. A mustache was proudly glued on his upper lip, and a small, black beard had been attached to his chin. When he smiled, two rows of perfect teeth were revealed, glued onto his crooked ones. New wrinkles stretched at the corners of his eyes and gave him an elderly appearance. He wore glasses with thick lenses on his nose. A white and black *keffiyeh* was wrapped around his neck, a sign of solidarity with the Palestinian people.

At the entrance to the Temple Mount, Gabby Ben-Jenou, the Jerusalem district's chief of police, wearing civilian clothes, waited for Arik and his guests. Beside him, wearing their ceremonial clothes, stood the Grand Mufti of Jerusalem and the head of the Waqf, the religious trust managing the Islamic sites on the Temple Mount.

They had been ordered to arrive to the mosque entrance to welcome an important Muslim oligarch from Turkmenistan. It was hinted to them that, should the oligarch be pleased, he might make a generous contribution to the Waqf's charity fund from which, as everyone knew, hefty amounts happened to end up in their own pockets.

Nur Sultan shook everyone's hands and greeted them in Russian. One of the Jerusalem precinct's general security servicemen translated their greetings from Arabic to Russian for the honorable guest's benefit. The Mufti beckoned with his hand respectfully, offering the guest to be the first to enter the holy place. Nur Sultan walked inside with small and humble steps. The other men of his entourage, including Arik, the chief of police, and the General Security Service guards, took off their shoes and placed them in a row next to the entrance.

Nur Sultan opened his eyes wide, trying to absorb the sight of colorful carpets, painted ceramic tiles, and the large foundation stone, on top of which, according to Islamic tradition, Al-Burāq, Muhammad's steed had once landed. The president's soul filled with ecstasy, and he smiled at everyone gratefully, telling them again and again how delighted he was to visit al-Aqsa for the first time in his life.

He had not told them the main reason for his sense of elation. On the previous day, before the operation, he had had a vision. He dreamed the angel Jibril was standing at his bedside, touching him. In an echoing voice, the angel told him it was not a Jewish doctor who would save him but Allah himself, who had flown him from Mecca, where the president prayed just a week before on his way to Dubai, to Jerusalem, just as He had done for the prophet Muhammad.

Nur Sultan was convinced it was a manifestation of a passage from the Surah al-Isra in the holy Koran: "Glory to Allah who did take His servant for a journey by night from the sacred mosque to the farthest mosque, whose precincts we did bless, in order that we might show Him some of our signs, for He is the one who heareth and seeth all things."

The other worshippers were removed to the sides of the hall. A few metal poles covered by a red drape offered Nur Sultan a private prayer area. The Mufti handed him a personal prayer mat as a present, then respectfully retreated to begin his own prayer. Nur Sultan placed the new mat beside him but did not make use of it. He preferred to have nothing separating his head and the earth to emphasize the humility of his spirit in the face of such divinity. Trembling with excitement, he began to mumble the words of the Surah al-Fatihah with great intent.

"In the name of God, the infinitely Compassionate and Merciful.

"Praise be to God, Lord of all the worlds. The Compassionate, the Merciful. Ruler on the Day of Reckoning. You alone do we worship, and You alone do we ask for help. Guide us on the straight path, the path of those who have received Your grace; not the path of those who have brought down wrath, nor of those who wander astray."[14]

Arik stood on the other side on the improvised private prayer area alongside a few security guards in civilian clothing and the president's personal and silent bodyguard who towered over them. Arik's eyes wandered across the hall. As far as he knew, everyone in the company of the president had been checked and didn't pose a threat, but he was worried about the other worshippers. When they bowed, he examined their backs, looking for any suspicious bulges. He needed to remind himself that securing the place wasn't his responsibility and that he should trust the chief of police. Reluctantly, he turned his eyes back to Nur Sultan, who appeared to be detached from his surroundings and in the midst of a deep, spiritual experience. In spite of the stitches of the operation, the president managed to perform

---

[14]Translated from Arabic by Kabir Helminski.

all the ritual prayer motions. The *Salah* included standing with raised hands; bowing, stretching the body forward while standing up; worshipping while kneeling; lowering the head until it touched the ground; and, finally, sitting on one's knees.

The cell phone in Arik's pocket vibrated once. He silently went out to the sun-washed square and bent to tie his shoelaces. A bothersome fly landed on his face. As he waved his hand to chase it away, he felt a hard object hit his shoulder. He dropped on his face and felt a wetness spreading from inside his shirt to the back of his neck. From behind him, he heard the sound of running police officers and security guards. Arik tried to get up on his hands and knees, but the pain in his shoulder proved to be insufferable, and he lay back on the cool stone floor. Ben-Jenou kneeled beside him, full of concern.

"I don't understand..." Arik mumbled.

"You've been shot. My men are scouring the area. Paramedics are on the way."

His phone vibrated again. "Could you take out my phone and put it on speaker?" Arik requested.

"What's going on?" Cornfield's gruff voice was heard. "I'm starting to get hungry. How much time before you get here with the guest?"

"Thirty minutes, I assume..." Arik struggled to speak. "He's almost finished praying."

"Why do you sound so funny?" Cornfield chuckled. "Sounds like you're talking from inside your grave."

"I've been shot," said Arik.

"You and your dramas again!" Cornfield shouted angrily and hung up.

Chapter 28

Arik was alert and hurting. The police paramedics placed him on a stretcher and brought him to the Temple Mount police checkpoint until an ambulance could come to evacuate him. The turmoil outside had not yet abated; police officers and General Security guards kept running around in and out of the complex. Arik lay on his back, his shirt unbuttoned, and his chest bare. He felt exposed and vulnerable. With an effort, he tried to raise his upper torso and push himself to a sitting position. A sharp pain cut through his back and shoulder. He dropped to the stretcher and this time turned around, leaned on his uninjured side, and tried again to sit. The pain worsened. Tears of effort welled in his eyes. "Don't feel sorry for yourself," he ordered himself. "Don't demonstrate any weakness. Get up!"

While Arik was trying to rise, the district chief of police came inside and kneeled beside the stretcher. Arik mainly saw his shoes and the edges of his pants. "Gabby, come closer, please," he asked in a hoarse voice.

The chief leaned toward him. Arik saw his reflection in Jenou's sunglasses and felt very vulnerable, definitely not as tough as he wanted everyone to think he was.

"You need to evacuate the guest immediately to the Presidential Suite at the King David Hotel," he ordered in the most authoritative voice he could muster. "Cornfield is waiting for him there."

"I'll give the order right away," said Ben-Jenou. Seconds later, Arik saw a terrified Nur Sultan Babayev, accompanied by his small entourage and surrounded by security guards holding automatic weapons, quickly being led to the gates of the Temple Mount. From then on, the images rushed quickly in front of Arik's eyes, as if time had quickened its pace.

An ambulance siren blared through the air, and he was finally evacuated.

When he was inside the ambulance, the paramedic told him, "You're lucky. It was a very small caliber bullet. There are clean entry and exit wounds." He stuck an IV needle in Arik's arm. Arik then felt another sting in his hip. "Morphine," the paramedic said, and the pain almost immediately disappeared. The officer in charge of the security team asked for his pistol and operational cell phone as required by regulations. Arik handed them to him.

It appeared the ambulance didn't miss a single bump on the roads surrounding the Temple Mount. Even later on, when they drove through the wide roads leading to the Hadassah Medical Center on Mount Scopus, the vehicle shook and jolted with the speed of the drive. Arik looked at the ceiling and tried to guess when the ambulance would pass by the military cemetery in which he'd met Eva just a few hours ago. He was wrong again and again, and when he gave up on his calculations, the ambulance came to a halt.

In the Emergency Room, he was rushed into the imaging room and placed in the CT scanner. While lying in the enclosed tunnel, he felt angry at himself. How come he hadn't recognized the assassin with his distinct oriental features among the other worshippers?

Suddenly, it occurred to him that the assassin had not even entered the mosque but simply waited outside. Now he wondered how come he hadn't seen him when he had remained by himself with the policemen and everyone else on the Temple Mount rushed inside to pray. Then he felt angry at the chief of police and his officers. Hadn't they searched the Temple Mount thoroughly? Patrolled its surroundings? Why had they broken the basic VIP protection regulations? Why had they even allowed worshippers to enter the Temple Mount during the president's visit? Why hadn't they stationed snipers?

The bed was pulled out of the tunnel with a buzzing, mechanical sound. A wheelchair waited for him outside. "I can walk," he almost screamed at the nurse.

"You're still sedated from the morphine," she answered with a coolness implying he wasn't the first who tried to play hero with her. "If you try standing up, you're simply going to fall."

He reluctantly obeyed her instructions and stayed in bed, allowing her to wrap his body with a hospital gown. Only now did he notice his shoes and pants had been taken off, and his shirt was gone. He was naked other than his underwear and the ridiculous gown with laces at its open back. The only time he had even seen such a hospital gown was when his ex-wife had given birth to their children.

An orderly helped him move to the wheelchair, then rolled him down the corridors, greeting almost everyone he encountered on his way with a hearty, "*Dobriy vecher.*"[15]

Ben-Jenou waited for him in the hospital room. "We've arranged a private room for you," he said with a proud smile. "At least for a few hours. You'll have some peace and quiet here."

He was the last person Arik wanted to see. "I don't want peace and quiet!" He erupted with rage. "I want to understand what the hell happened. Where was our security team? Where were all your police officers, the ones wearing uniforms and the ones undercover? How did it happen, and who was responsible for the security? Do you realize what the press will do with this story?"

"Don't worry, Cornfield already contacted the right people the whole thing will be silenced. And yes, heads are going to roll. Maybe mine as well. The police Commissioner has already announced a secret tribunal of inquiry."

"Who fucked up here?"

"Both you and us. We didn't have enough time to plan the security arrangements, and you classified the information and didn't provide details that could have allowed us to prepare a thorough VIP security plan. In a nutshell, you relied on us, we relied on you, and the assassin ended up slipping away."

"But how did *he* know we were coming? And don't try to cover your ass with the usual excuses. The way I see things, you're the ones who fucked up. I was told it was a twenty-two millimeter bullet that hit me. This could happen only

---

[15]Good evening. (Russian)

with close range shooting with a small handgun. On the other hand, a gun would have been detected at the entrance. You do perform a security check for every visitor with a magnetometer metal detector, I assume?"

"A metal gun would have been discovered for sure," Ben-Jenou said with lowered eyes, "but not one from other materials. We've found a cast plastic handgun next to one of the cypress trees with a zirconium barrel coated with graphite. It had two more homemade polymer bullets. If not for the turmoil around you after you had fallen he would have shot those as well."

Arik thought for a moment. "Only KGB assassins had such guns," he said. "Did you find any fingerprints? Did you arrest anyone?"

"No, but we've started an investigation."

"I know you guys. Two days from now you'll start a new investigation and drop this one. My guest will run away from Israel in a panic, and we'll all lose the opportunity to offer the people of Israel a great gift."

"The visitor won't run away. Cornfield is taking care of him."

"That's exactly what I'm worried about," Arik muttered and tried to get up again. "Do you have a shirt you could spare? Mine's torn and filthy."

"You can't leave before getting the CT scan results," Ben-Jenou said, as if he were his nurse. "And don't worry about the guest. I know Cornfield from my visits to the prime minister's office. He may be rough around the edges, but he's not an idiot. He's as ambitious as any other guy and wants to get the job done. Cornfield goes wild only when he knows there's someone to clean up his mess. When he's on his own and in charge, he knows how to behave himself. If something needs to happen with your guest, Cornfield will be able to handle it without you just as well."

"I want you to send a patrol car here with two officers to help me get out and rush me to the King David Hotel."

The chief of police shook his head and was rescued from another one of Arik's angry outbursts only thanks to the doctor, who entered the room with a smile. "Your scan came out perfect. The bone wasn't damaged; neither were the blood vessels and the nerves. Luckily, the bullet passed clean through your shoulder. A few stitches, some antibiotics, and you'll be as good as new."

Arik didn't answer, distracted by noises coming from the corridor. Ben-Jenou seized the moment and slipped out of the room.

Naomi entered, holding a square, plastic box. She patted his healthy shoulder and said, "I thought you'd prefer my stuffed vegetables with meat to the hospital food."

"How did you know?" Arik wondered with embarrassment. "How did you get here from Haifa so quickly?"

"Arik, it's five in the afternoon already. Claire called me more than three hours ago, and I immediately jumped into my car and rushed here."

Arik smiled. "You're good to me. I know you think I don't deserve any of this."

"You deserve everything, my dear brother. But perhaps you could help more with Mom instead of getting yourself injured in weird car accidents?"

Arik chuckled in agreement. "I'm trying," he said, waiting for her to approve he was indeed doing the best he could.

Naomi ignored his words and said with a smile. "Eva is on her way as well."

"Eva? Who asked her to come here?"

"I let her know, and she told me she'd come."

"How do you even know she exists?"

"When I came into the hospital and asked about you, the nurse called the security officer who asked who I was. I told him I'm your sister, and he gave me your belongings so they wouldn't get lost, including your cell phone. I wondered who else should be notified, so I checked your recent calls. Perhaps it's time you told me who this Eva is."

Arik felt grateful for the fact his operational phone had been taken away in the ambulance and hadn't fallen into her hands as well.

"She's a good friend of mine. A professor of theology who is spending her sabbatical in Israel."

"Eva doesn't sound like a Jewish name," Naomi said in an inquisitive tone.

"She's not Jewish. She's German," Arik mumbled.

"You're going to bring a German woman into our family?"

"There's nothing serious going on between us," said Arik.

"You don't sound too convincing." She glared at him.

Arik shrugged his single healthy shoulder.

"I called Nathalie as well."

"And?" Arik tensed up.

"She's on her way."

Eva stood at the doorway, prettier than ever, smiling at him and holding a bouquet of flowers.

"Pleased to meet you." Naomi offered Eva her hand.

Arik settled for saying, "Thanks for the flowers. You shouldn't have." Eva placed them on the windowsill.

"I'll ask for a vase from the nurse later on," she said cheerfully.

She's already rearranging my life, Arik thought bitterly.

"What happened to you?" asked Naomi. "What kind of accident? Were you in a car? On foot?"

Eva remained silent, and Arik imagined he saw a hint of understanding in her face. "I can't talk about it," he said darkly. "But yes, it was a vehicle accident."

"I understand," Naomi said, an expression of "you're playing secret agent again" on her face. "So what happened to you?"

"I fractured my shoulder."

"So why did they give you an antibiotics infusion?" She pointed at his medical chart.

"Stay out of my medical chart," Arik protested.

"Sometimes fractures are treated with preventive broad spectrum antibiotics and steroids," Eva said calmly.

"Oh," said Naomi. "I understand." Arik thought she remained just as naïve as she had been as a child. *But why is Eva covering for me?* he wondered.

Naomi's cell phone rang. She answered, listened for a moment and after hanging up asked Arik, "Nathalie is here. She asks if you're dressed and if she can come in."

Arik pulled the sheet tighter around his body. Eva grabbed Naomi's arm. "We'll wait outside," she said politely. When the two left, Arik heard Naomi introducing Eva to Nathalie in the hallway. Nathalie entered hesitantly, as if she were afraid of him. "Come. Come to Daddy," he called her. She stopped some distance from his bed. She was dressed in a long, black skirt and a white, long-sleeved shirt. Her hair was tied into a tight knot.

"Daddy!" she called emotionally.

The sound of that word immediately alleviated all the pains that began to awake as the morphine's influence began to wear down. He thought of asking her to come give him a hug, but feared it might be prohibited by religion and did not want to offend her.

"Does it hurt?" she asked.

"Now that you're here, it doesn't." He smiled at her.

She took an envelope out of her bag. "I brought you a surprise."

She placed the envelope on the bedside table and immediately returned to stand in the middle of the room. Arik barely tore the paper flap. The name of his ex-wife was the first thing his eyes caught under the words "the bride's parents," then he saw his own name, separately written. The names of the groom's parents, on the other hand, were written side by side, almost embracing.

He read the groom's name. "Haim Fischel?" He couldn't help himself and ended with a question mark.

"Yes, that's his name," Nathalie said, her eyes shining. "He's a great student of the Torah."

Arik nodded.

"It's very rare, you know, for a great student from a good family to marry a woman who has just found her faith, but…"

"But what?"

"We fell in love," she said emotionally. "His mother is my teacher, and once, when I spent the weekend there, he came back from the *yeshiva* because he was sick. I saw him, and he saw me, and…"

"That's how I fell in love with your mom. The only difference is it was at a campfire at the *kibbutz*."

Nathalie's face fell.

"All right. I hope you stay together longer than we did."

"Longer?" a hint of tears invaded her words. "We're going to be married forever and ever. Don't you get it? How insensitive can you be? What happened between you and Mom is exactly what I'm trying to run away from. It's the reason I turned to religion. I was seeking the purer side of life." The tears burst out of her all at once. "I came to see how you are and invite you to the wedding, and you... You always have to ruin everything."

She ran out of the room in tears, and Arik heard Eva trying to soothe her. He wondered where Naomi was, thinking only Nathalie's aunt could calm her down. To his surprise, the sound of crying gradually subsided.

Eva came into the room with her face beaming, much like Nathalie's before her crying fit. "Where's Naomi?" Arik asked angrily.

"She went to bring a vase. Are you all right?"

"That girl..." Arik motioned with his hands to indicate helplessness.

"That girl is wounded," said Eva softly. "She's afraid to get hurt again every time she's close to you. As far as she's concerned, the past is still here, and if you ask me, it looks like you haven't really changed."

"Tell me..." Arik erupted, then stopped himself and went silent.

"Tell you what?"

"How come you know so much about my life!"

She sat at his bedside and sought his hand with hers. He drew it away, and she didn't protest. "I don't *know*; I *understand*. I can read you, Arik, and believe me, it's not as hard as you think."

Chapter 29

A Profitable Investment

As usual, Ayalon Highway No. 20 was already jammed with traffic early in the morning. The cars moved slowly, bumper to bumper. Arik shifted uneasily in his chair. His shoulder still hurt. His cellular phone buzzed in his pocket. Arik slid his finger on the iPhone screen and saw the photo of a smiling woman. The *Arc de Triomphe* of Paris could be seen in the background. Mariam Halachi, or "Ruth the Moabitess" as she had been code-named in the operation's paperwork, waved at him, leaning on a brand new, white Mercedes-Maybach. Two grim-faced, muscular bodyguards flanked her.

Arik smiled with satisfaction. It was time to check whether the investment in Mariam Halachi had yielded the expected results. He pressed the buttons of the operational phone in his car and called, "Office." Claire answered and he asked her to connect him in an encrypted conference call with Albert Lev-Ari, the person responsible for Operation Flower Bud.

"Yes," a distracted voice answered.

"Albert, this is Arik Bar-Nathan. Am I disturbing you?"

"No, it's fine. I have a little electricity problem. I'm in the 'Pikpur' office." The officer used the code name for Kirkuk, a city in the Kurdish enclave in Iraq.

"What's going on with Ruth the Moabitess' guys?"

"They're very serious. The training and investment have definitely proven their worth. They're bringing in some good stuff."

"What about the nutcrackers?" asked Arik, actually speaking of the SIGINT[16] people drafted from among the Tabriz University students.

"Already working. We've equipped them with cutting-edge technology. They're proving to be fine students."

"What about the Ghostbusters on bikes?"

"Doing some fine and thorough cleaning and pest-control work."

"Excellent. Thank you," said Arik, finishing the conversation.

He stopped at the roadside and sent Mariam a smiley emoticon.

---

[16]Signals intelligence—Intelligence gathering by interception of signals.

Chapter 30

The Tehran Imam Khomeini International Airport teemed with human trafficking . Two men, supposedly strangers, sat next to a small table in a coffee shop at the corner of the terminal. One, wearing a turban and looking like a student from one of the religious seminaries, was reading the popular Al-Akhbar newspaper. Behind the newspaper, inside a backpack placed on his knees, rested a small submachine gun with a silencer and two hand grenades. The other one was dressed like a tourist with a large backpack placed beside him and a broad-brimmed Australian hat on his head, concealing most of his face. A powerful laptop sat on the coffee shop table in front of them, scanning the entire airport area in a phishing attempt—to collect information from other computers in the complex.

The hacker dressed like a tourist's eyes were restless. They moved back and forth from the computer screen on the table to the security cameras installed in every corner of the airport. Suddenly, he tensed up. The first data had been captured and a minute later was cast back into the net. It was a Facebook chat from a tourist from New Zealand on his way to visit India. The hacker emitted a silent curse and cast his virtual net back into the water.

Following an hour of failed attempts, his face brightened. He had found an Arabic-speaking computer. Within seconds, dozens of documents, including diagrams and construction plans on which the words "*natanz*," "*arak*," and "*fordow*" were written, among others, appeared on the screen in front of him. All the documents bore the title "Top Secret." There were also blueprint files bearing Chinese writing.

The laptop's owner sat only two tables away from the hacker. He was a big, burly man, wearing a suit that looked too small for him. A similar looking man, perhaps his bodyguard, sat beside him, they were watching an action movie. The hacker took out his cell phone and with a smile asked the turban-wearing student to take his photo. The young *Mullah*[17] complied with a smile.

The *Mullah* directed his cell phone camera at the burly man behind the hacker and sent the photo in an encrypted email to his own Gmail address. He knew that in one of Tehran's poor neighborhoods' Internet cafes, Ruth the Moabitess' people were sitting that very moment, monitoring his Google account. The moment the burly man's photo went on the Internet, it was sent to an email address in London and scrambled inside photos of a fictitious wedding. From there, it was automatically transferred to Mossad's research and intelligence center in Tel Aviv.

The computer on the desk of the Dr. Alex Abramovich, head of the Research and Analysis Division, woke up with a clicking sound. A message nervously jumped onto the screen. "Your attention is urgently required."

---

[17] A Muslim cleric.

The photo appeared on the screen and Alex immediately identified the burly man: General Ahmad Suleiman, the Syrian president's special advisor and chairman of the Syrian Atomic Energy Commission. A document written by the analyst team of the Levant Department was attached to the email, stating that, from checking the passenger lists of the various flight companies, the man appeared to be making his way from North Korea to Damascus and had a stopover in Tehran.

The hacker in the Tehran Airport received a message to his cell phone: "Personal pizza and drink for only ten *rial*. Free delivery anywhere in the airport area."

A great excitement overtook him. He lit a cigarette and took out a small USB stick. When he inserted it in the appointed slot in the computer, all the data phished out of the Syrian general's computer was transferred to the stick with an incredible speed. When the copying finished, the hacker concealed the USB stick in a hidden compartment in his pants and dialed his cell phone. "I'd like to order a personal pizza with mushrooms, onions, and olives. I'm sitting at the Departure Terminal lounge, section G, next to the bookstore. Please send a Coke and salsa with the pizza."

"The delivery man is on his way. He'll be there in fifteen minutes."

About forty minutes later, the *Mullah* rose from his seat and disappeared among the crowd of passengers. A golden-haired tourist dressed in an elegant suit with the symbol of the Red-Cross embroidered on its pocket took his place. The hacker shook, with a slight movement, the left side of his pocket. The USB stick dropped to the floor and almost vanished into the gray-black colors of the floor tiles. He waited a few more minutes, then rose and left the place. The tourist took her makeup bag from her suitcase and applied lipstick on her lips. An accidental movement caused her to drop it to the floor. She leaned to pick it up. When she rose, the USB stick was hidden in the palm of her hand as well. While the airplane took off for Paris, the hacker stood in front of the arrivals and departures board and looked with satisfaction at the Syrian general's flight number being erased.

He felt he had had an exceptionally successful day.

Chapter 31

Café de Flore—Boulevard Saint-Germain, Paris

It was an autumn Parisian morning. The skies were blue and cloudless, and a winter sun shone in the heavens, and the air was cold. Mariam Halachi sat in the old and prestigious café and drank a macchiato.

Since she'd met the stranger in Baku, the same stranger she was now supposed to meet, her life had changed beyond recognition. She returned to Paris and reopened the offices of the organizations she headed, this time with the full authorization of the French Deuxième Bureau[18]. Large amounts were deposited in her bank account every month, and her men were trained by "American" guides in Kirkuk or Azerbaijan and were equipped the newest weapons and technology. She often held press conferences, which were broadcast in Persian language radio stations via satellite and could be heard all over Iran. Her personal safety was assured. Her bodyguards held proper gun permits, and she drove around Paris in an armored Mercedes-Maybach with a diplomatic license plate.

She noticed two lovers sitting next to one of the tables. A suspicious bulge could be seen in the man's coat pocket.

---

[18]French security agency

Another couple sat next to another table and appeared to be interested in the surroundings more than in each other. She had no doubt they were actually Mossad agents securing the place for the important guest about to arrive and meet her. A man's image appeared in the café's door. Mariam recognized him immediately. She knew him as 'Raymundo', as he had introduced himself during their first and only meeting, would arrive. She had refused to speak with the Paris Mossad station manager and demanded to speak with 'Raymundo' alone, knowing he would not refuse. The message her cyber spies had sent her from Iran imbued her with a sense of power she hadn't felt for a long time.

She rose to him, and they exchanged kisses in the French style: cheek to cheek, then blowing a kiss in the air.

"You look wonderful," Arik flattered her. "I understand everything is in order."

"Everything is great, Raymundo. I've received everything we've agreed upon down to the last detail. I hope you are also satisfied from the level of service provided by my organization." Even though Mariam's French was excellent, her Persian accent was still very noticeable.

"Yes, absolutely." Arik beckoned the waiter to approach them. "Would you like to order?"

She smiled and shook her head no. Raymundo ordered an espresso and a plate of macaroons. He actually began to like her smile, which was warm yet restrained. He looked at her eyes, which sent him a look as bright and gray as the Parisian skies, and wondered how come he hadn't remembered just how beautiful she was. "You wanted to see me personally and urgently?"

She looked sideways and placed a narrow envelope inside the menu. "You'll find a USB stick here with photos of a huge complex under construction. It is hidden within a mountain. I have also included architectural plans and calculations written in Chinese."

Arik pulled the menu to him and placed the envelope in his coat pocket. Mariam gave him an expectant look, apparently seeking approval for her accomplishment. He merely gave her a polite smile of gratitude. Finally, she couldn't contain herself any more. "This arrived yesterday from Tehran. It appears the regime there has decided to aid the Syrians by funding a plutogenic nuclear reactor to be constructed with the aid of North Korean scientists. As you'll be able to see for yourself, construction is already underway."

"Thanks. Let me check it out," said Arik and rose from his seat.

Mariam stood as well and extended her hand.

"Well done." Raymundo finally managed to bring himself to praise her. He flagged the waiter, placed two ten-Euro bills on the table and went on his way.

Chapter 32

The House by the Lake—Creteil, East Paris

Arik had never felt lonely during his travels. He was curious by nature and loved to roam the streets of various cities, admire the architecture of ancient houses and buildings, meet people of different cultures, and taste ethnic and national dishes. He especially liked Paris for its parks and the way nature always managed to burst through the concrete armor of the city.

This time, though, a different kind of feeling nestled in him, a slight yearning for something he could not quite put his finger on.

Nathalie? No. She was a different person now. Different and far from him in her lifestyle. Michael? He missed him very much, but didn't have a real relationship with him either. Who was left then? Naomi and his mother, whose presence he has always taken for granted.

And Eva. He quickly chased the thought from his mind.

Eva was an attractive woman and a wonderful companion, but she was also an enigma, an unsolved mystery. Each time he thought he understood her personality and behavior, she managed to surprise him anew. One could not yearn for an enigma; they could only be troubled by it.

But he wasn't troubled. As he walked on the docks along the Seine, he thought what she would have said had she walked beside him that moment, and when he lay in his wide hotel bed, he found himself missing her wit, her body, her scent, and her laughter.

When his private cell phone rang, he hoped it would be her on the other line. But it was actually the duty officer at the Mossad's control center in Tel Aviv. "Your chameleon is sleeping?" he asked, reminding Arik that his operational cell phone was turned off.

"Its tail is in the cave," Arik replied, hinting that the phone was charging.

"Please talk to me on the secure line. I'll be calling in a minute."

Arik disconnected the operational cell phone from the charger and turned it on. The phone rang.

"I have some breaking news. The bastards have assassinated Ruth the Moabitess' brother. The boss thought it would be nice if you go pay a little condolence call before you come back."

"Roger that."

"Do you need company?" the officer asked, using the codename for bodyguards.

"I'll manage."

The house in Toison d'Or Alley in the Creteil neighborhood was modest when compared with the other mansions resting by the shore of the large, artificial lake yet was still highly impressive. Perhaps it was the small windows or the porch, protected by an iron grating, or maybe it was the steel door with its cast-iron decorations. When Arik approached it, an automatic spotlight turned on to illuminate his way. He pressed the doorbell bulging from a green copper frame. The ringing of a church bell sounded from inside the house. Two cameras moved with a slight whirr. The steel door opened, and Arik stepped inside only to find himself facing a semi-transparent glass door. Another light turned on, this time from inside the house, and the shadow of a feminine figure accompanied by three large dogs was seen on the other side of the door. Another camera examined him.

"Are you alone?" he heard Mariam's voice emerging from a hidden speaker.

"Yes."

"Are you afraid of dogs?"

Arik wasn't used to being in the company of dogs but still preferred to give Mariam a negative answer.

She opened the door, dressed in a close-fitting silk robe that complimented the curves of her body. Three giant *Dogue de Bordeaux* dogs drooled and exposed their fangs at him. Mariam uttered a command in Persian, and the dogs immediately dropped to the floor submissively.

"Why didn't you let me know you were coming?" she demanded. Arik saw a shadow passing behind one of the doors. Mariam noticed his stare. "A bodyguard," she explained.

"I came the moment I heard about your brother. I'm sorry for your loss."

She took his hand and led him to a large guest room whose floor was covered with soft carpets. Sofas stood across the walls, and an ornate cabinet was placed in the corner of the room. Mariam opened it and exposed a modest liquor cabinet. "Bourbon?" she pointed at a Jack Daniels bottle.

"Bourbon," Arik agreed. "How did it happen?"

"Like it always happens. Someone ratted him out." She blinked to fight the welling tears. "I've already lost my husband…ex-husband, actually, and now my brother. I'm fortunate not to have any children. Do you have children?"

"Two."

"A wife?"

"I used to. She left me."

Mariam sat on one of the sofas. "Are you angry at her?" Her voice softened.

"No, I was the one to blame. I had an affair. I started being angry only when she began using the children to get even with me."

"You can understand her, can't you? She was hurt by your betrayal. You strike the enemy where it hurts him the most, don't you?"

"I suppose you're right," Arik said. He felt a strong desire to avoid what he considered to be an overly intimate conversation, but Mariam was his most important trump card in the poker game against Iran and his most important accomplishment in quite some time, along with the Azerbaijan military bases Israel was leasing.

"Yes, I guess that's normally the case," he said bluntly, about to get up and leave.

Mariam had other plans. She went to the bar and refilled her glass. It was apparent it wasn't her second drink of the evening.

"Is there a woman in your life?"

"No one serious," he said decisively and immediately realized he was lying. Whether he wanted it or not, Eva had become a significant figure in his life.

She took his glass, intending to refill it with bourbon, but Arik raised his hand to stop her. "I really must be going. I need to get back to the hotel and prepare for the flight back home."

"I don't want to stay here by myself tonight. Why don't you stay? Don't worry; I'm not going to eat you." She pushed a few buttons inside the bar. Bossa nova music filled the room. Mariam kicked off her slippers and began to dance. The atmosphere of mourning immediately lifted.

"Don't look at me like that. Tonight, I'm honoring my brother, Massoud, hung by the bastards from a crane right in the middle of Tabriz. He was a man of the world. An atheist who knew how to live and drink, and I'm drinking in his honor just as the Irish drink and eat for their dead. A wake. That's what they call it, right?" She approached him and took his hand, trying to draw him into the dance. "Come, Arik! Let us celebrate the death of this great man."

The bourbon finally got the better of her, and she collapsed on the sofa, pulling him after her. Without any warning, she stretched out her hand and skillfully unzipped his pants, while passionately seeking his lips with hers. Arik resisted.

She was beautiful, and in her drunkenness, the tough and distant expression had been wiped out of her face. Her eyes pleaded him, but he had no intention of sleeping with her. He was on a mission.

The dogs had heard her cry came running, and looked at their mistress curiously. Arik got up and whispered, "Good night, Mariam."

He slipped to the door, bracing himself for a possible encounter with Mariam's bodyguards, but none of them showed up. Next to the front door, he saw a small restroom. He went inside, carefully washed his hands, zipped his pants and left.

The dogs followed him to the door, which closed after him with a click and automatically locked. He flagged a taxi that happened to pass in the cold street and returned to his hotel on the other side of the city.

Chapter 33

Special Operations Approval Meeting—Mossad Headquarters

Arik sat at the head of the table, trying to concentrate on the words of those surrounding him and, as usual, looking for a comfortable posture that wouldn't hurt his injured shoulder. The cold, air-conditioned air in the room awoke his injury pains, but he didn't ask to raise the temperatures so as not to make the other people in the room uncomfortable.

The internal phone suddenly buzzed. "I asked not to be disturbed!" he angrily whispered to Claire through the receiver.

"Don't yell at me! Alex is outside and asked that you come out and see him for a minute. Should I tell him to leave?"

Arik went out, not knowing at whom he should direct his anger. "What's so urgent, Alex? I'm in the middle of an SPA meeting."

"This is," said Alex and pushed a white envelope into Arik's hand. The words, "To General Arik Bar-Nathan—personal," were ornately written in French on the envelope.

"Was it checked?" asked Arik before tearing the sealed flap.

"While it was still in Paris. It was handed to Ruth the Moabitess' operator this morning at our embassy station. He sent it to me by diplomatic mail with a special courier."

Arik took a folded page from inside the envelope, opened it, and read its contents. Alex stood a short distance from him, his face flushed with curiosity. Arik handed him the page. The photo of a dark-haired man with a Caucasian visage stared from it in addition to a short letter.

Ruslan Akhmatov. Russian nationality. Chechen origins. Look for him in your own backyard. This is the man who has been trying to kill you. He was sent by the Hezbollah. He has a highly personal interest. You probably know what it is. Take care of yourself!

Mariam.

"We need to update Cornfield. You urgently need to get the personal protection unit involved."

Arik folded the document and placed it in the back pocket of his jeans. "We'll deal with this later. Right now, I'm in the middle of an operations approval meeting. Cornfield has a work meeting with the prime minister later this week and asked for my operative recommendations for actions against the Syrian plutogenic project."

"I'll summon an urgent meeting with Cornfield and the chief security officer."

"Thank you, Alex. You're a true friend," Arik said and hurried to get back to the meeting.

An hour and a half later, Cornfield's secretary called and asked Arik to come to an urgent meeting at the director's office. When he went inside, he saw that Alex and the redheaded chief security officer were already present.

Cornfield regarded him with his single eye, as sullen as ever. He reached inside his desk drawer, took out his whiskey bottle, and sent Arik a questioning look. Arik shook his head. Alex refused as well, and the chief security officer didn't even get an offer. Cornfield sighed, poured himself half a glass and tossed his head back to swallow it in a single gulp along with two pain killers he'd rescued from an aluminum tray. "My diabetes is always making me thirsty. Why is it suddenly so urgent to discuss a personal bodyguard for you?" he barked. "The prime minister is busting my balls every day. He wants to hear what we're doing to stop the Iranian-Syrian nuclear program, and you're wasting my time with this nonsense?"

Arik shrugged and said, "If you don't want to give me personal bodyguard, so be it. I'll manage on my own."

"Sir," the chief security officer tried, "with all due respect, we're not talking nonsense here. We've received information that includes the name and photo of the person who had tried to assassinate our Caesarea chief."

"What makes you think such an assassin exists?" Cornfield gave a derisive snort.

Arik couldn't control his temper anymore and shouted at Cornfield. "After everything I've been through, you still have doubts?"

Cornfield looked at him with mocking eyes. "Let's talk about what you've been through," he said, a sarcastic smile stretched on his lips. "First there was a shooting, supposedly aimed at your vehicle, at the entrance to the office along with a fire in a field of thorns. We've looked for the saboteur but couldn't find any trace of him, just some tire marks in a nearby orchard. The counterintelligence department couldn't report a group or an organization involved. One can only assume it was a single terrorist who had managed to escape, or perhaps a jealous husband? Am I right so far, Mr. Security Officer?"

The security officer nodded with embarrassment. "The police and General Security Service reports aren't conclusive," he admitted. "Empty vodka bottles were found in the bushes…."

"Muslim terrorists do not drink vodka…right? The second time, you told us someone had tried to run you over in Jerusalem, right? You've managed to escape unscathed thanks to an unidentified woman who appeared out of nowhere in a white vehicle. That is what you yourself reported. I can only assume the driver was the same jealous husband, and the unidentified woman was simply his wife who wanted to stop him. Am I right?"

"You're wrong," Arik spat, but Cornfield ignored him and continued.

"And the third time, you were shot on the Temple Mount right in the middle of a secret visit of the president of Azerbaijan. In the report, you yourself wrote, the weapon located at the scene was a ceramic gun manufactured for the exclusive use of Russian KGB assassins. Who knows? Maybe they were trying to assassinate President Nur Sultan and kill three birds with one stone: embarrassing us, finishing him off, and taking over his country."

"I sorry, sir," said Alex, not trying to hide his anger. "The name and the photo of the assassin we received this morning from Paris specifically indicate he is Ruslan Akhmatov, son of the Chechen Mafia boss who was killed during our failed operation in South America. Perhaps he has a personal score to settle with Arik, who was in charge of the operation. Akhmatov is known as a hired assassin who sometimes works for the Federal Russian security forces. He also has a long criminal record."

"And who, exactly, gave you this information?" Cornfield mockingly asked.

Arik and Alex exchanged glances. Since Mossad had been founded, the customary procedure was never to expose names or true identities of sources, even to the director, unless unusual circumstances demanded it.

Alex said, "I can't give you the source's real name. The code name is Ruth the Moabitess, and their information is credible."

"Really? And how many such alerts for possible hostile terrorist activities do you receive every day Dr. Alex?" asked Cornfield.

"Few of them are as credible as this information," Alex determined.

Cornfield silenced him with a flick of his hand. "You research and intelligence analysts always try to force the facts to fit with your anonymous tips and alerts so you can cover your ass just in case something really happens. Once more, I demand to know who gave you such detailed information that includes the name and photo of your would-be assassin?"

"We've already told you. Ruth the Moabitess," answered Arik.

"And that's your prostitute's fee for fucking her in Paris last week?" Cornfield exulted.

"I never fucked her." Arik looked Cornfield straight in the eye.

"In our code of ethics, fisting is also considered screwing. When an operator and an agent screw, we're talking about a serious violation of our ethical code, aren't we?"

Arik fell silent.

"You'd be surprised," Cornfield said. "We have ears everywhere. Cameras too."

Outside, on the way back to his office, Alex caught up with Arik. "Do you understand what's going on here?" he asked.

"Of course I understand. Mossad's Director is appointing agents to follow other senior members of Mossad. That's legal only if there's evidence or grounds for reasonable suspicion. That's why he's trying to frame me and prove that I have supposedly had an affair with an agent. I'm not worried. The law in on my side."

"What law?" Alex placed his hand on Arik's arm. "In case you haven't noticed, right now, Cornfield is the law in here."

Chapter 34

Beehive on the Cliff Neighborhood in the Palmachim Air Force Base

Arik was in a pensive mood as he drove down the roads of the vast military base. An uncomfortable feeling had plagued him all the way from Mossad Headquarters in Tel Aviv. Yet again, he thought he should have left Mossad the moment Cornfield stepped into office. His house at the Beehive on the Cliff neighborhood was dark. He threw the car keys on the kitchen table, went to the porch, and thoughtfully looked at the darkened sea. Long moments later, he went back inside the house, picked up the telephone receiver and dialed a number. After pressing the final digit, he changed his mind and hung up. He poured himself a glass of Armagnac and sat on the sofa. After minutes of sitting and musing, he redialed.

Nathalie didn't answer and her voicemail wasn't active.

He tried another number. His brother-in-law answered the call. "Ilush'ka," Arik called fondly. "How are you?"

Life was always simple and full of promise with Ilush'ka. He was a relentless optimist, and Arik sometimes envied him. "It's all good. Peaches." His brother-in-law summed up his state of mind. "How about you?"

"Everything's complicated, as usual. I need to speak with Naomi. She'll tell you about it later."

"She's out for her dance class. This is how we are. She's light-footed, and I'm overweight. An excellent recipe for a happy marriage." He laughed.

Arik was too tired for small talk. "Please ask Naomi to call me back."

Nathalie's approaching wedding awoke a bothersome sense of gloominess in him. He felt guilty for not being able to establish a fatherly relationship with his daughter. Once again, he wondered where he had gone wrong and what he could have done to prevent his mistakes. He suddenly felt a need to talk to someone who knew both Nathalie and him. Naomi, perhaps?

But Naomi wasn't available.

He looked for his ex-wife's phone number in his phone book. She answered after a few rings and her voice became aggressive as she recognized him. "What do you want?"

"To talk. I didn't call to argue. I assume you know about the wedding."

She chuckled. "Now you remember? The invitations were sent over two weeks ago. Where have you been for the past month? Hold on. I forgot. You probably went on another screwing trip abroad at the taxpayer's expense."

"I called to have a constructive conversation about Nathalie, our daughter, and about the wedding. Do you think we could please have this conversation without insulting each other?" he asked softly, overcoming the anger caused by her teasing.

"Oh please, let's have a constructive conversation about the pile of shit you've left me in. You've abandoned your wife and your children, claiming 'the security of the state of Israel,' no less, to justify your egotistical actions and disappearance.

My therapist says you have an infantile and egocentric personality, a man constantly busy with satisfying his own needs, entirely insensitive to his surroundings. You're a son of a bitch. A scumbag! Don't ever call me again!" she screamed and slammed the phone down.

Arik felt weak and humiliated when he called Eva.

"Hello, my beloved man." She immediately wrapped him with kind words that always embarrassed him. "What's up? Are you excited about the wedding yet? I'm sorry I haven't had the chance to talk to you about it yet. How do you Jewish people say it? *Mazel tof!*"

"*Mazal tov*," Arik corrected her and explained the expression's meaning to her. Then he asked if she'd like to go to the wedding with him.

"Are you sure you'd like me to come with you to a place where your ex-wife and your entire family are going to be? With your family's Holocaust history, do you think they'd be comfortable with you dating a German woman?"

"Yes," said Arik. "I need you here. Now. Beside me."

"Have you finally decided to give yourself to me?" she asked half-jokingly.

"Let's leave that for now," said Arik. The next sentence simply slipped from his mouth. "I've no one else…"

She was silent.

"Eva?"

"Let me finish with a few things here, and I'll let you know if I'll be coming or not. Sorry, but I can't make any promises. It's the end of the semester, and I have a lot of exams and papers to check. I'm committed to my students, you know."

"But it's right next to you. The wedding is on Tuesday in Jerusalem."

"All right. What about after the wedding? Will you spend the night?"

The sense of loneliness disappeared at once. Fear of commitment clutched at Arik again. "We'll see."

"A moment ago, you said you have no one else. Now you're avoiding me again," she said without anger or resentment, merely stating a fact.

"I'm not avoiding you. I'm just taking it slowly." A call came in on the other line. "I have to go. Kisses and… Yes, I'll spend the night."

"Wait a minute, what do I bring to a Jewish wedding? Is there a gift list somewhere?"

"Just bring yourself." Arik laughed and answered the other call. It was Naomi.

"I just spoke with Rachel," she said without introductions. "She's sorry for losing control. She just can't handle talking to you. She was also shocked to hear of Nathalie's wedding."

"Oh, well. I couldn't care less about her. She can call me back whenever she feels she can handle it."

"Arik! Enough!" Naomi scolded him.

"Does she have any idea where Michael is?" He cut her off.

"Yes, Rachel and I spoke two weeks ago. She told me he now lives in an *ashram* in Rishikesh in north India, studying yoga. The place is called Parmarth Niketan. I have the address. I sent him some money there. Here, write it down." She started dictating a long sentence which ended with the words "Rishikesh, India."

Arik had no intention of sending a letter there. It would take more than a letter to heal his relationship with his son. "Did she let him know about the wedding? Is he going to come?"

"She's left a couple of messages. He never got back to her. The hostel owner said he is probably in a *vipassana* workshop so no one would be able to reach him for ten days. She tried to get hold of him at the *ashram*, but they have a policy of not giving the guests any messages. Have you tried speaking with Mom?"

"I tried a few hours ago. She' can't really communicate. I spoke with the nurse and asked her to call me when Mom is more lucid. I really want her to be there at the wedding. It's important to me."

"With all due respect for what's important to you, dear brother, the question is whether Mom, in her current state of health, would be able to drive all the way from Haifa to Jerusalem just to attend some ultra-religious wedding ceremony. Do you think she'd even know where she was?"

Arik sighed with frustration.

Naomi tried to soften her words. "Arik, please understand, the wedding is going to involve tedious prayers and blessings and speeches given by rabbis. She will need to sit in a separate area for women, among women she doesn't even know, with the foreign nurse. It's not an easy situation to be in, even for a healthy woman."

"You and Rachel are going to be there too," Arik insisted. "It's important to me that we'll be there as a family. You know the saying we Ashkenazi Jews have. 'May you dance at your grandchildren's wedding.' I believe she wants to attend her eldest granddaughter's wedding."

"Oh, Arik," Naomi said with desperation. "When it comes to emotional matters, you still act like a little child."

"Thanks for your support," Arik hissed with irony.

"All right," Naomi relented, "a *beloved* little child."

Chapter 35

The building that housed the Breslov Yeshiva and Religious Seminary, Shuvu Banim, towered above the old city and the David citadel in Jerusalem. At the yeshiva entrance, a page containing the marriage ceremony prayers and blessings was handed out to the guests along with leaflets glorifying various Breslov orthodox institutions around the country. Men and women sat at separate tables and signed up guests for donations.

Eva walked next to Arik, modestly dressed and wearing a small, matching hat. Arik's knit yarmulke was immediately snatched by a burly man wearing Hassidic clothes and replaced with a black one.

"And you are?" the man asked.

"The father of the bride," said Arik trying to follow Eva, who was gently led to the women's section on the other end of the banquet hall.

The burly man led Arik to two elderly men who sat on ornate chairs. "This is the rabbi who will hold the wedding ceremony and join the couple in holy matrimony, and this is the groom's grandfather, Rebbe Nahman Feivish Steinsaltz," he said reverently.

Arik reluctantly shook both their hands.

"Come, Rabbi Arik Bar-Nathan," said one of the rabbis and rose from his seat, aided by the burly Hassid. "Come and say the evening *Maariv* with us."

The burly man aided the other elderly man to rise to his feet, and the two rabbis began to pray. A multitude of men wearing black surrounded them. They all rhythmically swayed back and forth with ritual movements and shouted their prayers to God in Heaven. A prayer book was placed in Arik's hands, and a finger showed up from nowhere to indicate the passage he should read from.

Arik, whose only visit to the synagogue had taken place during his son's Bar Mitzvah, felt like a complete alien. His Holocaust survivor parents had indeed come from religious families but blamed God for His indifference to the terrible fate of the chosen people during WWII and became complete atheists. Arik asked to be circumcised in a hospital when he was twelve, only after his classmates had pestered him endlessly, asking to see what a gentile's member looked like.

Now he felt like an anthropologist watching a strange tribal ritual. His eyes wandered and sought Naomi, Rachel, or Eva, but a crowd of people separated him from the partition dividing the men's and women's sections. As soon as the prayer finished, he hurried to make his way there. He lifted the curtain a bit and examined the forbidden area filled with women, most of them pregnant, all wearing head scarves or wigs. Small boys ran to and fro, knotted ritual fringes dangling from their pants. Little girls in puffed-up pink crinoline dresses stood next to their mothers. On a small stage, almost swallowed by a huge white armchair adorned with floral arrangements, sat his daughter. She wore a white, long, and loose dress that concealed her figure and looked completely different from the daughter he had once known. Her penitent friends were standing next to her, chatting excitedly, while she was entirely absorbed in a small leather-bound prayer book. His ex-wife stood to her right, mummified by a blue satin dress that was too tight and wearing a large, fashionable hat. Their eyes met, and she nodded with a sour expression.

Arik walked around the partition and approached his daughter. He tried to kiss her, but she gently pushed him away and told him in a foreign, Yiddish accent, "The father is allowed to kiss the bride, but he ought not do it in public." Tears of happiness welled in her eyes, but her expression told him his presence in the women's section troubled her.

He turned back and found Naomi standing beside Eva, who looked at him in embarrassment. Only then did Arik remember he had forgotten to tell her they'd sit separate from each other that entire evening. Lacking any other choice, he returned to the men's section.

A Hassidic song sounded from the speakers. "Come in peace, crown of her husband, both in happiness and in jubilation, amidst the faithful of the treasured nation. Come, O Bride! Come, O Bride!" The burly man who had placed the yarmulke on Arik's head approached him again and asked him to come to the dignitaries' table and witness the groom signing the *ketubah*.

At the table sat the two rabbis, the witnesses, and the groom, his body wrapped in a traditional white silk *kittel*, a large, white yarmulke on his head. Only the first traces of a beard could be seen on his face, and he looked thrilled—but exhausted by the traditional fast the bride and groom had to undergo on their wedding day.

Arik was invited to sit between the rabbi, the groom, and the groom's father. A long sheet of paper shaped like a parchment rested on the table. "What is the amount to be written on the marriage contract?" asked the rabbi and straightened his eyes to the groom.

The groom hesitated. He didn't want to appear poor or stingy but was afraid to put down an amount he would not be able to afford should he ever choose to separate from his future wife. Finally, he turned to the rabbi and asked, "*Rebbe*, what amount do we normally put down?"

"Based on the writings of the holy books, the amount for a Cohen's daughter is at least four thousand shekels which means a *yeshiva* student's yearly salary times eighteen."

Arik had forgotten he was the offspring of a Cohen family. He watched the groom's trembling hands. "Write one hundred and eighty thousand," said the groom with a faint smile. The rabbi noted the amount, and the groom signed along with two of his friends who served as witnesses.

"Do I need to sign anything?" Arik asked.

"No need," the rabbi ruled. "*Mazel tov*, congratulations!"

The groom looked at Arik in awe. "Which of the seven blessings should the father of the bride say?" he asked the rabbi, eager to please him.

"Unfortunately, the father of the bride does not uphold the commandments of the Torah," the rabbi mused aloud, completely ignoring Arik's presence. "So it is better that he doesn't say any blessings under the wedding canopy so as not to attract the evil spirits. In order to bless the newlyweds with success and prosperity, it is important that only the righteous would speak there." The groom submissively lowered his head before his spiritual teacher and mumbled a few words of apology to Arik.

The rabbi rose, supported by the burly man, to perform the wedding ceremony. The groom walked by his side, led by his father, who carried a lit candle in his hand. All the hundreds of men erupted into song and dance to please the groom. Arik lagged behind, angry and rejected. The groom and his entourage approached the women's section. Arik took a look and saw the groom covering Nathalie's face with an opaque veil. From there, the men continued to the wedding canopy. The song "*Eshet Chayil*" rose from the speakers. It was only after all the men had left the hall that the bride got down from her stage, accompanied by the rabbi's wife and Rachel, who each held one of her hands, their other hand holding a candle. They began to walk toward the wedding canopy as well while Nathalie's friends accompanied her by clapping their hands. Not one of them had joined the singing, as orthodox religion forbade the singing of women in public.

Arik's eyes chanced upon the image of Eva, standing on a chair, looking about her in wonder and photographing the Jewish wedding ceremony. To his surprise, it appeared that she liked what she saw.

Suddenly, he felt the familiar sensation that someone was staring at him. He looked around and his eyes caught the firm, somewhat familiar image of a man standing at the edge of the hall. He focused his eyes on him. It was a dark-haired waiter with slightly slanted eyes. A bulge was clearly visible above his belt. Arik tried to see if his fingers were tattooed, but they were covered by white gloves.

He was so focused on the waiter that he hadn't even noticed Claire, his secretary, slipping like an uninvited guest to the outskirts of the banquet hall, placing gift envelopes she had collected from Arik's office co-workers into the gift safe.

Arik was now fully alert. He had no doubt about the identity of the man and the reason he was there. He sent his hand to the phone in his pocket, wondering whether he should alert the General Security forces. The sound of the rabbi reading the marriage contract was heard from the speakers. Arik could only imagine what his ex-wife, sister, and daughter would say should the banquet hall be suddenly flooded by security forces. He decided to act alone.

Concealed by the corridor leading to the kitchens, Arik drew his Glock and covered it with a napkin he pulled from one of the tables. The man left the hall and headed to the kitchens, and Arik knew he was looking for him. When the waiter entered the corridor, Arik lunged at him, placed the pistol against his head, and dragged him into a darkened storage room with a choke hold.

The man gagged and tried to resist, but Arik held him tightly. He instructed him to take off his gloves, and the man obeyed. Arik examined his fingers. In the darkness of the storage room, he couldn't see any tattoos. He felt the bulge in the man's hip area. It was soft. Had he wrapped his weapon to conceal it better?

"What is your name?" Arik whispered.

"Misha Guryonov," the man answered with a slight Russian accent.

"What is this?" Arik pointed at the bulge.

"It's… I'm ashamed to say."

"I'm with the security forces. You'd better tell me the truth."

"I'm…I'm a disabled army veteran. I've had a colostomy, this is my stool drainage bag," the man muttered with embarrassment.

Arik sent a hand and dug the man's wallet out of his pocket. He closed the storage room's door and blocked it with his body. The man didn't attempt to run away. To the light of his cell phone flashlight, Arik checked the photo on the man's driver's license, then illuminated his face.

"What are you, a cop?" the man asked.

"I'm not a cop." Arik opened the door. "All right, you can go."

"You bastard!" the man said. "I'm going to call the police."

Arik slowly began to retreat out the banquet hall. From there, he decided he'd call Eva and ask her to meet him outside.

A hand suddenly tapped his shoulder. He turned around in panic. A young man stood in front of him, tall and lanky. His beard was trimmed and his tangled hair was rolled up behind his head. He wore amber-colored Indian *sharwal* pants and a traditional Indian shirt with a matching color. An earring twinkled in his earlobe, and a *rudraksha* prayer necklace hung around his neck. He looked at Arik, mummified in his suit, and smiled. "Hello, Dad. I came straight from the airport. The buses here are even slower than those in India."

A wave of happiness washed over Arik. He hugged the young man and said, "Michael, my dearest son, you're finally back home!"

Chapter 36

Hawarim Canyon—The Dead Sea Valley

It was Friday night. Arik loaded his H-D Night Rod Special motorcycle on a trailer and opened the SUV door for Michael. They were both silent during the drive south all the way to the Marlstone Canyon, next to the Sde Boker Field School. They were welcomed there by a vast and silent desert moon. Arik started the motorcycle, and Michael sat behind him. Hot desert dry air caressed their faces as they sped through hills and *wadi* sands. Mesa cliffs cast their shadows on the white marlstone rocks that gleamed in the light of the full moon.

When they returned to the SUV in the parking area, Arik took out two bottles of frozen beer from a small refrigerator in the trunk.

"Are you having a good time?" asked Arik.

"There are positive vibes in the air, and Nathalie's wedding this week was interesting and very moving," said Michael

"What I meant to ask was how do you like spending time with your old dad again?"

"It's not easy, but I'm glad we're doing it."

"Why isn't it easy?"

"Look, Dad, life for us children with you and Mom was no picnic. You weren't home most of the time, and you left us with a dysfunctional mother who closed herself up in the room most of the time, depressed and crying, consoling herself by eating Belgian chocolate. Whenever you were actually home, you preferred to run away from your endless arguments with her by going to play with your Harley Davidson toys. I can't judge your relationship with Mom. You're both adults, but you should have reached the decision to separate much sooner. Instead, you've used your children as tactical weapons in your war against each other."

Arik remained silent. He had never heard his son speaking so harshly.

"I'm sorry for bringing up such painful memories. I'm not doing it to settle a score. But it's time for us to talk. The last time we met, I was still a confused little boy. We hardly spoke to each other, just spent some time together, rode an ATV, had barbecues, watched action movies and westerns, or went to the zoo. It was as if we tried to do everything imaginable other than having a real conversation."

Arik nodded in agreement.

"You call yourselves 'second-generation Holocaust survivors,' but you know what? We third-generation Holocaust survivors have fought, struggled and got hurt too. I understand that you, as the son of parents who were mentally wounded by what they'd gone through, felt the need to compensate yourself by having fast cars, beautiful women, and lots of action. You felt like the world needed to compensate you for all injustices inflicted on your parents. Am I right?"

"Yes…in a way," Arik admitted.

"And I can't help but ask myself what for?" Michael pondered aloud. "I've had a lot of time to think about this in

India. We Israelis have become a neurotic nation that chooses to sanctify its Holocaust paranoia. We keep shedding tears while fighting. We think of all wars as 'wars of necessity,' as if the whole world is still against us. But there is no justification to conquering and ruling another nation—the Palestinians— just because we're an anxious people who do not trust Arabs or anyone else in this world. I keep asking myself, 'is it possible to break this vicious circle in which the victim becomes the victimizer? Must an abused child become an abusive parent?'"

Arik shuddered. He had never told anyone he'd been beaten as a child, most certainly not his son.

"I wish it were that simple." Arik sighed. "We live in a country which is a kind of villa in the middle of the jungle. And that jungle is the Eastern Mediterranean. When you live in the jungle, you can't ask a hungry tiger you happen to meet in the forest to spare you because you're a vegetarian or donate to the SPCA. In such an environment, a person who doesn't fight gets eaten alive."

"Let's not talk about high politics," said Michael. "Let's talk about us, your children. No one compensated us for the suffering you and Mom caused us. Do you even know how hard Nathalie took it when you went away? Did you ever know she tried to commit suicide in order to get your attention to her plight? You never listened to our troubles. You were always too busy fighting your wars."

Arik's heart lost a beat; he shed a tear and was happy the desert darkness concealed his face.

Michael kept pounding him with his words. "I ran as far as I could away from you so I'd have the opportunity to build my self-confidence after years of growing up as an insecure child with no parents. I've taken self-awareness and Tao workshops to learn to be able to objectively look at my inner world. Today, I'm able to look at you with compassion and without anger. You should know, though, that Nathalie is still very hurt. I think you should do more to heal her wounds."

"I've tried, but she won't let me," Arik whispered.

"Then keep trying, again and again. She needs to see that you care, that you're trying, that she means the world to you."

Michael placed his large hand on his father's shoulder, "Don't get me wrong, Dad. I love you very much. I'm happy to have you as my father, and I believe you're making a real effort to find a way back to our hearts, but there's something about your personality that doesn't know how to commit, that is afraid to give in to your emotions."

Arik smiled at Michael and couldn't help but wonder if he had failed in nurturing their relationship simply because Michael resembled Rachel, his ex-wife, in his appearance. His features and expressions were very similar to hers, as were his intonation and body language. Arik knew it was a dubious excuse, that the resemblance wasn't the real reason for his failure as a father; it was the constant need he felt to protect his comfort zone, his freedom.

He rose and threw his arms around his son. "I love you, my *boychik*," he mumbled.

Michael hugged him back with embarrassment.

The sound of falling rocks from behind them made them turn their eyes toward a couple of female tourists who rose from the *wadi*, chatting in Aussi English. One was tall and wore a pair of tiny shorts. Her ample bosom threatened to burst out of her shirt. The other one was chubby, bespectacled, and full of smiles.

"Hi, good evening. Do you mind if we set up our tent next to yours?" they asked in an Australian accent.

"With pleasure," Arik answered. "We've got some cold beer for you, if you'd like, and we were just about to put some juicy steaks on the fire. You're more than welcome to join us."

"We'd love that," said the handsomer of the two. "Can we use water from the jerrycan in your SUV to wash ourselves a little? It's really hot and humid today and we're very sweaty."

"No problem," said Arik and handed them the jerrycan. The two girls unabashedly took off their clothes and washed themselves naked, glowing like fireflies under the light of the full moon.

Arik looked at Michael, who examined their bodies. He had never thought of his son as a man. He'd always pictured him in his mind's eye as the little boy still riding his rocking horse in the living room of their first apartment. What happened after that? Had he become too absorbed in his work to notice his son had become a man?

"She's pretty hot, isn't she?" said Michael, eying the tall one.

"She sure is." Arik tried to go along, even though he felt increasingly uncomfortable.

He took the charcoal grill from the SUV and lit it. Michael took two cold beer bottles from the refrigerator. The smell of cooked meat attracted the two Australian girls who joined them, wearing light tunics, towels wrapped around their heads. Michael handed them the beers and they smiled gratefully.

Arik gave the three a dreamy look.

"Dad, I think it's time you left girls that age for me and concentrate on women your age. I saw Eva at Nathalie's wedding; I've spoken with her as well. She's a very impressive woman, if you don't mind me saying that."

"You two have spoken?"

"Yes. She asked me about my life and my future plans. Don't worry; we haven't spoken a word about you. Even though I have a feeling she knows a lot more than you think she does. She offered me her help in getting admitted to the Berlin or Heidelberg Universities."

"Why in Germany? Why can't you go to the Hebrew University, like I did? Like Nathalie?" Arik asked.

"Because there's no veterinary medicine department in Jerusalem," answered Michael. Then he teasingly added, "But of course, you had no idea what I want to learn."

Indeed, Arik didn't.

"But there is a veterinary department in the Hebrew University branch at Rehovot."

"Rehovot is not Jerusalem. I can't stand that boring city."

The thought of Michael was travelling to a far-off country again sent a wave of depression through Arik's mind. "And you think German cities aren't boring?"

"Berlin is a thriving cultural city, and Heidelberg is beautiful and peaceful. I like the idea of living in both of them, in spite of our family history. But I haven't decided to settle down yet. Maybe I'll end up studying international relations and business administration in Jerusalem, just like you did. Who knows?"

Michael rose to turn the steaks and offer the tourists more beer. He stayed with the girls. Arik continued to sit by himself, munching on a piece of steak without really being hungry.

An hour later, Arik napped on the SUV's backseat. In his ears echoed noises coming from the girls' tent. He recognized his son's laughter and felt old, but not so lonely any more.

Chapter 37

Specialists Clinic—Tzrifin Military Base

Arik returned from the desert exhausted. His pelvis kept sending waves of pain that pierced his back. He thought of David Fischer and the backaches he had had due to constant pressure from the prime minister's office. Fischer's ailing back had eventually brought about his retirement. Was he now suffering psychosomatic pains as well? He recalled the terrible weakness he had felt before the beginning of Operation Flower Bud and decided he shouldn't continue to ignore his pains.

His doctor referred him to the Department of Urology, where he described to the military physician, who was about Michael's age, how he woke up several times at night to go to urinate and how tired he felt during the day. "I'll have to perform a rectal examination," the doctor told him and motioned toward the bed at the other end of the room. A few minutes later, Arik was sprawled on a paper sheet, an oiled finger stuck up his backside. "Your prostate is fine, slightly enlarged, but that's only to be expected for a man your age. Still, I want you to undergo a urinary tract CT scan and run blood tests to check your PSA levels. Have you been suffering involuntary cramps and muscle spasms?"

"Yes."

"How severe?"

Arik shrugged.

"From one to ten?"

"Nine," Arik admitted. "But I've read on the Internet it could just be the result of prolonged sitting or overexertion of muscles during sportive activities."

"I see you've successfully graduated from the Google Academy of Medicine," the doctor joked, and Arik smiled in appreciation of his gesture.

Over the next few days, Arik's fatigue and pains worsened. His entire body ached with the pain. Ten days later, he returned to the urologist's clinic. "I'm concerned about the high levels of protein in your urine," said the doctor while examining the test results.

"What does it mean?" asked Arik with concern.

"It means that you may have a problem with your kidney function. I'll refer you to a nephrologist; he'll give you further tests to perform."

Arik needed to wait a whole month for his nephrology appointment. Eva took advantage of her semester break and travelled to Warsaw, where the Jewish Museum in Poland recruited her to serve as its advisor. He remained alone in the large house on the cliff. During the weekends, he tinkered with his motorcycle collection. Now and then, he took one of the motorcycles to the beach and roam the dirt roads between the cities of Ashkelon and Rishon LeZion. During those Saturdays, he felt the experience of existence like he'd never felt it before.

He roamed the orchards of abandoned, nameless villages that disappeared between the dunes, collected flattened figs dripping with honey, and picked prickly reddish *sabra* fruit, whose taste reminded him of yesteryears. Three such weekends later, Eva returned to Israel. He promised he would pick her up from the airport.

"What happened to you?" she asked when they met in the arrivals terminal. "You look sick."

He wanted to tell her he felt burdened by his life, but as usual, avoided exposing his sadness and distress. "I'm all right. Just a little tired, that's all."

She narrowed her eyes and looked at him. "You're hiding something."

"I'm just tired," he grumbled. "I'm under a lot of pressure at work. Don't make a big deal out of it."

She pulled her suitcase from the baggage carousel. "We're going to your place," she said.

"I don't think that's a good—"

"Your place!"

At night, every time he got up from bed to go to the restroom, or twitched in pain from leg cramps, she lay next to him in bed with her eyes open and attentively listened to his distress. She did not bother him with questions, and every time he got back to bed, she hurried to place her hand around him and her leg on his hip. They fell asleep spooning and snuggling together. Toward dawn, she whispered, "I don't want to lose you. What's going on? Please tell me."

Arik straightened up in bed. "I don't know. Something is happening, and it scares the hell out of me."

"I love you, and I want to have your child," she whispered longingly.

To her surprise, Arik did not erupt in anger. Instead, he turned to her and buried his face in her neck, weeping like a child.

"Love is the firm ground on which we tread," she whispered a line from an old German folksong in his ear and caressed his head, taking him to her bosom. Arik turned to her, and they joined in the act of love. Later on, they rested side by side, satisfied and thoughtful.

After preparing breakfast together, she joined him for an especially fast motorcycle ride on the beach. Before getting back into the military base, he stopped, turned and looked at her. "Did you enjoy it?"

"I enjoyed your enjoyment. I hate fast driving."

"I'm always embarrassed by your empathy."

She laughed.

"I'm serious."

"Learn to accept things, Arik. It might just help you give from yourself to others."

"Enough with your psychobabble," he protested.

She patted his leather-bound shoulder and smiled. "Just go."

Chapter 38

Hematology Ward—Sheba Medical Center

The next morning, Arik went to the nephrologist's clinic. The doctor, a middle-aged man with an Argentinean accent, looked at the medical examination results. "The protein in your urine indicates some sort of kidney dysfunction. I'd like you to see a hematologist."

"What does a hematologist have to do with the fact I get up several times at night to urinate?" Arik wondered aloud.

"I want you to do some more blood tests to rule out the possibility of other problems," the nephrologist explained with a straight face.

"Such as…leukemia?" Arik asked with concern.

"No, no, if you had leukemia, it would have been discovered in the first round of blood tests," the doctor answered reassuringly. Arik wasn't convinced.

The referral form for the Sheba Medical Center's hematology ward stated that he should arrive following thirteen hours of fasting and accompanied by another person. Eva demanded to come with him, but he adamantly refused and headed to the hospital early in the morning before she even woke up. When he waited in the polished corridor for his bone marrow examination, his mind was preoccupied by the latest incidents with Cornfield rather than his own health issues. The lack of trust demonstrated by his superior, along with the discovery he had been under surveillance while in Paris, made him feel like a stranger in the organization he loved so much. Thoughts of retirement rose in him again.

He began to feel pangs of hunger, and just as he thought of heading to the first-floor cafeteria, the door in front of him opened. A skeletal, yellow-faced girl came out, leaning on the shoulder of a man, perhaps her father, who looked older than Arik. A handsome, full-bodied woman with black hair followed. She was dressed in a green gown, and a stethoscope dangled around her neck. With a warm smile, she invited Arik to come inside the room.

"Good morning, my name is Dr. Alice Ben David." She motioned to the chair facing her desk. Arik sat and watched her closely as she examined the bundle of test results he had brought with him. He felt very lonely and didn't know how to shake off that burdening feeling. Sharing his pains and anxieties with others seemed like admitting defeat in his eyes. Ever since his first asthma attacks as a child, he had never demonstrated pain or weakness in front of strangers. The fact he had exposed his fears and weaknesses to Eva was a constant source of embarrassment.

"So, tell me how you are feeling." The doctor's pleasant voice dispersed the heavy cloud of his thoughts.

"I'm fine," he said with confidence.

"Are you sure? After all, you suffer from painful muscle spasms, bone pains in your hands, feet, and lower back…"

"How do you know?"

She gestured at the bundle of test results. "Based on your results, I know all about the symptoms."

"What do I have?" a question verging on a panicked sigh escaped from Arik's chest.

"It's too early to tell. Have you been fasting?"

"Since zero two hundred hours yesterday."

She smiled. "Are you a military man?"

"I used to be."

She didn't let go. "Where do you work?"

"The prime minister's office library."

She looked at his muscular body. "You? A librarian?" she asked with disbelief.

"I'm an information specialist," Arik lied. "I'm looking for researches, crosscheck data, statistics, information…"

The doctor leaned toward him. "I can recognize you people a mile away," she said in a low voice. "My dad was a department manager."

Arik didn't reply.

The doctor rose and opened a door that led to an adjoining room. A nurse in a white robe led him to a small dressing room. "Please, take off clothes," she asked in a heavy Russian accent.

"All of them?" Arik asked, shocked.

"All clothes," came the answer. "Then wear gown."

It was the twin brother of the hospital gown he had worn after getting injured at the Temple Mount. Once more, he felt very embarrassed as he came out of the small dressing room. The nurse was busy stretching a plastic sheet on a bed that looked like a small operating table with a large lighting fixture above it. "Please lie on side. Now give contrast agent. Just little pinprick."

Arik wanted to tell her he could take much more than a little pinprick, but kept quiet. It was indeed just a little pinprick. "Now the epidural." He heard the doctor's voice. The fact she had entered the room without him noticing enhanced the feeling of discomfort caused by the fact his buttocks were bare, and his testicles were crushed between his thighs.

"Why an epidural?" he tried to joke. "Am I about to give birth?"

The doctor didn't laugh. "Don't worry," she said. "You're just going to feel a little sting. After that, we'll wait a few minutes for the local anesthetic to take effect and take bone marrow fluid and tissue samples, as well as a pelvic bone sample—"

"Then we'll finally know what's going on?" Arik cut her short with an impatience that concealed his great concern.

"Not yet. I'll need to send everything to the pathology department. We'll have an answer in about a month. Perhaps a little longer with all the holidays on the way." Her touch was gentle and professional. He felt his legs drifting away from his body until they finally disappeared. "I'm going to insert a pressure-drilling needle into your pelvis. You can sigh or even scream if it helps." Arik felt something digging into his body. He didn't utter a sound and bit into his wrist. "I want you to rest a little before leaving the room," said the doctor and left the room. The anesthesia gradually wore off, and Arik felt intense pains in his lower body. He perspired and clenched his teeth. "We are not weak." His mother's voice echoed between the walls of his skull. "We mustn't show anyone that we're scared or frightened."

Half an hour later, the Russian nurse came inside and announced, "Now I help get up."

"No need," Arik grumbled. He tried to get up and fell back into bed.

"Perhaps you should rest a bit more. Strong anesthetic. Can't run your age."

Now he felt he simply must get up. He sat in bed, brought his feet down to the floor, and wobbled to the dressing room, expecting applause that never came. When he turned his face to the nurse, he saw that she was already busy with replacing the instruments on the tray next to the operating table.

He still found it difficult to walk and went out into the corridor and steadied himself against the wall.

For the first time, he thought he should have obeyed the medical instructions and brought Eva with him. He also immediately realized he could never have exposed himself to her in such a way.

He reached the cafeteria by limping painfully. With the last ounces of strength remaining in him, he bought himself some cheap coffee and a tasteless croissant and devoured them. When he tried to walk to the parking lot, he realized he'd never be able to drive in his condition. He decided to leave his car at the hospital and order a taxi. When it finally arrived, he dropped into the backseat, tired and hurting.

"I'm sick at home," he messaged Claire. "I left the car in the Sheba Medical Center parking lot. Level negative-two. Could you send someone to pick it up?"

Claire called him immediately. "What were you doing in the Sheba Medical Center?"

"Forget it. Is there anything important going on?"

"No, just a message from Alex. He says… Hold on…" The rustling sound of paper sounded. "Ruth the Moabitess…" She read with the acceptance of someone who had read hundreds messages that held no meaning to her. "…says that the time has come."

When he entered his house, he found out it was empty. Eva returned to the Jerusalem University and her apartment in the Belgium House on the campus, the guest house for guest professors.

Arik made a few calls in his secure line. He couldn't find the strength to climb to the bedroom floor and simply dropped on the living room sofa, curled up like a fetus, and covered himself with the quilt his daughter knitted him in better times.

Before falling asleep, he thought he was one of the few people in the country who could actually predict the next day's headlines: An Iranian ship full of weapons intended for the Hezbollah organization in Lebanon has sunk under mysterious circumstances off Port Sudan in the Red Sea.

Chapter 39

Cornfield wobbled into the room, late as usual to the division heads Monday morning meeting. His face looked tired and his artificial eye constantly shed tears. Hushed, scurrilous whispers accompanied his entrance. "He's all washed up," whispered the head of Tevel.

"That's what happens when you keep mixing amphetamines with alcohol," confided the head of Neviot.

Alex weighed in. "Don't celebrate just yet. Cornfield is like the phoenix. Every time people thought he was down, he managed to rise up and destroy his enemies. And I certainly don't intend to be one of them."

Cornfield heavily sat in his oversized chair, contemptuously rejecting the support offered him by his second in command, Mot'ke Hassin. "Gentlemen, life is an endless collection of unplanned circumstances, but we can't complain about presents that fall right into the web we've spent long years spinning and spreading."

The director's sudden outburst of poetic musing caused a surprised wave of whispered murmurs to pass through the room.

"I'm referring to the news about the Syrian plutogenic reactor brought to us to the head of Caesarea." Cornfield's voice now wore a tone of mockery. "Who literally sacrificed his body and soul to obtain this particular bit of intelligence, I must add." He snickered to leave no doubt as to his thoughts on the matter. "And, well, the prime minister is asking me to present him with operative recommendations. What do we know and what can we recommend?"

Alex, head of the Research and Intelligence Division, was the first to speak. "We already knew of surface-to-surface missiles being developed by the Syrians, aided by Iranian funding, but the fact the Syrians are about to have a nuclear reactor as well is both disturbing and surprising."

"What's surprising about it?" Mot'ke Steak face barked at him. "You guys have had almost a month to deal with this. Just give us your operative recommendation and spare us the empty speeches."

Alex looked at him with distaste.

Breiness, head of the Neviot Division tried to help. "The Directorate of Military Intelligence, with the approval of the prime minister, has been instructed to provide us with the intercepted communications between the Syrian president and his aides via ComInt."

"And?" Cornfield asked with impatience.

"Nothing. Nada. The bastards don't use cellular phones. They maintain radio silence and conduct their communications with extreme secrecy in private rooms."

"In other words, you have nothing," Cornfield summed up.

"It's not like we're not doing anything," Alex got back to the conversation. "The Military Intelligence's 8100 Unit has been instructed to change the course of the Ofek Nine satellite and start looking for dugouts and new constructions in the mountains close to Damascus to locate the whereabouts of a nuclear reactor under construction."

"And what have they found so far? Let me guess, nothing?"

"Not exactly," Jonathan Soudry, head of Tzomet, remarked. "A month ago, my reconnaissance officers sent out an urgent request to all agents in the field, asking them to keep an eye out and to send us any piece of information regarding large-scale digging and construction activities in the scope of moving a mountain."

"Moving a mountain?" Cornfield muttered.

"Yes, that's the amount of digging necessary for the construction of a plutogenic nuclear reactor. Ruth the Moabitess' men, who are training in the Kurdish enclave in northern Iraq, have spotted Iranian trucks headed to the Syrian border."

"So what? These could have been part of the convoys regularly transferring weapons to the Hezbollah," Cornfield yelled at him.

The head of Tzomet lingered for a brief second, preparing the surprise he had in store. "No! We are talking about double-trailer trucks carrying heavy machinery and engineering equipment," he said victoriously.

"Is that it?" Cornfield failed to be impressed. "Anybody else have some information? Recommendations?"

He looked at the Tevel Department head, who added, "We've asked the Americans to have their Icarus satellite pass over Syria to check for any large-scale, new dugouts. The answer we received was that it'd take them about a month to fit our request into their schedule."

"Those people would ask you to wait for an opening in their schedule even if the next World War started," Hassin remarked, and Cornfield silently answered him with a content smile. The remaining people in the room simply kept quiet.

"And what does our renowned Caesarea Division chief recommend that we do?" Cornfield wondered aloud without establishing eye contact with Arik.

Before Arik could answer, the door buzzed open, and a soldier secretary came into the room. She held a folded note that she presented to Shlomo Zimmer, Cornfield's bureau chief.

Zimmer opened the note, read it and transferred it to Cornfield with a big smile on his lips. Cornfield read it as quickly and said, "All right, this is the breakthrough we've been expecting and it happened no thanks to you. Our satellite, Ofek 9, has just discovered major earthworks taking place in the mountains near the Deir ez-Zor military base, next to the Iraq-Syria border."

He turned to Arik. "Yes, we're still waiting for Caesarea's operative angle on this. What do you have to say?"

"I met with the head of the IDF Operations Directorate and the head of the Directorate of Intelligence. Tonight, a unit of IDF agents, along with teams from the General Staff Reconnaissance Unit and the Navy Seals are supposed to infiltrate the area of the targets we've marked. They will penetrate the zone from the American Incirlik Air Base in southern Turkey. Their objective is to look for signs of new, special construction being built during the night. One of the places they'll check is the area in which earthworks are taking place near Deir ez-Zor."

"No! I won't authorize sending our soldiers over there," Cornfield erupted. "I don't want to take unnecessary risks. Send Tzomet's local agents over there. The Arabs who worked with us when we took out Husniyah."

"With all due respect, that's not your call to make," said Arik. "The chief of staff is the one authorizing IDF operations. Neither you nor I are the ones determining who to send to perform special military operations. In general, every cross-border military operation requires the authorization of the Security Cabinet. This is out of both our hands and responsibility."

Cornfield and Arik stared at each other like two stags in mating season about to lock antlers.

Alex hurried to try and get the discussion back to practical terms. "The IDF won't be enough in this case. We need to send our own people there to check the place and collect ground, water, and vegetation samples to determine whether any radioactive activity is taking place in the area. If the answer is positive, the reactor is already operational, and we have a big problem on our hands."

Cornfield wrinkled his forehead in an attempt to understand Alex's last remark.

"Supposedly, we have some leeway to operate while the reactor is still under construction," Alex explained, "but the minute it's operational, any strike would cause a vast ecological disaster. This is why we don't have any time to spare."

"Trying to cover your ass by saying opposite things in the same sentence again?" Cornfield scolded him.

Alex didn't reply, but a sarcastic smile snuck into the corners of his mouth.

"I'm against this entire thing," Cornfield said after thinking for another moment. "I'm not sure this is even something Mossad should handle. This is now strictly a military issue. They'd end up using the Air Force anyway. If it destroys the reactor, IDF and the chief of staff will get all the credit. But if something goes wrong, the politicians are going to blame it all on us."

Arik couldn't contain himself any longer. "Why can't you military men ever see the bigger picture?"

"What's all this talk about you and us?" Mot'ke Hassin shouted at him from the other end of the table. "Did you serve in another army? Weren't you a part of Flotilla Thirteen?"

"I think we need to take a look at the wider angle," Arik answered calmly. "If we nail down the plutogenic reactor along with the Syrian general in charge of it, we'll double our gain: eliminating the problem and discouraging the Iranians from further developing nuclear facilities at the same time."

Cornfield demonstrated his discomfort with a series of coughs. "Mossad won't take any action regarding this matter, and that's the end of it."

Everyone sitting around the table, other than Mot'ke Hassin, lowered their eyes.

As soon as he headed out of the meeting and retrieved his cell phone from security, Arik felt it buzzing in his hand. He took a look at the message Eva had sent him: *Darling, life is not measured by the number of breaths we take, but by the moments that take our breath away. Love, Eva.*"

At that particular moment, he liked the thought that he was loved.

Chapter 40

That very night, an Israeli Hercules transport aircraft took off from southern Turkey and headed south, toward the border of Iraq and Syria. A combined team of twenty-five IDF elite unit soldiers, commanded by Captain Yuval Ebenstein, was dropped by parachute next to Ras al-Ayn, about six miles off the city of Deir ez-Zor, off the banks of the Euphrates River. From afar, the lights of the hanging bridge could be seen above the river. The soldiers gathered in one of the *wadis*, buried their parachutes and started their dirt bikes, and sped east to the barren hills of the Syrian desert, toward the area in which the giant dugouts had been located. The force took well-concealed positions and prepared for a week-long stay in the field.

At the end of the week, the force returned to Israel with photos of the facility as well as ground and vegetation samples that were immediately sent to the Israel Institute for Biological Research in Ness Ziona.

The results weren't conclusive, but in the meantime, the Israeli satellite, Ofek, provided further photos of the site. Those were sent by the Tevel Division people to the CIA headquarters in Langley to be compared with photos the American Icarus satellites had taken across the world.

A day later, the deputy director of the CIA called Alex. "There's no doubt about it," he told his Israeli colleague. "This is a plutogenic reactor, the twin brother of the North Korean reactor in Yongbyon. We assume this isn't a strategic cooperation but a simple transaction. The motive is money. North Korea sells missile production and nuclear technologies to the highest bidder. We can only assume there are also North Korean scientists, engineers, and technicians in Syria to supervise the construction and create a training system."

Alex hurried to update Cornfield, who was on his way for his weekly meeting with Prime Minister Lolik.

Lolik, an experienced veteran, spat at him as soon as he entered the room. "Come on, spill the beans. I know you have something you can't wait to tell me."

Cornfield reported everything he knew. The prime minister listened and said, "We've declared more than once that we won't allow enemy countries to develop nuclear capabilities. So we definitely need to attack. The only question is when, and the answer depends on another question: Do we operate on our own or with the Americans?"

"We have a problem with the current American administration," Cornfield recited the summary he'd read in the intelligence reports Alex and his men had provided him. "It's the end of the current president's term, and he is busy with clearing his own table. It's not probable he'd be willing to get involved with another adventure in the Middle East. Especially after the mess the Americans had gotten themselves into during the wars in Afghanistan and Iraq. We think the Americans would only agree to take diplomatic actions against Syria."

"So we're completely on our own here?" the prime minister asked, and his little eyes sparked.

"Yes, and there's a price to pay. Should we attack on our own, without American involvement or assurances, Syria might attack our home front. They have missiles that cover most of the country's territory, not to mention the possibility of Hezbollah joining the party, along with Syria from the north, and possibly Hamas from Gaza. The entire country could be under attack. Besides, if we take out North Korean scientists and technicians, we'd be opening a new front and creating new enemies for ourselves."

The prime minister hesitated, but suddenly had an idea. "I'll turn to the chief of staff and ask him to conduct a 'war game' with your people and the IDF. The game is going to be based on the information you've given me without the people being involved knowing its real background. As far as they will be concerned, it will only be a theoretical game, but it will give us all options and situations we might be faced with should we decide to attack. Enlist the finest minds from the universities and research institutions and have them sign confidentiality statements. I want Alex Abramovich to be in charge of this operation, understood?"

Cornfield muttered something unintelligible.

"Wasn't Alex's division the one that conducted the evaluation you've based your survey on?" Lolik asked, although he already knew the answer.

"Yes, sort of," Cornfield had to admit.

The prime minister pressed the intercom button. "Ask Bar-Nathan to come in here."

Cornfield cringed in his chair. The motion had not gone unnoticed by the prime minister, and he flashed a mean smile. "Come in," he called with pronounced friendliness to Arik. "Arik and I have been discussing a few things. It'd be a shame to let him wait outside when he can contribute so much to our conversation."

"I…had no idea you two were having meetings." Cornfield gave Arik a menacing look.

"I meet with a lot of people," the prime minister said with exaggerated cheerfulness. "I'm allowed to do that, aren't I?"

All three of them knew the prime minister was allowed to meet with Arik. However, protocol demanded Arik to report the meeting invitation to his supervisor unless he had been specifically ordered not to do that. Cornfield wondered what could have caused his friend, the prime minister, to undermine him. Was it just Arik, or were there more people in the organization he was heading who were in direct contact with the prime minister?

"Sir," he said angrily, "you appointed me to—"

"Sure, sure. I appointed you to run Mossad, but this doesn't mean I can't pull my own weight in it, right? It's just that I had the impression—how can I say it?—that your organization wasn't willing to take some of the burden involved with the intelligence-gathering tasks and preferred the army to perform them with the Air Force and its elite units."

Cornfield felt furious. Who had leaked his position in the division heads meeting in which he had demanded the army would take care of the nuclear reactor problem? The only one who had something to gain from it was Arik. He must be the informer then, and both he and the prime minister had set him a trap. "I don't think Mossad is ready to undertake such a type of operation yet, Mr. Prime Minister," Cornfield tried to excuse his latest decisions. The prime minister rewarded him with a cynical smile.

"And in any case, Tzomet agents…weren't there," Cornfield mumbled. " It was the IDF's Magellan special forces unit who parachuted there and brought us the samples."

"Begging your pardon. That's not entirely true," Arik said with the generosity of winners. "It was our Tzomet people who brought and verified the initial information…"

"Brought by you," the prime minister hissed. Arik recalled all the times he had been told about the prime minister's tendency to turn his subordinates against each other so he could increase his level of control over them. This was the first time he encountered it firsthand. "Before you came into the room, I suggested to Cornfield we conduct a war game." The prime minister turned to Arik. "What do you say?"

"I don't know what the results of such a war game would be, but I believe it would show us our window of opportunity is quickly closing. If Israel wants to act, it needs to do it right away. We mustn't allow Syria to pass the threshold and possess an operational nuclear reactor. Should this happen, any attempt to attack it will cause a large-scale environmental disaster that might influence millions of people in Syria and Iraq, a disaster the entire world will blame us for."

"What are you suggesting, then?"

"Skip the war game. We've no time to spare."

Cornfield looked at Arik in amazement. He himself had never dared to contradict the ideas of his supreme commander in such a manner. Surprisingly, the prime minister smiled contentedly. "And why, pray tell, is that?" he asked in the sarcastic flowery language he loved so much.

"Because if it turns out the reactor isn't active, we'll have to attack anyway. I'm not especially worried about the American reaction. The American president is still furious at

Syria because it allowed terrorists to infiltrate Iraq from its territory last year and harm American soldiers."

"Good point." The prime minister flattered him.

"It's obvious to me we need to provide the Americans a general notification," Arik continued, encouraged. "But we mustn't share the details of the operation or the exact timing of the attack with them. Something like 'don't ask, don't tell.' This way, they'll be able to say, in retrospect, that they weren't asked and didn't know."

"Agreed!" The prime minister called and turned to Cornfield. "I want you to go and meet the head of the CIA and update him. If there'll be any problems, I'll talk to the president directly."

"All right," said the defeated Cornfield.

"Take Arik and Alex with you. They speak better English than you do."

Cornfield took the insult with a grim face. "I thought of taking Major General Hassin with me," he said quietly, but was completely ignored by the prime minister.

"Are we agreed, then?" the prime minister asked.

Arik rose to his feet. "Am I dismissed, sir?"

"Wait for me outside. Our real appointment hasn't started yet."

Cornfield followed him with his eyes as he crossed the large room, and Arik felt like a hunted animal escaping the clutches of a gliding hawk.

Chapter 41

Mossad H.Q

The Mossad director's car stopped at the entrance of a modern, pentagon-shaped office building located high on a hill facing the Tel Aviv-Haifa highway. Cornfield came out of it and headed straight to his office, crossing the secretariat and entering his private sitting room. He opened the wood globe and took out his favorite whiskey, Glenfiddich 21 Year Old Special Reserve, poured a glass, and gulped half of it. Shlomo Zimmer, his bureau chief, followed him into the room and asked with concern, "Cornfield, are you all right?"

Cornfield raised the glass toward him and said with a sad smile, "Not enough blood in my alcohol lately." Zimmer didn't reply. Like many others, he had been witnessing his commander falling into alcoholism and losing his concentration. There were those who excused Cornfield's behavior with the physical difficulties his new prosthetic leg made him suffer or with the dizzy spells caused by the diabetes medication he had to take. But Zimmer knew the real reason: the prime minister had been pestering his boss. *Why?* he asked himself. What reason could the person who had uplifted and promoted Cornfield now have to harass him?

With the whiskey glass in his hand, Cornfield went to his desk, took out a small phone book from the drawer, and dialed Admiral Jack Derby's classified phone number. A few moments later, the director of the CIA's voice sounded on the other line, full of cheer. "Yes, Cornfield, my friend."

"Jack, there's something urgent we need to discuss," said Cornfield with a heavy Israeli accent. "Are you in your headquarters?"

"Actually, I happen to be in your neighborhood."

"Then why don't you drop by for a brief meeting?" Cornfield asked hopefully. Since the two had met at the Washington National War College, they had developed a deep friendship. Both were disabled war veterans and decorated soldiers. "I'll finally be able to give you that tour of Tel Aviv I've been promising you for years."

Darby laughed. "I've seen enough of it."

"You were here?" asked Cornfield, surprised.

"You can say so. I was close enough to watch it through a submarine's periscope. Beautiful city. Especially at night with all the lights on."

"Oh, good, I thought you were closer."

"Is this something we could discuss on the phone? Or would you rather go to the American embassy in Tel Aviv and talk to me on the secure line?"

"No, no. It has to be a face-to-face meeting. I'll be bringing two of my men with me."

"Sorry, Cornfield, I'm busy these days. The president is about to finish his term, and I'm about to end mine with him. At the moment, we're conducting a series of meetings in Iraq. In two days, we'll be taking off to Afghanistan. Actually, why don't I send a plane to pick you up? We could meet midway in American territory."

"I don't understand."

"Hold on a minute," said the admiral. Two minutes later, he got back on the line. "Cornfield, I'm sending you a light aircraft. It could land in four and a half hours in the military airport near Eilat and bring you to the USS *Nimitz*, currently in the Gulf of Aden. What time is it in Israel?"

"Eighteen thirty," said Cornfield, still feeling reserved about the offer.

"Which means it's nineteen thirty in the Gulf of Aden. Five hours from now, it'll be after midnight over there. What do you think about meeting me tomorrow for breakfast at oh eight hundred hours?"

Cornfield thought about the difficulties involved with air travel, his new prosthetic leg, and insufferable headaches. "All right," he said reluctantly. "Should I bring you anything from the Holy Land?"

"Yes, you could, actually," Derby said happily. "My wife really liked that Gamla Chardonnay you brought me last time. If you could bring another bottle, that would be nice."

"No problem. See you tomorrow at breakfast," said Cornfield and hung up. He pressed the intercom and asked Shlomo Zimmer to come inside. "We're heading out tonight from Tel Aviv. We are leaving from Sde Dov Airport to meet the plane at the Ovda Military Airport and from there to another destination for a meeting with Derby. Have Alex and Arik be there on time and arrange a plane to take us from Sde Dov to Ovda. Arrange a trolley suitcase for me with a suit, tie, and a change of clothes. I also need a gift package containing six Chardonnay bottles from the Golan Heights winery in an olive wood box."

"Where am I supposed to get Chardonnay at this hour? Or an olive wood box?" Zimmer protested.

"I don't care. Call the winery and tell them it's a national emergency. Now you'll have to excuse me, I'm going to a concert. The Israeli SOS Mental First Aid Association has arranged one of those irritating fundraising concerts with Zubin Mehta, and Amira is on the board of directors and one of the organizers. Woe to me if I miss this concert or be late. There's a good chance I'd be spending the next couple of nights outside in the doghouse."

"I can still get you your whiskey there." Zimmer chuckled.

"Which reminds me, don't forget to pack that medicine in my trolley as well," he pointed at the Glenfiddich bottle.

"Don't worry. You'll have everything you asked for in Sde Dov at twenty-three hundred. The men, the Chardonnay, the suitcase, and the whiskey," Zimmer promised.

Cornfield teetered out of the room, thinking that of all the people around him, Shlomo Zimmer was the only one he could trust. In the elevator, he remembered to add General Hassin to that short list.

Chapter 42

USS Nimitz Supercarrier—Somewhere in the Gulf of Aden

A small American E-2 Hawkeye plane noisily landed at the Ovda Air Force Base in the Negev Desert near Eilat. A pilot, a copilot, a navigator, and an airborne mechanic immediately got off the plane. A car picked up the American team members and took them to the squadron club to meet their passengers.

About half an hour later, the team returned to the plane accompanied by three men. The air traffic controller who watched them chuckled to himself. They looked like a trio of clowns to him. One was short, the other was taller, and the third was a giant of a man. After they had disappeared inside the transport plane and the door closed behind them, the engines roared and it slowly took off, heading south to the Gulf of Aqaba.

Darkness lay inside the plane. The radios were silent. The airborne mechanic, a large-bodied African-American with the flat nose of a boxer, handed military blankets to the passengers. The plane's internal communication earphones were also meant to serve as earplugs but proved to be useless; the noise of the turboprop engines infiltrated all barriers. Numerous air pockets turned the passengers' stomachs upside-down. The coffee and wine Cornfield had drunk during the reception of the concert and later at the squadron club began to burden his bladder. "Excuse me, where can I take a leak around here?" he asked the mechanic.

"Follow me please, sir," the mechanic said. In a niche at the back of the plane, a long tube with a funnel at its end was installed. The mechanic presented it to Cornfield.

"What do I do with this?" Cornfield laughed, drunk from whiskey and swaying with the movements of the plane.

"Pull the fasteners on the funnel from both sides, sir, then place your penis inside, and let the laws of physics do the rest," said the mechanic with utter seriousness, as if giving flight instructions.

He retreated out of the niche and pulled a curtain after him. Cornfield remained by himself, trapped between three metal walls and a curtain. *How fitting to my situation in life, he thought. Walls closing on all sides, leaving me with my pants down.* He opened his zipper, and obeyed the airborne mechanic's instructions. The moment he pressed the fasteners, the thin air outside the plane sucked the urine out of his body within less than a second. The relief was complete and instantaneous, but lacked the sense of release that accompanied regular urination.

Dawn began to rise as the plane began to descend. The sea was the only thing seen through the windows. "May I have your attention, please," the pilot said on the internal communication system. "We'll be landing on the *USS Nimitz* shortly. I assume none of you have experienced a landing on a moving vessel before, so I'd like to brief you to avoid unpleasant incidents."

The three passengers straightened up with expectation.

"We are about to land on the USS *Nimitz* supercarrier, a nuclear warship sailing at its full speed of thirty-seven miles per hour. In order to land, we'll be using an arresting cable. It is connected to a hook installed in the rear and lower parts of the plane and slows it down to a complete halt. We'll be landing on board the USS *Nimitz* at maximum speed, so we can immediately take off and try to land again in case of a malfunction. During the landing and sudden arrest, an immense gravitational force is involved. Therefore, you might experience increased perspiration and find it difficult to maintain balance while standing on your feet. Please keep your seatbelts fastened during landing. Should we drop to sea, your life vests will be automatically inflated. I wish us all good luck."

Through the windows of the descending airplane, against the background of a spectacular sunset, the giant image of the aircraft carrier was revealed. It was accompanied by escort and supply ships and three destroyers. The plane touched the deck and was immediately arrested as if by an invisible hand. Two officers, dressed in gray overalls, stood at the end of the runway and waited for the Israeli delegation.

Cornfield came out first, sweating and swaying. He couldn't even reach out his hand to meet that of the admiral who stood in front of him, the Commander of the Fifth Fleet.

The admiral smiled. "General, I guess you're a landlubber. First time on an aircraft carrier?"

Cornfield nodded with embarrassment.

The delegation members were taken to the giant ship's guest cabins so they could shower and change clothes. Blue fleece jackets bearing the ship's insignia were placed on the guest beds along with baseball hats embroidered with the ship's name and gold laurel wreaths.

Cornfield, still dizzy, lost his footing, and Arik grabbed his arm a moment before he sprawled on the wet deck. Cornfield snatched his arm free. "You're the last person on earth I'd like to get help from," Cornfield hissed angrily.

Chapter 43

An Argument on the Nimitz

At seven in the morning, an American two-seater F-18 jet fighter landed on the aircraft carrier carrying Admiral Jack Derby, Director of the CIA. An American breakfast was served to the guests in the ship's club. The kitchen staff labored over the preparation of mountains of fresh pancakes with maple syrup and blueberry jam, omelets, bacon, toast, pitchers with preserved orange juice, and coffee. Two giant Marines stood at the club entrance, wearing a full combat uniform.

After breakfast, welcome addresses, and handshakes, the guests and the host moved to a square table and sat down, facing each other. A young female officer sat beside Admiral Jack Derby , recording the conversation and transcribing it in a small laptop. Cornfield began. "Thank you, Jack, for the great effort you've taken to come here and meet us."

Derby smiled politely.

"First, I'd like to introduce my team members. To my right is Arik Bar-Nathan, head of our operations division. To my left, Dr. Alex Abramovich, head of the Research and Intelligence Division. Now I'll show you two documents, which I hope will help you understand the urgency of the matter I'd like to discuss."

Alex took out the photos of the plutogenic reactor in Deir ez-Zor and placed them on the table next to close-up photos brought by the IDF taskforce that had been sent there.

Darby looked at them with interest. "Where did you get those?" he asked.

Cornfield looked at Arik. "You can tell him everything," he said. "We're among friends."

"The initial information was received by the leader of the Mujahideen al-Islamiyya."

Derby gave him a skeptical look. "Are you related to her?"

Arik didn't answer and simply added, "We've discovered the rest ourselves."

Darby shrugged. "I don't know if the people of the Revolutionary Guards and the Iranian leadership would be dumb enough to try such a stunt. They know the American position that opposes the transformation of Iran or one of its allies to a nuclear threshold country. We've imposed sanctions on them, and in my opinion, they're not looking for more trouble."

"In principle, you're right," said Alex, "but the Iranians are hiding behind the North Koreans and are merely funding the project. Besides, they know you're in the middle of a Presidential clearance sale. You're up to your necks in crumbling Iraq, not to mention what's happening to you guys in Afghanistan. Additionally, you need to take into account they are not directly provoking you. You are the Great Satan, and they're trying to harm us, the Little Satan."

"So what do you expect us to do?" asked Derby. "You know we won't get tangled up with a new military adventure. Not even for you."

"We know that," said Alex. "Our intention is to secretly update you that we are not going to sit idle about this.

Actually, you'll be able to claim you didn't know anything about it."

"That's fine as far as I'm concerned, and I assume the president would feel the same. But he's the one deciding, and I suggest you don't act before I give you an informal green light. I don't want to be in a situation in which we need to pull you out of a new Middle Eastern war, now of all times, with the elections up and coming. I hope I'm making myself clear."

The Israeli team, exhausted from the long night and the hardships of the flight, nodded as one.

"Gentlemen, I suggest we retire for a short rest and meet here again in two hours," Derby said and gallantly motioned toward the door.

On the way to the restroom, Cornfield and Derby disappeared into the Fifth Fleet Commander's empty cabin. Derby opened the bar. The bottle of Glenfiddich 21 Year Old Gran Reserva he took out of it made them both feel much more comfortable.

Cornfield took out a box of large Cuban cigars and a cigar cutter, cut the head of a cigar, and handed it to the admiral.

"Cohiba." Derby whistled in appreciation. "We don't have them because of the embargo."

Cornfield gallantly lit the cigar with his gold lighter. The two sat under the sign saying, "No Smoking in Public Places," placed their feet on the table, and exchanged memories and gossip. Arik's voice was heard from outside, speaking with the Marine who was guarding the cabin. "I need to speak to General Cornfield," Arik explained.

"You can't, sir. He's with Admiral Derby, and they're not to be disturbed."

"I have something important to say to him."

The same answer was repeated, polite, yet firm. "I'm afraid that's impossible, sir. He's with Admiral Derby and they're not to be disturbed."

Two hours later, Cornfield and Derby returned to the briefing room, all smiles and cheer.

"Cornfield!" Arik stretched up and said in Hebrew. "Now's the opportunity to update him about Ruth the Moabitess. I want him to recommend the Secretary of State to take her organization off the terrorist organizations list and allow the unfreezing of the organization's bank accounts in American and European banks."

"Forget it. What does your Iranian whore has to do with the reactor we came here to discuss?" Cornfield raised his voice.

Arik continued in Hebrew. "Cornfield, you're drunk. She's not a whore, and you're sabotaging my work. We may never have a better opportunity. This is a propitious time, and we need more things from him. For instance, an official approval for using American uniforms and identities to conceal those of Mossad instructors guiding the Mujahideen al-Islamiyya soldiers in Iraq."

Cornfield couldn't even hear him anymore. The blood rushed up to his alcohol drenched brain. He was furious. "I'm drunk? How dare you talk to me like that! Shut up and get the fuck out of here!" he screamed at Arik.

Darby turned his face away from them, embarrassed.

"Cornfield, let's go outside. You're embarrassing our host," Arik tried to appease Cornfield and held his arm.

Cornfield lost control. He violently pushed Arik away from him and roared angrily. "I told you not to touch me, didn't I? You're through with me, you hear? You ungrateful son of a bitch. You think I don't know about you and Amira? You arrogant prick. Who do you think you are? You and your dramas. You're nothing but a pathetic *gigolo*! I should have kicked you out of Mossad on my first day on the job."

Arik looked at their host, who rose and gazed outside through the porthole window. "I beg your pardon, sir."

Darby nodded, and Arik stepped outside.

Alex, who wanted to leave with him, was ordered to remain in the room for the continuation of the briefing. But Derby rose from his seat and said, "Cornfield, I apologize, I must join my boss on Air Force One. Perhaps we could meet at your place or mine with the wives sometime in the near future?" He shook Cornfield's hand, then Alex's, and hurriedly left.

Cornfield wasn't able to rise from his chair. He was weak and dizzy, as if in the middle of a hypoglycemic attack. In the dimness of his mind, he recalled he had forgotten to take his pills. Neither Shlomo Zimmer, his bureau chief, nor his wife were there to remind him.

Alex called for help. "He's diabetic," he worriedly said to the naval doctor, who injected the unconscious Cornfield with a glucose solution.

The flight back to Israel passed in an uncomfortable silence. As the plane began to descend for landing, Cornfield spoke for the first time and said, "Bar-Nathan, get your stuff. You have thirty days to transfer all your files to Mot'ke Hassin. I don't want to see your face during that time in any of my meetings. You're through. You're fired. Get out of my face. Understood? And you, Dr. Abramovich, breathe one word about my medical incident and you'll be next. Am I making myself clear?"

Chapter 44

Up the Descending Stairs

About two hours after he had landed, Arik sat upset in his house. He felt trapped in one of M. C. Escher's *Trompe L'oeil* paintings.

He tried to call Eva, but was directed to a voicemail again and again.

After some hesitations, he called Michael. In his heart, he thanked his son for choosing to study in Jerusalem and not abroad. Surprisingly, he was answered after the first ring.

"Hey, Pops. What's up?"

"I'm fine, how are you?" Arik mumbled the necessary words of politeness.

"I'm all right. Crazy busy in school. Anything special going on?"

Arik was silent. He couldn't possibly expose his distress, and suddenly felt sorry for calling his son.

"I can hear you're in trouble, Dad."

"I had a fight with my boss," he said slowly. "As far as he's concerned, I'm out. I wanted to ask your opinion. Should I go to our big boss and ask him to get me back to work? What do you say?" he couldn't believe he was having such a conversation with his young son.

"In India, I studied the way of the Tao. My guru explained that when we are angry at other people because of their behavior, we are usually angry at them for reflecting our own flaws in an unflattering way."

"Your advice may be great for India with its slow shanty mentality. Unfortunately, I'm living in adrenaline-drenched Israel, where things never slow down. Your guru may be right in theory, but right now, I need some practical advice."

"Dad, you live in the western world in which the general belief is that action is always the best cure for anxiety, right?"

Arik grunted in hesitated consent.

"So if we go along with this concept, you have two options: go home quietly, like your boss wants, or turn to the big boss and ask him to decide. Now tell me, what course of action leaves you with the narrowest margin of error?"

Arik was amazed. That was exactly the train of thought he needed. "My *boychik*. Now I'm very happy I called you. Thanks."

"Hold on." Michael kept him on the line. "Do you have direct contact with the prime minister? Have you ever spoken with him?"

Arik was astonished to discover how little his son knew of his life. *Actually,* he thought, *how could he know?* Everything was top secret—his actions, anxieties, accomplishments, even his actual job title. "I have a good and direct contact with him," he said. "I visited his office just a few days ago regarding another matter. He's on my side."

"Great. Good luck, Dad!" said Michael with genuine joy in his voice.

Arik called Major General Amishav, the prime minister's military secretary. "I need to schedule an urgent private meeting with the boss."

"Oh really? You've got some nerve, Arik! I still remember how you just happened to 'forget' your meeting with the prime minister during Fischer's time. What happened? Cornfield kicked your ass so now you suddenly need a private meeting?"

"All right, at least let me explain—" Arik tried.

"I don't think so. You're done here in the prime minister's office! Just retire quietly and be thankful for not having to stand trial before Mossad's ethics committee for screwing one of your agents and humiliating your boss in front of the CIA director. You're lucky you weren't dismissed for misconduct and still get to keep your pension rights. Just sit quietly, and don't make people angrier than they already are."

Arik hung up the phone, sat on the porch and gazed into the sea, defeated.

The phone rang. "Hi, Arik!" Eve called cheerfully.

"Where are you?"

"Jerusalem, of course. The school year has started, remember?"

"All right," he said, disappointed.

"Is anything the matter?"

Arik tried to hold on with all his might to the image he had spent a lifetime preserving but finally gave up and said, "Problems with my boss."

"Tell me."

Arik hesitated.

"Tell me only what you're allowed to."

"I wanted to promote something, and he was drunk and drugged from medication and stopped me by screaming and shouting at me in front of guests from abroad. I tried to explain, and he just fired me."

"Go to the big boss. He appreciates you very much, doesn't he?" Once more, the mysterious Eva emerged from the one he was familiar with.

"How do you know?"

"You told me so, remember?"

Arik didn't. But at that moment, was desperate enough to agree. Perhaps he had simply forgotten; perhaps she had imagined it. "They won't let me through to him."

She remained quiet for a long time. "Is there anything I can do?" she finally asked.

"Yes. If you could get here early."

"I'll leave right after class. Meanwhile, be strong and remember that I love you. Kisses."

An hour later, the phone rang again. Major General Amishav was on the line. "The prime minister instructed me to summon you and Cornfield to a meeting tomorrow at nine AM."

"How come?"

"I don't know," Amishav muttered. "Perhaps you have a guardian angel."

Chapter 45

Good Evening, Despair—Good Night, Hope

At exactly nine AM, Prime Minister Lolik Kenan moved from the conference room to his personal office and found Arik in the waiting room. "Come," he told him. Then to his secretary, he said, "Where's Cornfield?"

"He's not feeling well and sent Major General Hassin to replace him."

"And where's Hassin?"

"The elevator's out of service. He's coming up the stairs, slowly."

The prime minister's face lit with a vicious smile. He pictured Hassin in his mind, holding the rail with his hook, intimidating the receptionists with his burned steak face on each and every floor. He stepped into his office, and Arik followed.

"I've known Cornfield for thirty years." He chuckled. "If he doesn't even want to see me just because I agreed to meet with you, then you must have managed to piss the hell out of him."

The intercom buzzed. "Hassin is here," said the secretary, and the prime minister instructed her to let him in.

"So, I have a new job now? Mossad babysitter?" the prime minister said as soon as Hassin entered and refused the curved hook extended for a handshake.

Hassin gave Arik a menacing look. "You thought you could go behind our backs to the prime minister and get your job back?"

Arik ignored him. "Sir," he said to the prime minister, "my motives are related only with state security. I never had any intention of undermining my superior or indulging in self-promotion."

"Don't you want to be promoted?" asked Kenan with a smile.

"No, I don't. Not in the current organizational climate, which revolves around insults and personal antagonism. I'm not the only one suffering from this attitude. The poisonous head is infecting all the lower levels of the organization, affecting each division head and department manager—"

"That's an inexcusable insult! You're a liar!" Hassin called.

"Shh. Let him talk." The prime minister silenced him with a wave of his hand. "Why do you think Cornfield and Hassin are acting this way?" He turned to Arik.

"They come from a different organizational culture; one that leaves subordinates no personal freedom. Mossad has always been a creative organization that promotes alternative thinking. People are supposed to think and present their ideas to their superiors without fear, not simply obey orders."

The prime minister's face turned serious. He took out a pencil and a notebook with the title "BA Cornfield" from one of the drawers and started scribbling remarks.

"Do you have anything to say?" he asked Hassin.

"Bar-Nathan's behavior is outrageous."

"What has he done? I've read the report. Cornfield claims he teased and insulted him during their meeting with Admiral Derby Derby. Tell me, what exactly happened there?" He turned to Arik again.

"I can't, sir. That wouldn't be right. I don't want to shame anyone."

Lolik Kenan gave Hassin a slight smile, awaiting his reaction.

"Can I speak openly, as a soldier?" the deputy director of Mossad asked.

"We're all soldiers here, speak freely."

"Sir," Hassin said excitedly and pointed at Arik, "that man has violated all the ethical codes expected from a Mossad division head to follow. He has some Persian whore in Paris. She gives him reasonable intelligence information, and her men are not doing a bad job, I'll admit that, but we're the ones who need to pay the bill for everything this *gigolo* is doing with her."

"*Gigolo*?" The prime minister released a mock whistle of admiration and smiled at Arik. "And what bills did he ask you to pay, soldier?"

"He bought her a white Mercedes-Maybach, even though the Mossad director has specifically instructed—"

Kenan's cheeks tightened in anger. "Enough with your bullshit. Do you know any good agents who don't ask for money? An agent not getting money will end up costing us in gold. There are no volunteers in espionage. It's in our best interest that she and her men depend on favors we provide them. You yourself just said they were doing a good job."

"But—" Hassin protested.

"No buts. This is all bullshit!" the prime minister shouted, and his little eyes spat fire. "This man has brought us our bases in Azerbaijan; this man took out Imad Husniyah; this man has given us information that will aid us to perform an important preventative operation in Syria. Did you forget why Cornfield flew to meet Derby in the first place? So he has a woman in Paris, and he authorized buying her a Mercedes something…"

"Mercedes-Maybach," Hassin offered his help.

"Maybach, shmaybach," the prime minister muttered contemptuously. "You think I give a shit? And let's assume that he fucked her. So what? Why do I even need to hear about it?"

"If you bring him back into the system, it will be over my dead body." Hassin stood on his feet, leaning his hooks on the shiny mahogany table and scratching it.

The prime minister laughed. "Don't fret. As far as I'm concerned, if you don't like it, you can leave your keys on your way out. From what I hear, you're doing more harm than good."

Hassin left the room, slamming the door and muttering, "You son of a bitch!" at the laughing Kenan.

"He's allowed to curse me," Kenan explained to the astonished Arik. "We shared the same foxhole. Now, about you."

Arik prepared himself for the worst.

"I'm going to merge the National Security Council and the Counterterrorism Office into a single body, and I want you to manage it and serve as my right hand and help with the coordination of all security agencies. We'll give you the title of Prime Minister Intelligence Advisor. As far as I'm concerned, you can also serve as Chairman of Intelligence and Security Services."

"And how do you think Cornfield would react when he hears I'm now above him in the chain of command?" asked Arik.

"Don't worry about Cornfield. He's a practical old dog who just wants to finish his term." The prime minister's eyes wandered to the large clock hanging on the wall, indicating to Arik that his time was up.

Arik rose, shook the prime minister's hand, and discovered his grip was as firm as a farmer's.

"By the way," said Kenan, "I really appreciated the fact you chose to remain professional and didn't speak about Cornfield's drinking problem and diabetes attacks."

Arik kept a straight face.

"You thought I didn't know?" the prime minister asked and emitted another one of his sour little laughs.

Chapter 46

Meiersdorf Dormitories. Mount Scopus—Jerusalem

It was early morning and Michael Bar-Nathan walked from the student village in Mount Scopus to the bus station to wait for the shuttle bus transporting students between the two Hebrew University campuses in the capital. The chill of the Jerusalem morning made him shiver. He missed his warm bed and his beloved girlfriend, Michal, who still slept there, snuggled in his shirt.

The station was empty. According the timetable, the bus was supposed to arrive any minute. Michael stood on the curb, waiting.

A cry of, "*Allahu Akbar*" suddenly rose from a small car that climbed on the sidewalk with dizzying speed. Michael jumped back, but his leg got hit by the vehicle's bumper. He collapsed to the sidewalk, watching with horror as the vehicle turned back and sped toward him again. He crawled beneath the bench. The car smashed into the station, and its glass, decorated with the emblem of Jerusalem municipality, smashed into a thousand pieces. The car stopped.

From the window, Michael could see a head completely covered by a black ski mask and the barrel of a gun. A pair of slanted eyes gave him a blank stare. The bullet was fired almost without a sound, a second before Michael rolled himself under the bench and down the steep slope behind the station. Two bystanders came running.

Michael shouted, "Look out, he's got a gun!" but they didn't hear him. The man got out of the car and shot at them. One fell, and the other jumped into the bushes. The man got back to his car and tried to reverse. The smell of charred tires rose in the air. After several such attempts, the car came down from the sidewalk, and the terrorist escaped with the front bumper of his vehicle dragging on the road.

It was only then that Michael took a moment to inspect his body. His clothes were torn and a deep, bleeding cut opened across his arm. His right foot was stretched aside at an unnatural angle, like the broken leg of a doll. He fumbled in his pockets and was relieved to discover his cell phone intact. He heard the sirens of emergency vehicles approaching, so he assumed someone had already called the police. He dialed his dad's number and Arik answered right away.

"I got run over," Michael cried with pain.

"Where are you?"

"In the slope behind the station next to the student village. Someone else got killed or injured… Wait, the police are here. Maybe they won't see me…I am behind the big bush……"

"I'm on it," Arik told him in a reassuring voice. He attached the red and blue police strobe to the roof of the BMW he still possessed and sped down the fast lane to Jerusalem, zigzagging on the wayside and activating the siren to make his way through the endless traffic jam.

While maneuvering on the road, Arik called the Jerusalem district's chief of general security agency . He updated the officer who answered about the exact location of the incident, then called Claire at the office, and finally Naomi.

"Michael's been in an accident. He's all right, just injured his leg," he said. "Please let Rachel know. They'll probably take him to the Hadassah Medical Center in Mt. Scopus."

When he reached Sho'eva Junction , the phone rang. He recognized the Jerusalem Precinct chief's private number. "Your son, Michael, has been injured in a hit and run terrorist attack in Mount Scopus about half an hour ago," the officer immediately said.

"I know—I was the one who reported the attack. Where is he?"

"In an ambulance on the way to the Emergency Room at Hadassah Medical Center. The paramedics diagnosed a compound fracture in his leg."

"What else?"

"Abrasions on his hand. Nothing serious."

"Is there any information regarding the terrorist?" asked Arik.

"The university's security cameras show a masked attacker exiting the car and firing. The attacking vehicle was leased in the old city under a false identity and was found deserted in the Ramat Eshkol neighborhood. Are you coming here?"

"I'm on my way."

The moment he finished the call, Claire, his longtime secretary who had been transferred with him to the new office, called him. "Alex wants to talk to you," she said and he immediately heard Alex's unique accent.

"Arik?"

"Yes, it's me," Arik responded nervously.

"All right, we've identified the attacker. It must be your Temple Mount assassin. I'm hanging up because Shlomo Zimmer is about to call you any minute."

"What does he want?" asked Arik, but Alex had already hung up. And indeed the phone immediately rang for the third time. "Arik, it's Shlomo Zimmer. I understand you're on your way to Jerusalem. Stop at the Castel Shopping Center, and a General Security agency bodyguard will join you. He's already on his way."

"Why?"

"Because we think this is a trap like the one we prepared for Imad Husniyah at his brother's funeral in Lebanon. We have reason to suspect the assassin is preparing an ambush for you at the hospital."

"What happened? Cornfield's finally convinced this is not about a jealous husband?"

"Cornfield isn't here. He's on vacation in the US , and Gideon Perry has been called back to serve as his temporary replacement. Now you're part of the prime minister's office personnel and should be protected accordingly."

"So why are you handling it?" asked Arik with suspicion. "Why can't the prime minister's office security officer take care of this?"

"Because, officially, you're still on a leave of absence from Mossad and just temporarily employed by the prime minister's office."

"In that case, place security guards next to my son's hospital bed. That is where the assassin will go if he goes there at all."

"I ask that you wait for the bodyguard at Castel," Zimmer repeated.

"Forget about it. Send him to my son, I haven't got time to wait or lose. I can take care of myself," Arik said and hung up.

Half an hour later, Arik arrived at the hospital compound. As usual, the parking lot was full and he parked on the sidewalk, hurried inside to the Emergency Room, and rushed through the cubicles separated by curtains until he found his son.

Michael lay on an elevated hospital bed, his leg and hand bandaged and bleeding. His face was expressionless, and he seemed dazed from the morphine injection. He recognized Arik's face and smiled. Arik fondly ruffled his hair. "How are you, my *boychik*?"

Michael smiled an "everything will be all right" smile.

"Did you get a good look at him?"

"I did. He wasn't Arabic," he whispered. "He had Mongolian eyes."

"Have you told this to anyone?"

"No one asked."

Arik wondered where the General Security agency agents and police personnel who were supposed to interrogate Michael were. Where was the bodyguard he had been promised?

"I'm going out for a moment to ask that you be transferred to a secure room. It could very well be they hurt you just to set a trap for me here."

"Enough with the paranoia, Dad. Not everything is part of a conspiracy, you know," Michael whispered.

Arik went outside into the corridor. The commotion and shouts of the sick, wounded and their escorts filled the air. He found a quiet corner and called Claire. "Hi, I'm at—" he managed to say before a thin metal wire was wrapped around his neck from behind, and two strong hands dragged him to a nearby laundry room.

Arik choked and gurgled, and his consciousness began to dim. He allowed his body to drop down and back. The attacker leaned over him, and Arik took advantage of the opportunity and slammed his head back against the assassin's. The sound of a smashing bone was heard, followed by a short cry of pain. The assassin let go of the wire and grabbed his bleeding nose. Arik turned around. The dim light in the corridor was enough for him to identify his attacker. Ruslan Akhmatov stood in front of him, wearing a green surgeon's gown, a white, blood-drenched mask on his face. Ruslan took a scalpel from his pocket and reached forward with his hand to slash Arik's throat.

Arik kicked Ruslan's hand. Ruslan dodged the kick with the agility of an acrobat and cut Arik's forehead with his knife. Arik drew his Glock, but Ruslan sent a quick and precise kick to Arik's right shoulder exactly where he had shot him on the Temple Mount. Arik screamed with pain and dropped the pistol. Ruslan jumped on his back, grabbed his hair and pulled up his head, readying Arik for the slaughter. Arik tried to break free, but Ruslan wrapped his legs around his ribs and they both fell.

Was it all over? The desperate thought passed through Arik's mind.

Barely conscious, he saw a hand reaching out, from beyond the curtain covering the laundry room's doorway, and slamming a blunt object against the back of Ruslan's head. Arik felt the full weight of Ruslan's body falling on his. He gathered his remaining strength and rose all at once, kicking back the semi-conscious Ruslan. Arik lunged toward the pistol still resting on the floor. His right hand hurt badly, yet he still managed to aim and fire three bullets in Ruslan's head.

Two hospital guards heard the screams of panic emitted by the people in the corridor and rushed inside the laundry room with their guns in their hands. "Police!" one of them shouted. "Put down your weapon and get your hands up!"

"You're not police, and I'm Arik Bar-Nathan from the prime minister's office." He tried to take out his wallet from his pocket to show the guards his ID. The guard nearest to him raised his gun towards his Arik's head . "If you pull out my wallet," Arik said, "you'll be able to easily identify me."

"Toss your gun first," the officer insisted. "Do it now, or I'll shoot."

"You're not going to shoot," Arik said calmly. "You're going to pull out my wallet—"

Before he could finish the sentence, two General Security Agency men from the Jerusalem District appeared at the entrance. "Lower your weapon," they instructed the guard and presented him with their IDs.

"It's about time." Arik complained and used a handkerchief to wipe the blood pouring from his forehead and staining his face and shirt.

"We received the call over an hour ago," one of them explained apologetically. "But we got stuck in morning traffic in the old city . Sorry."

Arik leaned toward Ruslan and closely examined his fingers. The thin slivers of light that barely penetrated the laundry room from the corridor were enough to reveal tattooed crosses and stars. He grabbed the dead man's right hand sleeve and tore it, exposing the tattoo of an eagle, skull, and sword. He turned the body and revealed a gaping hole at the back of the skull, oozing blood. Arik closed the curtain and moved to the back of the room. His hands fumbled across the wall, seeking the light switch. He felt wrinkled fabrics, iron cart frames and exposed pipes. Finally, he found the switch and turned on the light. Hundreds of towels, gowns, blankets, pillows, pillowcases and sheets filled giant carts. A large metal hammer rested between two of them, stained with blood.

The handle of the door at the end of the room was also stained with blood. A slight rustling sound was heard behind it. Arik drew his pistol and turned to the side of the door. A few seconds later, he opened it with a kick. In the dim light coming from behind the open door, he recognized a mountain of scraps: bed parts, old metal cabinets and broken chairs. He slammed the door shut behind him and shouted in English, "There's nowhere to run to! The place is crawling with cops. Get out with your hands up."

No answer came.

The sound of muffled breathing was heard. It came from the corner of the room. He advanced carefully. Another rustle was heard, nearer and stronger this time. "I'm about to fire," he said. "This is your final warning."

A dark figure hesitantly rose from behind a table lying on its side. Its hands were raised in the air, weaponless. Arik still feared an explosive vest or a charge concealed in the room. With one hand, he grabbed the terrorist's wrists, which surprised him with their slenderness. His other hand, he squeezed into a fist and slammed it between the terrorist's ribs. The terrorist collapsed behind the table with a sigh of pain, but offered no resistance.

Arik dragged him across the floor to the laundry room, slamming his face against every piece of furniture on the way. To Arik's surprise, the terrorist continued to show no resistance at all. When they passed the storage room opening, he tossed him onto a pile of laundry with his face down, pressed his knee against the terrorist's back and pinned him to the floor.

The terrorist groaned with pain. Arik tied his arms back with a shirt that was lying on the floor.

When he finally turned him and saw his face, he froze, dumbfounded. "Eva?"

Chapter 47

A Fateful Encounter. Hadassah Medical Center's Emergency Room—Mount Scopus

Eva was badly bruised and partially conscious. An orderly and a nurse moved her to the Emergency Room and adamantly refused Arik's request to question her. "You can question her only after a doctor authorizes it," the nurse said angrily and led him outside. She then added, "You need stitches in your forehead."

Arik's gaze followed them. Then he went to wash his face before rushing to see his son in the orthopedic department. Michael lay with his eyes open, his plastered leg tied to a splint and elevated, and his entire hand bandaged. His mother stood beside the bed, her hand resting on the armrest to indicate she was now the one in control. They exchanged cold glances.

"Son, are you all right?"

"Getting better. What happened to your forehead?"

"I ran into a wall," Arik said and placed an alcohol pad against his forehead to stop the bleeding.

Michael laughed. Before he could question him any further, Arik asked, "Do you need anything?"

"Same old Arik," said his ex-wife. "Keeping things practical so you don't really need to give of yourself."

"Mom, stop. Dad, don't answer her. Please don't start fighting here."

"I'll come back later," said Arik and left the room, washed with a feeling of disgust and an uncontrollable urge to question Eva. He found her in the Emergency Room. A hospital security guard blocked his way. "Can't now," the guard said in broken Hebrew. "Police come soon."

Arik's nerves were shot. He took out his ID and waved it in front of the guard's nose. "I've had enough of you people," he said and pushed him beyond the curtain. To his surprise, the guard simply gave up and stayed behind. Eva looked at him with sad eyes, hands resting on her painful ribs. "No more games now," Arik said. "I want to know everything."

"I'm sure you already know..."

"No, I don't!" Arik called angrily. The expression, "I'm sure you already know," was one Rachel, his ex-wife, had often used. "I don't know anything anymore. I want to know here and now. Who are you?"

She closed her eyes and tiredly said: "I'm Agent Three-Six-Two of Tzomet Division. I was drafted to Mossad by David Fischer about twelve years ago and underwent a field agent training course. If you call Fischer, he'll confirm my story."

"And this whole cover story, your university titles, the lecture at the Van Leer Institute..."

"Officially, I'm really a professor of theology and German philosophy at the Heidelberg University, and today I'm also an associate professor at the Hebrew University's department of philosophy. I first arrived in Israel while a student during my summer vacation after finding out about the crimes my beloved grandfather had committed during the Holocaust.

"I volunteered in a *kibbutz* and lived with a German-speaking family, refugees from Germany whose son worked for the Mossad. A short while after I had arrived, Mossad agents came to see me. They asked for my German passport and used it. I don't know for what purpose, and I don't really want to know. When I got back to Germany to continue my studies, Fischer, who was Head of Mossad's Bonn Station at the time, approached me and recruited me to perform small errands and courier tasks.

"While working for Fischer, I developed a deep sense of love and admiration for Israel in general and Mossad in particular. David noticed it and, after I had finished my studies, suggested that I come to Israel and undergo an agent training course. I took part in several missions in Europe and the Middle East, but at a certain point I decided I want to concentrate on my studies and became a sleeper agent that could be activated only in cases of emergency."

"And what was the emergency that brought you back?"

"After your operation in South America, Alex shared his fears that the Chechens might seek revenge on Fischer. It all happened at the same time I came to Israel to visit my adoptive family. I dropped by to say 'hi' to Fischer, who was just finishing his term as Mossad Director. He asked me to volunteer for a special mission—protecting you. This is why he had arranged the sabbatical for me here at the Hebrew University.

"I guess I've done a good job; the university management has already asked me to remain for three more years, and now I'm an associate professor of humanities. I'm still officially on unpaid vacation from the Heidelberg University, for the time being."

"Why on earth would he recruit you? Did Mossad suddenly run out of bodyguards?"

"He knew Cornfield would never authorize security measures for you. That's why he wanted someone unknown. Alex recognized the terrible danger you were in. He was afraid the incident at the triple frontier would lead to an attempt on your life and shared his concerns with Fischer. Just to be on the safe side, Alex had registered me as a senior analyst for Europe One." A hint of her familiar smile rose to her lips. "Cornfield doesn't know anything about it, obviously."

"So when you came to my party and went to bed with me it was all part of the job?" Arik asked indignantly.

"Partly," Eva's lips stretched into a painful smile. "I came to check things out, familiarize myself with the person I needed to keep safe. But I chose to stay that night, and be with you in all the days that followed out of… You know…"

"You were the one who rescued me from the biker's assassination attempt in Jerusalem?"

"Yes. During the lecture, I noticed a Chechen man who matched the general description Alex had given me and saw that you were looking at him as well. After you'd left, I followed him to the parking lot. He went to his motorcycle, and I got into my car. He drove around the gate, but I had to use my parking ticket to open it. This is why I arrived at the scene a few seconds after him and didn't have a chance to shoot him."

"You're able to fire precise shots while driving?" Arik wondered and gave her a skeptical look.

"I'm an expert markswoman, specializing in the use of Sig-Sauer guns. I have a second *dan* black belt."

Arik tensed up. "Are you still carrying your weapon?"

She rolled up the right sleeve of her pants, exposing a leather holster attached to her ankle and containing a small, yet deadly, P250 Sig-Sauer pistol.

"How did you get to pass the idiot standing outside?"

"The Hospital's chief security officer came to see me, and I showed him this." She took an ID, very similar to his from her pocket. "This is why the guard gave you no arguments when you showed him your ID."

Arik felt stupid. So many things had taken place around him without him having even the slightest idea of their existence. He thought about everything Eva had just told him about herself, then thought back to the various incidents of the past few weeks. "You were really there when I visited my mother in Haifa, weren't you?"

She nodded.

"How could this be? I dialed your Jerusalem hotel number."

"It's the oldest trick in the book. Your phone was programmed to transfer calls to my hotel to a Mossad operator. She simply transferred the call to my cell phone."

Arik sighed with frustration. "What else don't I know?"

"How did you manage to go over the head of the prime minister's military secretary and get a personal meeting with Kenan?"

"I honestly don't know. How?"

"After you told me he was blocking you, I called David Fischer, who called Kenan." Her eyes sparkled.

"And now, after you helped me take out the assassin, why did you hide from me?"

"You were pumped up with adrenaline, and I was afraid you might instinctively shoot me, thinking I was the assassin's accomplice."

Arik thought aloud. "So actually, you've been running my life for the past few months."

"You almost sound like you're complaining. Don't forget I saved your life today, and remember what I told you. Learning to accept from others is not a weakness."

He sat by the edge of the bed and took her hand in his. "So where is our relationship headed now?"

"It's up to you, my dear. I've been much more than your bodyguard for quite some time now, but you're a tough customer who doesn't commit easily."

Chapter 48

Deir ez-Zor—North Eastern Syria

Eight F-16 fighter jets took off minutes after midnight from the 'Khinkali' military base in South Azerbaijan, a base given on lease to the Israeli Air Force by Nur Sultan Babayev, President of the Republic, upon his return from Jerusalem. The eight fighter jets were accompanied by F-15 tactical fighters, and the entire squadron flew west south toward the border of Turkey and Syria. Electronic warfare surveillance aircraft flew high above them.

On the ground, at a safe distance of about half a mile from the reactor, hidden beneath thorn bushes, were two teams of soldiers from the IAF special Shaldag unit, specializing in marking targets for airstrikes. Complete radio silence was maintained. Electronic warfare aircraft flew at a high altitude and blocked the Turkish and Syrian air defense radar systems. In mid-sea, north of Cyprus, a tanker aircraft awaited for the squadron jets to return from their silent attack.

Eight maverick missiles and bunker buster bombs silently slid from above, and the Syrian reactor went up in flames and crumbled in a series of blasts. The pillars of smoke could be seen for miles all around.

From the moment the planes had entered Syrian airspace until the moment they left, leaving the blasted reactor behind them, the jets weren't discovered by the cutting-edge Syrian radar systems, which included Pechora 2A missile launchers. These were advanced and highly sensitive systems that had recently been bought from the Russians with Iranian funding and were the source of the Syrians' pride and sense of security. Even after the attack finished and the jets left Syrian airspace, the systems remained inoperative. The Syrians were shocked. The Russians' shock was even greater upon discovering their systems had not worked at all. The Iranians received a clear and immediate message that their nuclear facilities were not protected from the Israeli Army's technology and military might.

In the Israeli Military's underground command center in Camp Rabin, 100 feet below the streets of Tel Aviv, the members of the Security Cabinet sat along with the Heads of Intelligence and Security Services, headed by Arik Bar-Nathan, the prime minister's office new intelligence consultant. Everyone sat in tense silence. The radio silence made it impossible to follow the results of the bombing in real time. Eight green dots were seen on a huge screen with the middle eastern map moving south . It was only half an hour later that the squadron commander reported to the chief of staff in an encrypted message. "Red onion. I repeat, red onion."

Shouts of joy echoed between the reinforced concrete walls. Glasses of cognac were poured, shoulders were clapped, and hugs were exchanged. But as far as the commanders of the Israeli Mossad, the score had not yet fully been settled. Cornfield wanted to make sure General Ahmad Suleiman, the Syrian president's special advisor and chairman of the Syrian Atomic Energy Commission, would completely disappear from the pages of history, thereby sending the Syrian president a clear and unambiguous message.

The very next day, a tiny tracking device was attached to the general's car while it was in his secret HQ in Damascus, allowing a satellite to monitor it. Meanwhile, Alex examined Suleimani's personal file and analyzed it with a Mossad psychiatrist. It appeared that the general had a weakness for young boys. Those were brought from refugee camps in Bosnia and Moldova for him and his friends to pleasure themselves with. The children were transferred to Syria with the aid of a network of Balkan Mafia smugglers specializing in supplying prostitutes and sex slaves to Europe in return for drugs cultivated in the Beka'a valley in Lebanon. . Now and then, the general and his friends would hold wild parties in his villa in the luxurious Sabatan neighborhood, off the shore of Latakia, not far from the Presidential beach Resort .

On a full moon night, when the Syrian general and his friends partied on the villa's porch, the dim shadow of a Dolphin submarine emerged from the sea. Half a dozen Flotilla Thirteen seals, dressed in black diving suits, headed out from the submarine toward the shore in two tiny Zodiac boats. They sped along until they were about 6,000 feet from the porch, far from the light of the boardwalk street lamps on the beach. A man holding an elongated object lay on one of the boats. He slammed a cartridge with 8.59 mm bullets into a L115A3 sniper rifle, cocked it, and placed a silencer and a dimmer on the barrel. The men in the water supported the boat on both sides to make it stable and unmoving. The rifle was directed to the porch of the house on the beach. General Suleimani's head filled the large telescopic lens, and the crosshair was placed on his forehead.

The marksman held his breath for half a second and gently squeezed the trigger. A slight rustle sounded in the air. On the porch, General Suleimani's skull exploded. No one noticed the black shadow of the submarine that hurried to admit the Zodiac boats into its escape hatch. Within less than a minute, the submarine sank below the surface of the water, on its way back to the Port of Haifa.

The phone rang in Cornfield's house. A young soldier working in Mossad's control center let him know, "The black goat is out."

Cornfield bit his lower lip, knowing it was Arik who would be credited by the prime minister for the operation's success. In his heart of hearts, he had to admit Arik indeed deserved it.

Chapter 49

"Heaven can Wait"—A Rehab Resort, Malibu Beach, Florida

The clock showed the time to be one after midnight. In his house, in the village of Kfar HaNagid, near the city of Yavne, Cornfield sat in his favorite battered leather armchair. He took off the prosthetic leg from his aching knee and allowed it to slide to the floor. The stump of his leg was swollen all the way up to the hip, and he felt intense pains in his phantom limb.

Aided by his crutch, he stumbled to the bar, took out a bottle of Glenfiddich 30 Year Old single malt he had saved for special occasions and poured himself half a glass. Then he raised it, saluting the enemy who had just been killed in Operation Black Goat and draining it with a single gulp.

"What's going on, Cornfield?" he heard Amira calling him from their bedroom on the upstairs floor.

"Everything is fine, dear. Good night," he shouted back.

Before he could pour himself another drink, he saw her standing in front of him in her transparent nightgown that exposed her still firm and supple breasts and the curves of her thighs. She scolded him. "That's enough, Cornfield. Put that glass down. You're like a little child; someone always needs to keep an eye on you. You're your own worst enemy."

He reluctantly put down the glass and sank into his soft armchair.

"Do you want to end up like your dad?" Amira continued in the same scolding tone.

"My father had both legs amputated because of diabetes. I'm making it easier on the doctors; I've already done half the job for them."

"No, dear, I'm talking about the blindness and stroke he had to live with for ten years before he finally died. Is that how you want to end your life?"

He didn't answer. In his mind, he saw the image of his father, a farmer and a giant of a man, who ended up a blind, wheelchair-bound amputee.

"You're not eating well. Most of your diet is composed of coffee and cookies. You smoke cigars all day and consume enough alcohol to make an elephant drunk. You're not doing any physical exercise. If you want to go to hell, you're on the right path, Cornfield."

"You don't know what I'm going through. The pains in my leg, the pressure at work, the headaches..." he argued tiredly.

"I know only one thing: There are no desperate situations, only desperate people. If you don't take some time off and start taking care of yourself, you're done for."

Cornfield's silence expressed his agreement.

A week later, again with a glass of whiskey in his hand, he let her know in a cheerful voice, "You got what you wanted. I got sick leave for a month. Kenan found me a great place. The Malibu Beach Recovery Center. The wife of another prime minister spent some time there."

"You're talking about the wife of—"

"Don't you dare say the name. Some things you just don't talk about. Will you come with me?" he asked hopefully.

"I really think you need to go on your own."

"But I need you." Cornfield tried hard to sound confident, but his voice was cracked and pleading. "I'm dizzy most of the time. It's hard for me to even walk straight, and I keep forgetting to take my medication. Come with me, please."

Three days later, when they boarded the flight, he thought how lost he would truly be without her. He suffered pains and shivers, and the medication only served to make him weaker. She had to support his large body during the long journey from Tel Aviv to New York, then to Miami. After two days of torturous travel, they finally found themselves at the reception desk of a private rehab located in a remote corner of Malibu Beach.

From a safe distance, and without his knowledge, two Israeli General Security Agency bodyguards kept a close eye on the couple, backed up by a local team of US Secret Service.

A young doctor welcomed them. "Hello. I'm Dr. Brian Strum . I'll be your medical consultant for the rehabilitation process. It's not going to be an easy experience, and I'd like to salute you for your courage and for agreeing to join our intensive program."

"What can I expect here?" asked Cornfield. "I don't like surprises. I'm a man who likes to prepare and know what the future has in store for him."

"Well, I can't promise you a rose garden," the doctor joked and immediately regretted his humorous remark when faced with the angry and tough expression on Cornfield's face. He immediately began to describe the details of the rehab program. "You'll experience all the alcohol withdrawal symptoms: shakiness, increased heartbeat rate and high blood pressure. Then you'll have severe seizures and, finally, during the last week, psychotic attacks that normally include delusions and shivers as well as nausea."

"Is that it?" Cornfield asked with a bitter smile.

"Actually, no. As you are diabetic, we'll need to add a rehab treatment based on medications from the benzodiazepine class of psychoactive drugs. Their effect on the brain is very similar to that of alcohol. We'll also need to restrict and balance your diet. You can undergo the most difficult parts of the treatment under sedation, if you'd prefer that."

"And miss out all the fun?" Cornfield laughed bitterly and signed the consent forms.

During the next few nights, his body thirsted for alcohol. He shouted in his sleep, cursed, raged, and threatened in every language he knew until the resort staff had no choice but to strap him to his bed. Yet he still refused to take any sedatives. He didn't know that Amira visited the rehab center every day, and her heart went out to him when she heard his screams from the hall, just as it had gone out to him twenty years before when he had been injured and lost his eye and leg. It was only during the last two days of his stay that she was allowed to visit him in his room. He looked calm, the color returned to his cheeks, and he gained a few pounds. He appeared to be genuinely healthier.

"The past few days have made me think a lot about myself and our relationship. I got the opportunity to spend a lot of quality time with myself." He chuckled cynically.

"And what did you come up with?" asked Amira and sat by the side of his bed."

"Perhaps I should finally retire."

"Are you asking for my opinion, or have you made up your mind?" She rose and looked into his eyes.

Cornfield's eyes clouded. "I haven't finished my term as Mossad Director yet, and I want to end it properly. On the other hand…"

"Cornfield, there's no 'other hand' here. If you retire now, you'll never forgive yourself. Go back to your job and finish your illustrious career in the best possible way. The fact you insist on keeping one foot in the grave doesn't mean you need to let people step on the other. Just don't kill yourself, learn to delegate responsibility, and spend more time with me and the children."

The sound of ocean waves breaking against the rocky shoreline could be heard from below the cliff, rising and falling. The Cornfields snuggled together, he in his pajamas and she in a tiny summer dress. She smelled wonderful. Cornfield felt the old emotions rise in him and was intensely attracted to his wife again.

A Mexican nurse came into the room and disturbed their rare moment of intimacy. She checked Cornfield's blood sugar levels and prepared a cocktail of medications that slowly dripped into his veins through a thin cannula. He looked tired, and the nurse asked Amira to leave and return at a later time.

"From now on, we'll be together forever," Amira said and kissed her husband's forehead. But there was still one thing Cornfield wanted to ask her before their reunion could be complete.

From the verge of sleep, he heard himself saying, "Darling, I have a personal question for you, one that has troubled me for the past few years now," he barely muttered. "That business between you and Arik. When I openly accused him of having had an affair with you, he didn't deny it. On the other hand, I've no right to criticize you. I wasn't exactly the ideal husband, and you were on your own with the children and the household chores—"

The medication cocktail finally got the better of him and he fell asleep. In his dream, he felt the soft, warm touch of Amira's body and saw her climbing on his bed, placing her lips close to his ear and whispering, "Come to me, my silly goose." Her lips fluttered on his face with little kisses, as she confessed, "You're my champion, the only one I've ever loved. And that's all you need to know."

Chapter 50

The House at 12 Maimon Street—Neve Sha'anan Neighborhood, Haifa

"This is the voice of Israel broadcasting from Jerusalem…" The familiar voice of the announcer rose from the radio in Arik's new car. Heading to Jerusalem, he sat comfortably in the backseat of his black Audi 6 and listened to the lead story on the morning news.

"During a meeting held yesterday, the government has approved the appointment of Mr. Arik Bar-Nathan to the role of Prime Minister Intelligence Advisor and Chairman of Intelligence and Security Services joint committee."

Within less than a minute, his phone began to ring. Arik ignored the calls and kept reading intelligence reports and researches. The only call he answered was from his sister, Naomi. "Too bad our parents are no longer with us to see how far you've come. It would make them feel incredibly proud." She sighed.

"Mom's still with us," he reminded her.

"Only in body," she answered sadly. "And we need to take care of it instead of her. You need to come here urgently to sign the guardianship forms for the judge. Mom is no longer able to eat by herself, and the hospital won't use a gastric feeding tube without our signature."

"What's a gastric feeding tube?" Arik asked in horror.

"A tube inserted through a small incision in the abdomen into the stomach to allow feeding," she answered.

"When would you like me to come?"

"Yesterday! I have a lawyer friend who can see you anytime. He just needs your signature to present the forms to the court."

"How about this evening?"

"Perfect!"

Arik hung up and immediately called Eva. "I want us to go to Haifa this evening to visit my mom," he said briefly. "It's important for me that she'll see you before the end."

That very same evening, Arik's car stopped at the Ziv commercial center in the Neve Sha'anan neighborhood. Arik and Eva got out of the car and both walked toward the neighborhood flower shop.

"Mom loves daffodils," said Arik. "I hope they have some."

On the flower shop's floor, buttercup and anemone bouquets rested inside water-filled buckets. Arik was overwhelmed by childhood memories. He recalled the weekly ceremony of picking wild flowers and bringing them to his mother every Saturday. Eva, as practical as ever, began to scour the flower shop for the right bouquet and found it. A last bouquet of delicate scented daffodils was hidden in the corner.

"As lucky as ever." Eva laughed and rescued him from his memories. Arik thanked her with a smile and asked the seller to enrich the bouquet with a variety of winter flowers.

A few minutes later, the car parked next to Arik's mother's house. The two of them crossed the street and turned toward a long Soviet-style apartment building, one of many that had been built during the mass immigration period of the fifties. Eva lingered at the entrance for a moment and looked at the apartment building.

The soot coming from the factories of the Gulf of Haifa had made the stairwell walls turn gray. A stranger opened the door for them. She gave them a questioning look. Arik was surprised as well. He couldn't recall his sister telling him anything about a new nurse.

"I'm her son," he explained in English and encountered a blank stare and an embarrassed smile.

To his surprise, Eva translated his words and the nurse immediately replied, "Ja Marushka."

"She says her name is Marushka," Eva translated.

"Is there anything you don't know?" Arik appreciatively teased her.

"Lots of things, but I still needed to learn some basic Russian for my PhD thesis."

"Excuse me, where are the restrooms?" Eva asked the nurse with urgency and quickly disappeared. The muffled sound of vomiting was heard from inside the restrooms. Arik stood behind the door and asked with concern, "Is everything all right?"

"Yes, yes, don't worry, I'm fine," shouted Eva from within.

Arik suddenly noticed the great change around him. The house had never looked so neat and tidy. Pleasant scents rose from the kitchen, accompanied by the familiar smell of *borscht*.

His eyes sought his mother and found her sitting in the armchair, thinner than he had remembered her, wearing a colorful dressing gown. Her hair had been dyed in eggplant shades and gathered up in a way that did not suit the fact it was thinning. She completely ignored him and continued staring at the cartoon characters running on the television screen and squeaking in Russian.

He noticed that what first appeared to him as a colorful dressing gown was actually a large sheet wrapped around her hips and shoulders, holding her body to the couch. Now and then, she slid hither and thither, unable to control her own movements. She looked as small and fragile as a rag doll.

Marushka tried to take the flowers from him, but Arik ignored her presence and kneeled next to his mother. He handed her the bouquet, bringing the daffodils, whose scent she loved so much, closer to her face. She looked at him with the curiosity of a woman meeting a suitor for the first time and flashed a toothless smile. "*Sheyn, zeyer sheyn,*"[19] she said about the flowers. "*Und ver bist du?*"[20]

"*Mamele,*" Arik said with tears choking this throat, "*ikh bin deyne zun.*"[21]

She replied with the embarrassed smile of a child. Her green eyes, once bright and beautiful, were now covered with a veil that distanced her from him. She held his hand tightly, but was immediately distracted, and her eyes wandered to the cartoon characters on the television screen.

Eva came into the living room, pale, her hair disheveled. The nurse immediately realized the source of her distress and gave her the mysterious and knowing smile of rural women.

"This is how it is. Mother's condition is changing every day." She spoke to Eva, then waited for her to translate her words before continuing. "Naomi is in contact with Mother

---

[19]Beautiful, very beautiful.
[20]And who are you?
[21]I am your son.

every day. She probably doesn't understand you are her son…"

"I haven't been here in a long time," Arik admitted and his heart was immediately filled with guilt.

The nurse continued to speak, and Eva translated. "She will bring a vase and take care of the flowers. They have such flowers in her village back home. She suggests that you sit and talk to your mother for a little while. She'll set the table so we could all sit down and eat some Ukrainian *borscht*."

Within a few minutes, the table was set, and a large pot of borscht was placed in its center. Marushka sat Arik's mom at the head of the table, much like a kindergarten teacher seating a small child. She tied a large bib around her neck and secured her to the chair with a harness. Arik averted his eyes, embarrassed.

"*Malorussiski borscht*," said Marushka with pride and filled deep bowls with a thick, reddish soup with meat cubes, grated beets and carrot cubes. The smell of apple vinegar and lots of garlic rose from the stew. Next to the soup bowls, the nurse placed a saucer heaped with sour cream and chopped dill. She beckoned Arik with her hand to place a spoonful of sour cream and dill in his soup.

Even though she had not eaten anything since morning, Eva didn't touch any of the food. It was apparent the sour smell of the soup repelled her. She drank some water and munched on a piece of brown bread.

His mother did not eat either. All the nurse's attempts to feed her were in vain. His mother clenched her lips and stared at the nurse with distant eyes. Marushka smiled at her, cleaned her face patiently, spoke comforting words in Russian, and repeatedly tried to make her drink from the spoon she held close to her mouth. Finally, she slapped her own hips in frustration and said something long to Eva.

"Things aren't good," Eva translated, halfheartedly this time. "Your mother won't allow the nurse help her eat, but might starve without her help. She needs this gastric feeding tube operation urgently "

Arik shed tears in silence. Marushka handed him some tissues. Eva rose and placed her hands around his shoulders. "What happened to you earlier?" he asked.

She shook her head, as if rejecting his question. "Can I see your room?"

"Of course, but I hardly lived in this house. My parents had moved here when I was a young soldier. But there's all this junk my parents brought from my childhood home in the poor Halissa neighborhood."

When they entered his room, she stood next to the spartan wooden bed he had used to sleep in as a child and youth, facing the bookcase containing old and yellowing books. Certificates and awards of excellence hung on the wall as well as photos from which peeked the face of a chubby boy dressed up like a Cossack and playing an accordion beside a girl dressed in a traditional Chinese suit and holding a yellow bamboo parasol. "Is this a photo of you and Naomi at the Purim Festival?" Eva laughed and hugged him. Arik nodded in embarrassment. The small apartment suddenly seemed extremely crowded and pitiably old.

"Did you own a grocery store?" she asked and pointed at the sacks of rice, sugar, and flour placed in the corner of the room beside cases full of oil bottles and various types of canned food.

"No, dear. What you see are the traces of World War II hunger. In 1991, Saddam Hussein of Iraq attacked Israel and launched rocket attacks against Haifa as well. From the moment the first siren and the first blasts sounded, my mother regressed back to all her Holocaust trauma and started hoarding basic commodities again."

Arik returned to the living room, sat beside his mother, and stroked her hands. She did not respond, her eyes hypnotized and fixed on the television screen again. Eva knelt beside her and stroked her emaciated and transparent hand as well. "I'm so ashamed of my grandfather and his generation for what they've done to you," she said quietly in German and wiped a tear. A wave of compassion washed over Arik. Not only had Eva saved his life, twice, she also loved him with all her heart.

"Tell me what happened to you earlier during dinner," he asked again gently. "You hardly touched the food."

"It's hard for me to explain, even to myself. I guess it's something that has to do with your mother, my grandfather, and the sense of responsibility I feel for all of us as a nation. I don't know, and I don't want to talk about it now." She held his arm. "Come, we need to go meet Naomi. The lawyer is waiting for you."

Arik went to his mother, kissed her head and stroked her wrinkled face. She turned her eyes to him, yet her face was still expressionless, as if she was seeing a complete stranger. He inhaled deeply, wishing to smell her old motherly scents but finding only the sour smell of an ancient body. He realized, in the sharpest and most immediate way, that the motherly figure of his memories was forever gone, and shed bitter tears without a sound.

"You're quite the crybaby for a tough Mossad warrior ," Eva told him fondly and placed her hand on his shoulder.

"The older I become, the more I realize how I've repressed my emotions over the years. Now I finally realize a powerful man is measured by his ability to reveal his so-called weaknesses, by his ability to express his emotions," he said quietly.

Eva smiled at him and went to Marushka. "Thank you for taking such good care of Mother," she said in Russian and placed two €100 bills in her hand.

Arik slowly descended down the stairs. In his heart he knew he had just bid his mother a last farewell.

When they sat in the car, he suddenly said, "When Mother celebrated her seventy-fifth birthday, Naomi and I wanted to take her to Poland so she could revisit her native village. When we told her about our idea, she spat contemptuously and said the day she had left Poland, she swore never to set foot again on the soil of that accursed country soaked with the blood of her family. Then she told us, for the first time, her personal Holocaust story.

"At the end of the war, she returned from the Auschwitz labor camp to her home village of Sarnaki, not far from Warsaw. She was twenty-five, a *muselmann*, a human skeleton, a young widow and a bereaved mother. She was naïve enough to think she could reclaim her family's lumber mill. When she finally arrived in the village, she discovered the Polish laborers who had worked for her family now ran the business. To her great fortune, the foreman's daughter, who was about my mother's age, whispered to her that her father and brother, at that very moment, sharpening the knives they normally used to gut pigs with so they could murder her and hide her body in the forest."

Arik gasped with excitement. "But we still wanted to give Mother a trip abroad as a present and asked her where she would like to go. She said she had always wanted to see Vienna, Prague, and Budapest. Our first stop was Prague. On the first day of our stay there, we hired a local guide with a vehicle to take us for a tour of the city, but my mother remained inside the Hilton Hotel's lobby and refused to go outside. A strange and distant expression lay on her face.

"We asked her, gently, if she wasn't feeling well, and she commanded us in Yiddish, in a voice that seemed to come from another world, 'Leibele, you sit on my right, close to me. Naomile, sit on my left. Now, hold each other's hands and look straight ahead. Do you see the Nazis right in front of us?' There was a group of German tourists in the lobby, chatting loudly and happily ignoring us.

"Mother said with excitement, 'The Nazis tried to kill me, and so did the Polish. Now I'm back in Europe with my two children. Both of them big, strong, educated, married, and both of them gave me grandchildren. I want these Nazis to know this is my victory over them, this is my vengeance— life!' She burst into an emotional crying fit. Pretty soon, we were crying with her. Just imagine it: three people sitting in a hotel lobby, crying their hearts out. The reception manager came running to ask us if everything was all right, and our tears quickly turned to laughter."

Eva kept quiet, and Arik joined her silence. After a few minutes of driving down Haifa's emptying streets, Eva said, "I've witnessed your special relationship with your mother and heard a lot about it, but you've never said a word about your father. Leon, right?"

Arik hesitated before answering. "My father was a simple man who used to beat and humiliate me. He didn't want me to grow up and outshine him, and he did his best to keep me small and under his control. But I was a rebellious child. And so our relationship was mainly comprised of an endless series of conflicts."

"I'm sad to hear that."

"The funny thing is that he turned out to be a warm and loving grandfather. His grandchildren loved him very much. Somehow, being such a good grandfather was a sort of compensation for being such a lousy father." He shrugged. "I think I hated him."

"What about me? Do you love me?"

"Can't you feel that?"

"I feel that you're fond of me, but I don't know if you have deeper emotions for me." She smiled. "Do you know what's the difference between, 'I love you,' and 'I like you,' in Buddhist philosophy?"

"No, I don't."

"When you see a flower you like, you just pluck it, but when you love a flower you love, you water it daily."

"What are you trying to say?"

"That perhaps it's time we moved in together."

Chapter 51

"Operation Survival"

Arik dragged the phone closer to him across the large desk in his bureau and dialed the Sheba Medical Center's hematology ward. "My name is Arik Bar-Nathan. I'd like to check if my test results are back."

A rustling sound was heard from the earpiece as the nurse sorted through some paperwork. Finally, she said, "Yes, but you'll have to talk to Dr. Ben David about it."

Arik felt a pang of anxiety. "Any particular reason?"

"No, not really. She'll give you a call back."

The doctor called after two nerve-wracking hours and immediately said, "Mr. Bar-Nathan, we need to meet as soon possible."

"It sounds like an introduction to a requiem."

"It's definitely not an introduction to a requiem, but if you insist on hearing about it over the phone, it seems that you have advanced multiple myeloma. We need to speak about the medical protocol urgently."

"What's multiple myeloma?" asked Arik.

"I don't think this is a conversation we should be having over the phone. I see that you have a routine appointment scheduled a month from now, but I'd like to see you before that."

"If you say it's urgent, I'd like to come right now."

"How soon can you get to the Sheba Medical Center?"

"I'm in Jerusalem at the moment. If I leave now, considering the traffic, about two hours."

"I'll wait for you."

Arik quickly went to a special room, which contained a computer station with a regular Internet connection.[22] With trembling hands, he typed the words "multiple myeloma" into the white and inviting rectangle of the search box.

His heart sank as he read the words.

Multiple myeloma is a malignant disease involving abnormal plasma cells that accumulate in the bone marrow, where they interfere with the production of normal blood cells. The disease may cause multiple organ failure and takes a different course in every individual. With conventional treatment, median survival is 3–4 years, which may be extended to 5–7 years or longer with advanced treatments.

He froze in front of the screen. *All right*, he thought. *If this is war, then I'm going to fight.*

---

[22]As a general rule, the Israeli security forces' intranet computers are not connected to the Internet.

Chapter 52

Onco-Hematology Clinic—Sheba Medical Center

Reception hours were already over. The clinic lobby was deserted, and Arik's quick footsteps emitted a muffled, echoing sound. Dr. Ben David waited for him in her room, a look that spelled bad tidings in her eyes.

"Sit down, please. I'm sorry I gave you the diagnosis of multiple myeloma over the phone. I assume you've already rushed to check it out on the Internet. Am I right?"

Arik nodded.

"The information on the Internet might be shocking, especially because the illness is described as incurable. In my experience, it can be treated with effectiveness. In recent years, clinical research has considerably advanced, and there are now plenty of medications and treatments at our disposal. As a result, the life expectancy of multiple myeloma patients is steadily rising. Today, myeloma can almost be regarded as a chronic illness."

"Cut the medical bullshit, Doctor," Arik said with a bitter smile. "Since you've already guessed what my profession is, you know that I regularly deal with matters of life and death. I just want to know when I could expect to retire from this life with some dignity."

"I have some young patients, like you, who expected to live about three years before the treatment. Thanks to the treatment, they've all been with us for over ten years now and enjoy a reasonable quality of life."

"I come from a house in which being weak or exposing your weaknesses was strictly forbidden." Arik stripped himself of all defenses. "I live in an environment which has very clear rules: when a chicken demonstrates weakness, the rest of the chickens in the coop peck it to death. Do you have any idea what my life would look like if people discover I'm about to die?" His hands trembled. He had always assumed he would die during combat or in a special operation and had imagined a short, sharp death for himself. He had never imagined a slow, agonizing death without being able to be in control over his final destiny.

"Look, Arik... May I call you Arik?"

Arik nodded. His face was frozen, and his thoughts drifted elsewhere.

"Arik, try to think of it in a different way. It's not that you have cancer. The cancer has Arik. And this means the cancer is in deep trouble because Arik is a real soldier, a shark who won't let cancer get the upper hand, right?"

Arik smiled and regained his composure. "That's all right—I don't need any encouragement. I just want to know what the test results are and what can be done."

"Unfortunately, the myeloma has spread through your body for quite some time. I assume you've noticed the fact you're getting tired much faster than before?"

"Yes, maybe. I was very busy with work and other things. I've always maintained a peaceful coexistence with my illnesses. I just suppress them."

"Your illness is at an advanced stage and mustn't be suppressed. You also have severe anemia, and I'm afraid the myeloma has started attacking your pelvic bones. We've diagnosed a few lytic lesions in the pelvic area. The excessive protein in your urine, because of which you visited a urologist and a nephrologist before returning to us, results from damage to the kidneys."

"It sounds like multi-system failure," Arik said with a calmness that surprised him as well. "So how long do I have left?"

"No one can tell for sure. The effects of multiple myeloma are different from patient to patient. The most important thing is to start treatment immediately. I consulted with some of my colleagues in the department, and we all agree there can be no delays."

"What does the treatment involve?"

"You are going to get different medications, possibly radiation therapy, and maybe surgical intervention. We'll begin by prescribing a cocktail of medication. Later on, based on your condition, we will be able to determine the next stages of the treatment. We may end up implanting bone marrow to arrest the development of the disease."

"Will I still be able to work?" Arik asked.

"I don't see any reason why not," said Dr. Ben David. "Except for about two to three weeks of absence, which you'll be able to excuse as a vacation abroad" She held his hand. "Arik, you must be confused by all the new terms and the new reality you've suddenly found yourself in. We have an excellent service of social workers here, all specializing in clinical practice. They'll be able to help you with all the important questions you must be asking yourself now, such as how will the illness influence your life, who should you share this new reality with, how should you tell your wife, your family, your children..."

The small office closed in on Arik, and he wanted to run away, as far as possible. "I need to go outside and get some fresh air," he said with honesty.

"I'm going to tell you something which may sound completely absurd. You need to be healthy in order to be sick. Get it? You need to be mentally strong and stay physically fit. It's the only way you could win. Here, take my card. It has my private cell phone number. Call me soon so we can get started with the treatment."

Arik took the card, placed it in his pocket, shook the doctor's hand quickly, and went outside into the cold corridor.

Chapter 53

Beehive on the Cliff Neighborhood in the Palmachim Air Force Base

The phones kept ringing, but he didn't answer. Sitting in the iron chair next to his basement work table, he looked at his motorcycle collection and the ancient motorcycle parts he had collected over the years in the hope of fixing, assembling and riding them into the horizon with his son after his retirement.

Just before midnight, he finished writing a will in which he had equally divided all his possessions among his children. He added letters addressed to each of them. In the letters, he apologized for not being a perfect father and accepted full responsibility for divorcing their mother He admitted he felt very proud of them and that he was sorry he did not tell them that before. Then he wrote letters to Claire, his sister, and Eva.

He felt he lost control over his mood. He was overpowered by emotions. He felt sorry for himself and angry at his cruel fate.

At the first light of dawn, Arik found himself sitting in the enclosed porch, his eyes turned westward and watching the winter sun playing games of light and shadow across the surface of the sea. All the letters he had written and his will were placed in front of him on the table, the topmost was a love letter to Eva. He placed them all in a large envelope and sealed it.

Chapter 54

The National Security Council Offices in the Prime Minister's bureau—Jerusalem

That morning, Arik arrived earlier than usual at his office, tired, unshaven, and pale. He was extremely serious and hardly smiled or joked with the security guards at the entrance or with the division receptionists. When Claire arrived, Arik asked her to come into his office.

She went inside with a stony expression on her face. "What's up with you?" Arik scolded her when he noticed she was giving him a strange look.

"What's up with me?" Claire yelled at him. "What's up with you!"

Arik was silent. He didn't know he was so easy to read.

Claire wouldn't let go. "You're hiding things from me! You constantly disappear without letting me know where you're at. Just before the last operation you called me from the hospital and asked me to send someone to pick up your car. Now you have the nerve to ask me what's up with me? It's time you tell me everything, Arik. Other than fucking you, I'm virtually your wife. A ghost wife. I took care of your dirty laundry, I had your house cleaned, I filled your refrigerator with food while you were abroad, and I shared all your moments of happiness and those in which you were sad and depressed because of your miserable divorce. I briefly attended Nathalie's wedding and was happy to see your son, Michael, getting close to you again. For a time, I was also happy to see you getting your life back on track with Eva. Talk to me! I'm not a stranger!" she screamed with desperation.

"What I'm about to tell you needs to stay in this room," Arik whispered and looked around nervously.

She nodded.

"I've been diagnosed with blood cancer," he told her in a whisper.

"What? What did you say?"

"Blood cancer."

"Leukemia?" she almost shouted the word.

"No, myeloma. It's a type of bone marrow cancer that attacks the white blood cells." Arik said with confidence, even though it was only yesterday that he had heard the disease's name and symptoms for the first time.

"What are you going to do?" she asked quietly.

"I'm going to undergo an intensive medical treatment. This large envelope contains a will and letters addressed to my children and the most meaningful people in my life, which means there's a letter there for you as well. I want you to serve as my witness and sign the will after I sign it in front of you. Right now. I want you to serve as my trustee and hand all the letters to their addressees after I'm gone."

Claire began to wail.

"Claire, dear, please don't cry. I need you beside me now, stronger than ever."

She tried, unsuccessfully, to overcome her tears. She sniffled and a series of sighs escaped her chest.

"There's a chance I'll be much weaker soon, perhaps even unable to control my physical reactions and going in and out of consciousness. I trust you to take care of every legal aspect of things"

"What about your job?"

"I'm about to go into the prime minister's office and ask him for six months of unpaid vacation. After that, we'll just have to see."

Clair burst into bitter tears again. Arik hugged her fondly, then gently pushed her away from him. He took out the will and signed it. Then Claire signed it as his witness. The angry and confused eyes of the receptionists accompanied him on his way out of the office. They all wondered how he had insulted Claire again and why she ran out of his office in tears holding a large envelope.

He went up to the prime minister's office and asked Raaya, Kenan's personal secretary, for permission to go into the aquarium for a few minutes and give the prime minister a personal and urgent update.

"The prime minister has a meeting with his chief of staff regarding coalition problems," said Raaya. "I'll give you a call the moment they're finished. You can wait in your office."

When Arik was called inside, he spoke straight and to the point. He briefly gave some details about his illness and added that he thought it would be unwise to leave this important and dynamic government office without a commander for the foreseeable future.

The prime minister vigorously patted his shoulder, and Arik remembered an insight he had learned while a young flotilla officer: "Most people who pat your shoulder aren't really fond of you. They're merely seeking the easiest spot to stick you with a dagger once you turn your back on them."

"Let me take care of the office. You need to take care of yourself and be healthy now. Keep in contact, you hear?"

Two minutes with his new boss were enough for Arik to understand thirty-three years of service, fifteen of them in Mossad, had vanished into thin air. The huge investment in his various roles, the fact he had to neglect his family, the personal price he needed to pay, the injuries he suffered, all simply vanished.

For a moment, a great sadness overcame him, but the very next he was surprised to feel an immense sense of relief. He remembered the Roman phrase, "Sic transit gloria mundi."

Chapter 55

The Guardians of Faith Quarter—Jerusalem

Nathalie woke up toward dawn, suddenly feeling extremely nauseated. She ran to the restrooms and threw up for long minutes. She was gripped with fear. It has been months since her husband, yeshiva student Haim Fishel, had returned from his visit to Rabbi Nachman of Breslov's grave in the Ukraine. Indeed, his good deed had born fruit. She was in the third month of her pregnancy.

In the dim light of the emergency bulb, she returned to bed and sank into a restless sleep. Suddenly, she saw her father in her dreams, pale, old, tired, and unshaven. He held his hands to her and called her name.

She had been seeing visions since she was a child, and, amazingly enough, most of them turned out to be detailed images of future events.

The sickly sight of her father made her forego her anger about his broken promises and the fact he had left the house while she was a teenager. The rage was now transformed into sadness and empathy. They had lost so much time together by arguing and blaming each other. She sat in her bed, and large tears rolled down her cheeks and fell to her buttoned nightgown. She recalled how her father had carried her in his arms as a child, then hurled her up into the air while she screamed with joy mixed with fear. She recalled how he stood by her side every time she would have one of her endless adolescent arguments with her mother and how generous he had been financially, supporting her over the years, depositing an amount that was enough for her rent and living expenses each and every month. Now her father's image called her from the darkness. Was he sick and in need of her? She sank into a nightmarish sleep again. Her last waking thought was that she must call her brother first thing in the morning and ask him if he knows anything about an illness suffered by their father.

Chapter 56

The Cancer Center and Hemato-Oncology Institute, located at the southernmost end of the giant Sheba Medical Center, looked like a resort in the middle of a remote and secluded island. Densely-foliaged *poinciana* trees, whose branches were adorned with beautiful red flowers, formed a shaded boulevard. Hairless patients sat on wood benches, wearing hospital pajamas with a portable IV drip line attached to their arm and quietly spoke with their visitors. A flock of *myna* birds wandered on the grass, pecking food scraps and chirping loudly.

A large sign hung on Arik's door: "Isolation Room— Entry Permitted to Medical Staff Only!" A picc line had been inserted into his chest, and the chemotherapy substances were administered through it into his superior vena cava. He was exhausted. He suffered from abscesses that formed inside his mouth. He needed to wear a diaper and suffered from involuntary spells of diarrhea. A bedpan was placed next to his bed because he frequently vomited. The lower end of his stomach was hurting from anticoagulant injections. His calf muscles suffered frequent and sudden spasms. His hair grayed and began to fall. His consciousness drifted between dreamless sleep and nightmares. He tried to hold on to a solid object so he could find some security and rest but to no avail. He rocked back and forth between floating and slowly and uncontrollably sinking into an ice-cold bottomless pit.

At a certain point of time, between exhaustion and incontinence, one reaches a point of deep detachment filled with simple clarity. At that point, Arik felt a sense of pure and impenetrable tranquility. It was a defining moment in which Arik understood who he really was and that nothing really mattered. Everything suddenly appeared unimportant and miniscule. His senior position at Mossad and the prime minister's office, Cornfield's and the prime minister's clashes of ego, Israel's strategic problems, the Iranian nuclear threat, the operations against the enemies of Israel that still awaited execution… They all dwarfed next to the most important battle of his life.

He missed Michael and Nathalie. Barely conscious, he called their names again and again. They didn't answer. He tried to scream, but was barely able to utter a sound and sank back into the exhausted drowsy sleep induced by his medication cocktail.

Ten days had passed, and the chemotherapy treatments stopped. Gradually, his body began to recuperate before the autologous bone marrow transplant could take place.

Arik was lost in a temporary blindness. Every attempt to open his eyes caused severe spells of vertigo-like dizziness. A female hand tried to help him drink lukewarm tea, which he immediately vomited. Through the haze of pain, he felt a gentle hand washing his body with a soft washcloth. He smelled the familiar scent of *ylang-ylang* soap, lifted his hand, and grabbed the soft hand that caressed his head. Soft lips kissed his eyes, just as his mother had done when he was a sick little child.

From afar, he could hear someone calling his name. Was it his daughter who had heard his call? His sister, Naomi? Eva? His mother? Was he dreaming? Dead? Was he still alive?

He was the young asthmatic boy from the poor Halissa neighborhood in downtown Haifa again. Little *Leibele*, who beat his own chest with his fist during severe asthma attacks and shouted at his body, "You're not going to rule me!" Now he wanted to rule his own body and destiny again but was simply too weak to do that. This was very frustrating for him.

A few days later, when he woke from the effects of the medication and painkillers, he saw Eva next to his bed, dressed in a green nurse's gown, a surgical mask on her face and a plastic cap covering her beautiful hair. She combed his thin hair and beard with a little comb.

"How long have you been here?" he asked in a cracked voice.

"More than two weeks. I sleep right over there." She motioned with her head toward the large armchair that had been brought into the room for her. "But I'm not the only one." She pointed at the round window, through which he could see the worried faces of Naomi, Michael, and Nathalie. "You're in the isolation room and entry is forbidden, especially for Nathalie. She's been put on bed rest because of pregnancy complications." She subdued a smile.

"You speak Hebrew?" Arik was surprised.

Eva smiled and said, "Yes, and I've started the process of converting to Judaism."

The door opened, and the chubby Dr. Alice Ben David

entered the room, along with the hospital manager and the prime minister's military secretary Major General Amishav. They all wore plastic caps, hospital gowns, masks and shoe covers. "Good news," Dr. Ben David announced. "The biomarker we sent to the medical center in America indicates that you can be treated by an innovative and groundbreaking new medicine developed there."

"What kind of medicine?" asked Eva, taking command over Arik's destiny.

"They've developed a biological substance that manages to make the cancerous growths myeloma patients suffer from disappear," said Dr. Alice, while placing a bundle of papers on Arik's bed and asking for his signature. "You'll need to appoint a legal guardian to handle all the travelling arrangements."

"That would be Eva," Arik whispered, and both women answered with a wide smile that stretched to the edges of the surgical masks.

Epilogue

April 2008. Beneath a pair of coconut trees, in Manuel Antonio National Park in Costa Rica, facing a red sunset, two vacationers swung in a large hammock.

To their great delight, the beach was silent and empty of tourists. It was a wise decision to travel to such a popular tourist destination off-season.

Their naked feet splashed in the clear water of the Pacific Ocean, and vast, green expanses lay behind them. The woman embraced a baby that enthusiastically suckled from her exposed breast. She leaned her head on the shoulder of a skinny man whose face was adorned by a whitening beard.

"*Pina colada, señora?*" asked the waiter who roamed the beach idly, trying to fish for tips.

The woman shook her head no, and the man said, "Why don't you bring me a *caipirinha?*"

Six months had passed since Arik had signed the medical approval forms at the clinic and a month since he had been released, healthy, yet extremely weak, from the Mayo Clinic in Minnesota, following his treatment. He was grateful to Lolik Kenan, the prime minister, for breathing down the necks of the Minister of Health and his team until they finally gave up and approved the funding of the innovative medicine for myeloma. Kenan also made sure all the payments for the trip and the expensive treatment would be taken care of by the government. Some Ministry of Finance officials muttered complaints about the fact an ordinary citizen would have never received such treatment. But Kenan answered them all that most ordinary citizens had never risked their lives for the sake of their country like Arik had.

Eva gave birth to their son in the same hospital in which Arik was admitted. They decided, at Eva's request, to name the boy Leon Hai Junior after Arik's father, as a gesture of compassion and forgiveness.

They spent their recovery vacation in a small ecological hotel called Clandestino Beach Resort, which was actually a handful of large wooden huts paved with black slate, in the middle of a rainforest clearing. The huts were built around a large pool whose sweet, warm water gushed from a hidden volcanic spring. In the mornings, Arik and Eva woke to the sound of colorful parrots screaming. Capuchin monkeys jumped down from the treetops onto their porch to give them a curious morning greeting, and giant, red-green iguana lizards fearlessly drowsed on the tanning chairs lining the swimming pool.

Jorge, the French landlady's young lover, served as the hotel's chef and trained Arik in yoga exercises on the beach every sunset to strengthen his body.

One morning, their peaceful vacation was disturbed by a phone call. "*Señor*, you have a call," the waiter announced and pointed at the office.

"Arik Bar-Nathan?" Major General Amishav's voice was heard through the earpiece.

Arik knew it was pointless to ask how Amishav had located him and confirmed his identity.

"This is Amishav. How are you, Arik? We've been worried about you," the prime minister's military secretary, continued with trivial politeness.

Arik smiled. He knew the polite exchange was just an introduction and waited with newfound patience.

"The prime minister would like to speak with you," said Amishav.

A muffled click was heard, followed by the prime minister's exuberant voice. "How are you, Arik?"

"I'm fine, sir. Still a little weak, but getting better every day."

"Perfect!" said Kenan and Arik, as usual, had no idea what he was getting at.

"When are you coming back to work? I still haven't appointed a replacement. I'm filling in for you as Chairman of Intelligence and Security Services."

"I'm grateful, sir, for everything. For your friendship and for the backup," said Arik with suppressed excitement.

"Make no mistake—I did it all out of sheer egotistical reasons. I need you here."

This time, the expressed irony in Kenan's words made Arik sympathize with the man.

"Cornfield is getting old, and I'm looking for a replacement. He's going to finish his term in December. What do you say? You think you're strong enough for the job?"

"What about Gideon Perry, the Mossad deputy director you brought back after you had fired Mot'ke Hassin?"

"No, he's too old and is a wonderful number two."

"Thank you, sir. I'll think about it and get back to you," said Arik.

"You've got a month."

Arik took a large glass of cold milk and a plate of cookies from the bar and started walking back to the beach. He knew it would be difficult for him to convince Eva but also recognized the fact he wouldn't be able to refuse the offer of the man who had rescued him from certain death.

Acknowledgments

First and foremost, I'd like to thank my wife, Denise Abensour Ronen, for her active participation, her wise insights, her suggestions for the twists and turns of the plot, her encouragement, and her constructive criticism regarding the writing of this book. I'd also like to ask her forgiveness for not always being there for her while my mind was preoccupied with the characters of this book who forced me to sit down and write their story for over three and a half years.

A special thanks to my dear friends for their remarks and insights for the first drafts of the book and for finding plot holes and pointing out unrealistic dialogue: Shlomo Zimmer, Gideon Perry, Lina Sharon, Ra'aya Soudery, Jo Amar, Abigail Urman, Genya Shafir, Nava Gad, Eli Nemzer, Edna Kalef, Tani Geva, Shlomo Tobi, Elie Parkal, and to H.D., who asked to remain anonymous, as he is still active in the system.

To my dear children: Ariel, Nathalie, Michal, Yuval, and Galit and their spouses for their support and encouragement.

Last, but not least, my deepest gratitude to the book's editor, Dr. Amnon Jackont, an author and historian without whom the book would not possess its correct pace, tight plot, dramatic twists and turns, and what I regard as the right combination between a human drama and an espionage thriller.

I'd love to hear your comments and insights at: **arikbarnathan@gmail.com**

Made in the USA
Middletown, DE
04 May 2017